CROSSING THE LINE

By Isabella Muir

Saluti e baci !

Isabella

x

July 2020

Published in Great Britain
By Outset Publishing Ltd

Published July 2020

ISBN:978-1-872889-32-0

www.isabellamuir.com

Cover photo: by Erda Estremera on Unsplash
Cover design: by Christoffer Petersen

'People glorify all sorts of bravery, except the bravery they might show on behalf of their nearest neighbours.'
Middlemarch, George Eliot, 1871

1964

CHAPTER 1
Sunday, 5th July
Morning

When Rose was a child, she liked to play a game on the street outside her home. She dared herself to run from the lamppost at one end of Factory Road to the telephone box at the far end. As she ran, she kept her eyes focused on the ground, taking great care to place her feet in the centre of each paving slab, never stepping on the lines. Touching the lines meant a chasm opened into which she was swallowed up and lost forever.

Now, as an adult, Rose Walker had discovered it was the lines and boundaries in her life that kept her safe.

Her home was a cottage that stood alone on the stretch of Beach Walk leading to the railway crossing. The densely packed privet hedge edging the front garden created a boundary from the single track road. Tamarisk bushes provided a windbreak down one side of the cottage and on the other two sides was a low picket fence. Beyond the fence, sheep grazed.

The shingle beach was fifty paces from her front door. Rose knew it was fifty paces because she'd counted the steps many times. But since the caravan arrived some weeks earlier, Rose hadn't walked down to the shoreline. Instead, she opened her front room window and listened to the rhythmic sound of the sea. There was a comfort in the regular pattern of tides, controlled by the moon and the changing seasons; seasons she saw reflected in the flowers she tended.

There was order inside the cottage too, everything in its proper place. If she remained focused on the structure she'd created, the patterns she repeated day after day, then she could always be prepared for what might happen next.

1

Until that Sunday morning.

Rose wasn't one for superstition. As she went about her routine, she had no premonition of the event that would change her life. Again.

The gilt carriage clock that stood in the centre of the tiled mantelpiece kept perfect time. The wireless was tuned to the BBC Light Programme. Just before the hourly news broadcast Rose listened to the chimes of Big Ben, then switched her gaze to the carriage clock, comforted to see the position of the clock hands edge forward to confirm the time.

11am.

She relaxed a little, her breathing settling. Each weekday, at 11.05, the Hastings to Eastbourne train passed to the rear of the cottage, winding its way past the fields. The track swerved to the right where the crossing gate was, before heading straight again and on into the distance. By standing to the far right-hand side of her front room window, she could see the train as it passed through the crossing. The carriages were too far away for her to see the passengers, but the rattle of the windows and slight shaking of the floor beneath her feet were, in themselves, reassuring.

But today was Sunday, so her weekday routine had to alter. There was no 11.05 train. Nevertheless, there were elements to the regular pattern of her day that she could keep the same. At 11am she went into the kitchen, filled the kettle and set it on the gas. She prepared a tray, covering it with a white lace square, before selecting her favourite blue china cup and saucer, matching milk jug and sugar bowl. She picked two digestives from the biscuit barrel and placed them on a tea plate. It was important to present the right image should she receive a visitor. Although the thought of a visitor - any visitor - brought back the breathlessness, the griping sensation in her stomach.

While she waited for the kettle to boil, she returned to the front room. And that was the moment she saw them.

Two teenage boys were walking up the front path towards her cottage. She felt a confusion of emotions; exhilaration, mixed with fear. She heard the boys' laughter, and then their whispers as they stood at her front door. She stayed in the front room, standing back from the window, so she could see them, but they couldn't see her. At least she thought that was the case until one of the boys caught her gaze. Seconds later there was a loud rap on the door. *Should she open it?* It was too late to pretend she wasn't at home. There was a pushing and pulling inside herself, in the pit of her stomach.

Moments later, she had decided. She walked to the front door and opened it. The boys looked at her, then at each other.

In all her life Rose had never taken the drugs that young people took nowadays. She had enjoyed an alcoholic drink on occasion, but never experienced what it was to be so drunk you couldn't focus. She imagined the effect of such intoxication might resemble the way she felt now, as she looked at the two boys standing on her front doorstep who were almost identical in every way. It was as if she had double vision. Her hands went to her spectacles. They'd slipped down her nose a little. She should try to tighten the arms. The tiny screwdriver she kept in the kitchen cutlery drawer would do the job. The spectacles were forgotten as she refocused on the boys.

They stared at her, then grinned, dimples appearing in their cheeks. Some of their baby fat still lingering. She wanted to reach forward and touch their faces, push back the fringe from the boy whose hair was more windswept than his twin.

'Come in,' she said. 'I've got the kettle on.'

For all her anxiety a few moments ago, it seemed the easiest of actions to invite them in. The boys grinned again and stepped into the small hallway. She pointed towards the front room and followed them.

'What's your favourite kind of biscuits?' She would put out a selection, open the tin of Crawford's Assorted biscuits she'd bought around Easter time. It had been on special offer, and she'd succumbed to the temptation to buy it. Since then it had remained in the larder.

The boys shared a look before flopping down, side by side on the settee. Rose wanted to apologise. The settee was old and worn. She never sat on it, it was there for visitors. Although the boys were her first visitors.

'You might prefer a cold drink. What about some lemon barley water?' She always kept a bottle of squash in the larder, especially during these hot days. There was a glass jug in the sideboard, although it would need rinsing out.

As she studied the boys more closely, she noticed differences between them. It wasn't just their hair, but something about their faces too. Or perhaps their expressions. The windswept boy had an ease about him, his posture relaxed as he rested his arm along the back of the settee. The other boy sat upright, closer to the edge of the settee and was constantly glancing around the room.

'I've seen you before,' she said, immediately wishing the words had stayed inside her head. They would wonder why she'd been watching. They wouldn't understand.

Then there was a scratching at the door.

'It's Tabitha,' she said, standing back as the ginger cat ran in from the kitchen.

One of the boys bent down to stroke it, receiving a hiss for his trouble.

'She's frightened of strangers.' Rose felt the need to apologise for the cat's behaviour.

'We always cycle this way at the weekend,' the windswept

boy said, patting his lap by way of encouragement to Tabitha. The cat remained a distance away, eying him suspiciously.

'What about those biscuits then,' his brother said, stretching his legs out, almost kicking over the coffee table.

Rose noticed mud on the bottom of his jeans. She wondered if his mother would be cross.

'I'm Paul and he's my brother, George. And your kettle's whistling.' He spoke as if he was giving Rose an instruction.

She was so absorbed in her thoughts, she hadn't heard the noise, which was now piercing the silence.

'I'll help if you like.' George followed her into the kitchen. She tried to guess at his age. The angry pimples across his forehead, the merest dark shadow on his chin, suggested fourteen or fifteen. No longer a child and yet not quite a man. She imagined preparing meals for him, teenage lads had healthy appetites. She took two more cups and saucers from the top shelf of the dresser.

'Lucky you're so tall,' he said. 'I'd have to get on a step to reach, same as Mum and Dad. We're all short my lot.'

She blushed. It was a reminder of her own teenage years when a growth spurt had sent her skyward, making her several inches taller than the rest of her class. The teasing continued for years.

'It's good being short though, makes me lighter on my feet at footie,' George was speaking again. There was a quiet confidence about him. She wondered how it might feel to have certainty. She realised she couldn't imagine it.

Each time he spoke he smiled at her in a way that suggested they could be friends. Rose dwelled on the thought for a moment. Having a friend, even a young friend like George, could open up such opportunities. There would be a chance for conversations, a sharing of ideas about books and music. It was the kind of relationship she dreamed of having with

Vincent. Not friends exactly, but something close to that.

'Your parents must be very proud of you both,' she said.

He picked a digestive biscuit from the plate, broke it in two, letting the crumbs fall to the floor.

'Not when we get on their nerves,' he said and laughed.

'I would be proud of you,' she said and then blushed again.

She remembered the tin of assorted biscuits. She opened the door to the larder, lifting the tin down from the top shelf, placing it on the kitchen table. But before she put the biscuits onto the plate, Paul was in the doorway saying they should leave. Within moments they were gone.

She called out to them as they ran down the path, their laughter loud and coarse. 'You haven't had your tea.'

She heard Paul call out to his brother. 'Race you.' Then she watched them jump on their bikes and cycle back along Beach Walk until they turned the corner and were out of sight.

CHAPTER 2
Saturday, 4th July to Sunday, 5th July

Giuseppe Bianchi had never mastered the art of packing. His suitcase laid open on the blanket box in his bedroom for two weeks before his planned departure. At random times of the day and night he went to his wardrobe or chest of drawers and pulled out a shirt or a pair of trousers, tossing them into the case. As a result, the clothes were piled high in the centre, leaving gaps around the sides.

The evening before leaving, he tried to inject some urgency into his preparations. He wandered from room to room in his flat, opening cupboards and drawers, hoping to catch sight of an item of clothing, or toiletries, that might act as a reminder about what to include.

He would be arriving in England in July. He knew it would be colder than Rome, but not as cold as his previous visit ten years earlier. That had been for a two-week Christmas holiday. On that occasion he thought his repeated words of persuasion for Rosalia to accompany him might have worked. In the end she remained resolute. She planned to stay at home, spend Christmas with friends. An English Christmas was not for her. On his return he spent most of January back home in Rome, trying to thaw out. This visit would be different for many reasons, not just the weather.

When he visited Roma Termini to buy the train ticket, he couldn't decide on his return date. It was easier to buy a one-way ticket, but it meant packing was even more challenging. If he was uncertain how long he might stay with his cousin, how could he know how many belongings he should take?

On the morning of his departure, after a sleepless night, he added two cotton jumpers to the top of his case. They were still in their shop wrapping, never worn. Whenever he wore a jumper he felt constricted, as he did when he had to wear a tie. He wasn't oblivious to the admiring glances he received from women, but had no patience for preening in front of the mirror. He'd inherited his good looks from his father, the natural curls, dark brown eyes and olive skin. He could have his pick of women, but he was a married man. Even though it was almost three years since Rosalia walked away from their life together.

An hour later, as he stood on the pavement outside his *palazzo,* he couldn't recall if he'd turned the gas off. He'd wasted most of the morning, spending it gazing out of his kitchen window at the skyline. In the distance he could catch a glimpse of the cupola of St Peter's Basilica. That view was one of the reasons he'd chosen to stay in the flat, despite all the negative memories it held for him. The minutes he'd spent gazing meant little time to wash or shave and no time to double check the gas feed to the cooker.

The taxi arrived five minutes late. It was only as Giuseppe handed over his suitcase to be put in the boot of the car, he realised he had never turned the gas on. He no longer prepared his morning coffee. He'd grab one at the station before catching the train.

The taxi driver muttered to himself throughout the journey towards Roma Termini. Giuseppe was so used to the cacophony of sounds, the chaos of traffic, the frequent ambulance and police sirens. He barely heard any of it. Citizens of Rome were impatient to get on with their day.

Once on the platform he let the porter load his suitcase onto a flatbed trolley, along with the leather holdall Giuseppe grabbed almost as an afterthought. In contrast to the hustle and bustle all around him, the porter walked slowly, pushing the heavy trolley ahead of him, weaving in and out of the crowds of people arriving and departing.

Minutes later Giuseppe stood on the platform next to the sleeper train that would take him all the way to Paris. Before climbing into the carriage he took a deep breath, in an attempt to hold onto the smells of his beloved city. The mix of fresh coffee and cigarette smoke, citrus and basil, all reminders of the place he would soon leave behind. Even now, as he walked through to his seat, he had doubts about the decision he'd taken. It was tempting to pretend he could run away from his troubles, when in reality he knew enough about life to know they would remain with him, wherever he ran to.

He'd bought a first-class ticket. It was an extravagance, although easily justified now he was retired. His police pension was generous. For years he'd done nothing but work, his money accumulating, with little time to spend it.

He had the carriage to himself for the first part of the journey down to the Swiss border He read and dozed alternately. Then at Basel the carriage door slid open and a couple entered. He nodded. They smiled. The man wore a suit, the woman a silk jacket over a matching dress, a luxurious fabric Rosalia would adore. It seemed to Giuseppe an entirely inappropriate outfit for travelling, but then clothes fashion had always irritated him. Many a time his wife had paraded in front of him in one outfit, then another, asking for his thoughts. He'd find himself drifting off, thinking about an ongoing case, that elusive piece of evidence that confirmed the identity of the criminal. His work colleagues spent much of their wages on the finest suits, handmade shoes. When off duty they dressed up to take the evening *passeggiata,* pausing at a bar to enjoy an aperitif or an espresso. Italian design was renowned the world over. Giuseppe could see no sense in it. His usual attire was an open-necked blue shirt, a dark blue jacket and cream linen trousers. All his shirts were blue. He wasn't one for favourite colours, but if he had to choose, yes, it would be *blu.* And this time grey trousers. Cream trousers for travelling was madness.

'Do you mind if we move your suitcase over?' The man was speaking to him in English. It was a reminder that soon Giuseppe would have to get used to conversing in a foreign language. He had a good command of English but little chance to practise. Some words were hard to pronounce and many were impossible to remember. He would find the first few days with his cousin and family tiring, having to translate phrases in his head before speaking.

The English couple seemed content with each other's company. A relief for Giuseppe, who kept his eyes closed much of the time to avoid any attempts at conversation. His visits to the dining car were brief and solitary. His friends weren't surprised to hear of his plans. Travel was a good thing, they said, it broadens the mind. He shrugged off their words. His mind had been broadened enough with crimes of every kind. He had looked into the dark minds of criminals and shuddered at what he'd seen.

Early evening the attendant came through the train, making up the beds and advising passengers the dining car would open again for breakfast at 6am. Giuseppe did not expect to sleep, but the train's repetitive movement lulled him into a deep slumber. It was only the voices of the English couple that woke him just after 6.30am.

'Are you stopping in Paris, or going on to England? On holiday are you?' the man asked.

'England. But it is not an 'oliday.' He spoke slowly, enunciating each word, enjoying the strangeness of the sounds, making a mental note about the English 'h' - it always caught him out. It was only when he said the word that it was confirmed in his mind. Not a holiday, then what? A visit to family? An escape?

When the train arrived in Paris Giuseppe was ready at the door to the carriage, leaving the English couple fiddling with their luggage. He had crossed Paris on his last trip to England. He knew it was important to have francs ready and to be alert to the taxi driver overcharging him. It was the same the world over, he was sure of it.

The last leg of the journey passed quickly. He was a good sailor so the ferry crossing caused him no problems, but there was a sense of relief when the White Cliffs appeared out of the mist.

He was to take a train from Dover and Mario had told him to ring on his arrival in Eastbourne. 'I'll collect you, save you getting a taxi.'

He'd told his cousin, 'I will arrive when I arrive. There is no need for any fuss. It is better you do not leave Anne alone in the café.'

'You don't change,' his cousin had said.

'Why would I want to change?' It was a conversation they'd had many times over the years and one he reflected on often. Who was the most stubborn - his cousin or him? Perhaps both of them in their own way. Mario had spent half his lifetime in England, forgoing his childhood home in Rome, refusing to return even for a visit. Giuseppe knew the reasons Mario gave for not returning, but now that so much time had passed they sounded more and more like excuses.

Leaving Dover behind, the train meandered through the leafy green of Kent and on into East Sussex. As Giuseppe looked out of the train window he was struck by the stark comparisons. July in Rome meant hot, dusty streets, yet here it was as though the route had been selected to show off trees in full leaf and fields ripe for harvest. An artist's palette filled with every shade of green, scattered everywhere to create the most exquisite painting.

After a change in Ashford and another in Hastings, the final part of Giuseppe's journey followed the coast, heading for Eastbourne. He caught glimpses of shingle beaches and a murky coloured sea. Despite it being a summer's day, the sky was a milky white, much of the sunlight filtered through a blanket of cloud.

He was due to arrive in Eastbourne at 6.05pm. Giuseppe glanced at his watch. He was fifteen minutes away from his final destination. Suddenly the train screeched to a halt, Giuseppe pushed his face close to the window, trying to focus. It was as if the clouds had descended. All he saw were shapes, movements in the mist. A sea fret had drifted in, hiding the sun, giving the view from the window an almost dream-like quality.

He was alone in his carriage, but as he slid the door open, he heard raised voices. Many of the other passengers had left their seats to congregate in the corridor.

'Why have we stopped?' shouted one elderly man, waving his walking stick at his companion.

'Find the guard,' wailed another passenger, a young woman, her hands clasped to her face.

'Maybe someone pulled the emergency cord,' the elderly man said, the authority in his voice a clear attempt at trying to calm the situation.

Within moments, before the guard instructed him to do otherwise, Giuseppe seized his opportunity, opened the door nearest to him, and jumped down onto the railway track.

He didn't turn to see the shocked expressions of his fellow passengers, but climbed over the track, walked across the railway crossing and towards the emergency sirens that were approaching.

CHAPTER 3
Sunday, 5th July
Afternoon

When Christina Rossi secured her job as junior reporter for the *Eastbourne Herald* she promised herself she would remain 'junior' for as short a time as possible. Her editor, Charles, was encouraging, but in a patronising way. His attitude made Christina even more determined to prove she was more than an eager twenty-three-year-old who dealt with the births, marriages and deaths column, interspersed with regular reports on the local Women's Institute meetings.

Her determination to make her mark didn't stop when she left the office on a Friday evening. Most weekends, when she wasn't looking after her six-year-old nephew, Stevie, or helping her parents - Mario and Anne - with an occasional shift in their seafront café, she was writing. Her transistor radio was on in the background. *The House of the Rising Sun* had just finished playing, her foot tapping away to the rhythm.

Her mind was still buzzing with the arrival of their first television the day before. After months of pleading, she'd finally persuaded her dad to rent one. His argument was that there would be no time to watch it, so what was the point. But when the Rediffusion van pulled up on Saturday afternoon, she was almost as excited as Stevie.

'Don't think you'll be allowed to watch it every day, Stevie,' Mario told him. 'It's more for grown-ups than for you.'

But Christina had bought a copy of the *Radio Times* in readiness. She'd found children's programmes that Stevie would love, and a listing showing that The Rolling Stones would be on the panel for *Juke Box Jury* at 7pm. Her Saturday night was sorted. Once the programme ended she switched the television off, but was drawn back to it for the late evening news.

For weeks all the nationals had been reporting the news about a missing boy in Manchester. Twelve-year-old Keith Bennett had been on his way to his grandmother's house, but never arrived. Seeing the report on the television screen made the dreadful incident more real. It was difficult to concentrate on her writing after that. The phrase 'stranger danger' had been picked up by some of the papers and she'd heard it repeated by some of the mothers when she dropped Stevie at school. The feature article she'd been working on wasn't about the dangers children might experience, but now she wondered if it should be. Instead, her article focused on the way persistent injustice could control someone's life, remove their voice, steal their freedom, all written from a woman's viewpoint. She'd been researching and planning it for weeks and, as a result, had been thinking dark thoughts about the inequalities that seemed to be all around her.

Charles had said he'd look at any feature article she drafted, but made no promises he would print it. Plus he made it clear she should work on it in her own time.

She'd promised Stevie they could spend Sunday afternoon on the beach, but was so focused on redrafting her article for the hundredth time that before she knew it, the afternoon was almost over.

Stevie had spent most of the day in the café, being spoilt by the customers. Two slices of lemon sponge and a piece of shortbread had distracted him enough to leave Christina in peace, but boredom had finally set in.

With his granddad, Mario, busy chatting to one of the regulars, and his grandmother, Anne, wiping tables and refilling the sugar bowls, Stevie was able to slip up the back stairs to Christina's bedroom without anyone noticing.

'Can we go to the beach now, please?' Despite being only

six years old, Stevie had already discovered how to produce a winning smile to order. 'I've been very patient.'

He sidled over to Christina's dressing table, which doubled as a desk, and picked up the top sheet from a pile of discarded drafts, waving it around as though it was a bird in flight. 'You said I could take my bucket and spade.'

A few days earlier Stevie had taken a bite of an apple and one of his front milk teeth had come out. The gap it left not only resulted in a slight lisp, but made his cherubic face even more endearing.

'Stevie is spirted,' his class teacher told Christina at the first parent's evening. The description made her smile. Knowing all Stevie had to cope with, she was relieved the report was so positive. There was no doubt he was bright, but he was often wilful too. Her greatest fear was that he would turn out like his mother.

'It's too late now, Stevie, the best of the sunshine is gone. We'll go next weekend, I promise.' As she spoke she watched his mouth droop and his chin wobble. She pulled him towards her, pushing his fringe away from his eyes.

'Don't cry, a trip to the beach is not worth crying about. Trust me.'

There was so much of Stevie that reminded Christina of her sister. The stubbornness, petulance and, when needed, the ability to turn on the tears. Her sister, Flavia, had a self-destruct button, which she operated at every opportunity.

When Stevie was born Flavia announced she wasn't cut out to be a mother. Soon after Stevie's second birthday, Flavia left the family home and headed north, leaving Christina and her parents to care for him. There was no mention of Stevie's father, or even if Flavia knew who he was. She'd returned on a few occasions, but each time she came back she had another tale of woe, one more failed relationship, money troubles, being sacked. The list was endless. Flavia's last visit coincided with Stevie's first week at school, maybe by intention, more likely by chance. Her presence merely added to the emotions already present for any child starting primary school. Long after her visit Stevie woke from vivid dreams, only settling after comfort and reassurance from his aunt.

As soon as Stevie was old enough to understand, Anne had explained to him that Flavia was his mother, but that she had a very busy job and couldn't look after him. The truth was Flavia had no job at all. Christina had helped to raise him, and now their relationship was more akin to parent and child than aunt and nephew. Christina couldn't decide how she felt about that.

'Okay, you win,' Christina said, pulling Stevie towards her for a hug.

'Really? Can we go, really?'

'Yes, we can go really. Fetch your swimming trunks and find your sandals. Last time I saw them they were in the middle of the back lawn.'

Half an hour later Stevie was sitting in the back of Christina's Mini, clutching his bucket and spade, all grumpiness replaced by a broad grin. Christina wound one of the back windows down, before sliding into the driver's seat, turning the key in the ignition, starting the engine and pulling away.

All along Bexhill seafront people were ambling, focused on their own conversations. A woman in her Sunday best summer frock, a pale blue cardigan draped over her shoulders, strolled hand in hand with her husband. Another couple, younger, were showing off sunburnt arms, the girl in the shortest of miniskirts, the boy in drainpipe trousers.

The day was warm, humid, rather than a blistering heat. Christina opened her own window as far as possible, willing

16

the through draught to blow away the stuffiness in the car. Her Mini had been parked up opposite the café since Saturday evening and had the lingering smell of the sixpenny worth of chips she had treated herself to on her way home from a friend's house. The stale odour of frying, mingled with vinegar, made her feel queasy, distracting her from any thoughts about the unfinished newspaper article she'd left behind on her dressing table.

She glanced in the rear-view mirror, catching Stevie's look of concentration as he hummed a tune. Christina recognised the beat of *Can't Buy me Love,* the last record she'd listened to before turning her transistor off, grabbing her swimming costume and swapping her favourite strappy silver sandals for a battered pair of plimsolls. Aunt and nephew hummed along in harmony, with Christina adding in the words.

Her eyes returned to the road ahead. She glanced at the landmarks she'd passed countless times in all the years she'd lived in the seaside town. Bexhill-on-Sea was once a favoured resort for families from London and beyond. But in recent years, holidaymakers seemed to prefer the nearby towns of Hastings and Eastbourne, with their amusement arcades and funfairs. In the main, the residents of Bexhill saw the drop-off of tourists as a bonus, it meant the community had the town to themselves. Nothing much happened, and the locals liked it that way. Winter and summer they could enjoy the Victorian beach shelters, weathered by the constant battering of salty rain; the ice-cream van that rarely moved pitch, ready to sell a '99' even on the chilliest day.

As Christina reached the end of the seafront, her concentration was needed as she crossed the Little Common roundabout, past the village shops, and down towards the sea. She'd never been a confident driver, despite surprising everyone by passing her test first time.

Minutes later she turned right onto Beach Walk, the narrow back road that formed a short cut for locals who chose to avoid the busier Marsh Road. Beach Walk ran close to the shingle and after a winter storm, combined with a high tide, waves threw up clusters of stones, bringing them crashing down onto the tarmac, making it difficult to drive along. On such days, the locals knew to avoid the route for fear of getting a smashed windscreen or worse.

But this July day followed weeks of dry weather, leaving the road free of shingle. Earlier, the beach would have been crowded with families enjoying a Sunday together, a brief respite before the new working week began.

When the tide was out a wide stretch of sand was exposed and on the odd occasion that Christina had visited the beach early evening she'd watched men digging for lugworm. It looked like such a peaceful pursuit, although the thought of picking up the wriggly creatures turned her stomach.

Christina had checked the tide tables and knew the tide would be half in, half out, by the time they reached the beach and she was thinking about the best spot for her and Stevie to lay out their towels. She glanced to the left, towards the horizon and that was when she noticed the low rolling clouds of mist advancing towards her.

Anyone who had been on the beach earlier would have seen the sea fret approaching. The children would have needed no persuasion to leave their sandcastles. As the sun became covered by the thick haze, so too the warmth would have been replaced with a chill.

As she progressed, the mist thickened. It was as though a giant walrus was lumbering across the water and up over the beach, removing all colours from the sea, the sky, transforming everything to grey. She was being swallowed by a force that obliterated all her senses. Gone were the familiar smells, the

18

tang of salt, the mustiness of seaweed, almost ubiquitous on this stretch of coast. She had stopped singing minutes earlier, but now Stevie stopped humming too. Despite the car windows being open, the repetitive movement of the seawater on shingle had been silenced. It was as if she had lost her hearing.

The sticky perspiration she felt on her face earlier as she passed the ice-cream van, was replaced by a cold chill of sweat. Her pulse was racing. She slowed the car, turning on the wipers, hoping it might help her see ahead more clearly. She sat forward, her fingers gripping the steering wheel, her face pressed close to the windscreen. The mist was at its most dense here, swirling past the car as she advanced as carefully as possible. It was like driving through clouds. It made the place seem eerie, as though mystical creatures might emerge from the sea to engulf them.

Christina knew from the curve in the road that she was close to the railway crossing, although now she could see barely ten feet in front of her. There was nowhere to turn the car here. She must keep moving forward. At the same time she was preparing herself for Stevie's outburst when he realised there would be no swimming today after all.

She remembered from previous visits to this favourite spot that to the right of the single lane track, and maybe fifty yards before the crossing, was a solitary cottage. A few weeks earlier an old caravan had turned up, remaining there on the beach, directly opposite the cottage. Now, in the murky light, she could detect little, except for vague outlines, shapes in the mist. As the Mini crept forward Christina felt increasingly disorientated. It was as if she was in a foreign land.

Suddenly she saw something ahead of her on the ground. Braking, she brought the car to a complete stop. She peered through the windscreen, trying desperately to focus.

She turned to her nephew. 'I'm going to stop the car here. But I don't want you to move. Do you understand, Stevie? It's important you stay in the car.' Hearing the urgency in her voice made her heart beat faster still.

The child nodded, sensing a change to the mood of the afternoon.

Then Christina got out of the safety of the car and walked towards the motionless form that was lying partly on the road and partly on the edge of the shingle. A teenage boy, his body twisted, misshapen. And blood, so much blood.

CHAPTER 4
Sunday, 5th July
Afternoon

At 5pm on Sunday afternoon, Rose Walker sat at the kitchen table to have her tea. Two slices of bread, with Shippam's fish paste spread between them, the sandwich cut neatly into four. Rose had never been a big eater. Some days she had to force herself to eat all four quarters. She couldn't bear to have leftovers in the fridge and she never threw food away. She remembered a time when there was little enough to eat. There were mornings, as a child, when she'd woken with hunger gripping her stomach and bedtimes when she tossed and turned, dreaming of cake and biscuits.

Alongside her sandwich she had a pot of tea, large enough for two cups. She left the leaves stewing for exactly five minutes. She wasn't one for weak or milky tea and sugar only spoiled a brew. She liked to taste the sharp tang of tannin.

After the brief visit from the two boys earlier that day, Rose spent the afternoon reading. It was the third time she'd read *The Lion, the Witch and the Wardrobe*, the third time she'd worked her way through all of *The Chronicles of Narnia*. Each time she turned the pages she discovered more layers to the stories. Sometimes the land of *Narnia* filled her imagination. It was as though she'd visited it in person. A place where a wicked witch enslaved people, where people waited to be set free.

She wished the boys had stayed longer. She could have had a conversation with them about the books. One of the boys - George - the boy who followed her into the kitchen, had a gentleness about him. She could imagine him understanding the themes of the *Narnia* books, perhaps he'd also read them. The thought made her smile. It was more likely that he would choose *The Lord of the Flies* or something of that ilk; stories where danger and violence lurked. Images flashed through her mind. She tried to shake them away.

Too much time to think. If it wasn't a Sunday she could launch into her housework routine. But Sunday was a day of rest, a holiday. She rolled the word around, saying it aloud slowly. Holy day, holiday. She enjoyed thinking about words and how they gained their meanings. She read all the time now and yet when she was at school the other children laughed at her, called her a dunce. She wanted to tell them she knew the answers to all the questions the teachers asked, but was too scared to raise her hand. She was always trying to merge into any crowd unnoticed, but being so tall made it difficult. There had only ever been one person who understood.

Having finished her sandwich and tea, she cleared away the dishes and wiped down the wooden kitchen table. She'd taken her Sunday apron off before sitting down to her meal, but before doing the washing-up she put it back on again, tying it around her waist in a double bow.

By 5.20pm her chores were complete. She went into the front room, anticipating the arrival of the next train. It was one of the trains that remained unchanged on the Sunday timetable and was due into Eastbourne at 6.05pm.

She stood at the window and edged the net curtain to one side for a clearer view. But a sea fret bleached everything outside, removing all the colours. It was as if she was still looking through the net. She pressed her face against the window, removing her spectacles, then putting them on again. She'd got used to wearing them all the time, even though the optician had told her she hardly needed them. It was the constant headaches that led her to visit the optician. He told her that her eyesight was good. Nevertheless, the spectacles made her feel protected, a shield from the outside world.

Something caught her eye and as she looked to the left she

saw a car moving slowly along Beach Walk towards the cottage. Despite only being able to see vague shapes in the mist, she was certain she wasn't imagining it. Then, as the car was a few yards away, it stopped. Moments later she saw a woman get out of the car. The mist was too dense for Rose to see the woman's face. She continued to watch, transfixed, as though watching a film in slow motion.

The woman moved forward, towards a bundle on the ground. On reaching the bundle the woman seemed distressed, her hands raised up and then down. Her movements juddering, uncontrolled. Rose couldn't hear any sound, but she was certain the woman was shouting.

Then Rose watched in horror as the woman pushed open the gate and ran up the front path. Rose was seized by a sense of panic. The woman was approaching the front door and Rose saw her face more clearly. She'd seen the woman before. She often came to the beach at the weekend, accompanied by a little boy. They sat beside one of the groynes, the woman reading, while the boy collected shells in a bucket. Rose had spoken to the boy on one occasion. She always carried a sweet or two in her apron pocket and one morning Rose had been out in the front garden and the boy had run up her front path. Rose had said, 'Hello', but then the woman had called him. Rose hadn't liked the way the woman grabbed the boy's hand and dragged him away. Perhaps now the woman was coming to berate her for talking to the child. She meant no harm, but there were rules. Children were warned not to speak to strangers. She heard them talk about it on the wireless.

Rose had seconds to decide what to do. She thought about hiding out the back. She had done that a few days earlier when there was a loud banging on the front door and a voice she recognised. Somehow he'd tracked her down, she didn't know how. On that occasion she'd stayed crouching in the kitchen, underneath the kitchen table until long after the banging and shouting had stopped. She was terrified to emerge in case he was still there, waiting. The whole experience reminded her of days during the war when the sirens went off and there was no time to reach a shelter. Of course now she realised how pointless that had been, hiding underneath a table to avoid the bombs. If there was a direct hit, your house would fall around you and a kitchen table would form little or no protection. On the contrary, it would more than likely create a trap, a kind of makeshift coffin.

There was no more time to hide. The woman was banging and banging on her front door. She must have seen Rose at the front room window. Rose had been brave before, she'd discovered a strength inside herself. She could summon it up again now, giving her the courage to open the door. She stood tall, taking a deep breath, then slowed her approach, sliding her slippers along the hall carpet, preparing her defence. She would explain that she only wanted to give the child a sweet, surely there was no harm in that. Perhaps the child was waiting in the car. She could ask them both in for a drink and a biscuit. She wondered if he'd had his tea, he would be hungry. Perhaps she could offer him a sandwich.

Rose slid the chain across, opening the door a couple of inches. She saw the woman's face was pale, drained of blood. Something was very wrong, and now Rose realised it must be to do with the bundle that was lying on the ground, yards from her front door.

'Please, you must come. I need help.' The woman had her arms outstretched in a plea to Rose. 'Dial 999. Do it now and then come and help me. There's a boy, he's been badly hurt, I think he might be dead.'

CHAPTER 5
Sunday, 5th July
Afternoon

Christina didn't wait at the cottage. She left the woman standing at the front door, still gaping at her. She had asked the woman to dial 999, but it was as if the woman was frozen, unable to move or react.

Christina ran back to the boy and knelt beside him. He was lying on his left side, his leg twisted at a strange angle, a tear in the right leg of his jeans. Blood seeped from a gash at the back of his head, his thick hair was matted with it, the collar of his tee-shirt patched with dark red. The blood stained the tarmac beneath him. His eyes were closed, but there was tension in his face. This was no peaceful slumber.

She crouched down, careful where she put her hands as there were pieces of broken glass close to the body. She put her face close to his mouth, praying she would feel his breath, however shallow. She stared at his chest, willing it to rise and fall, to show any sign of life. If she touched him, it could make matters worse.

She couldn't think straight. The woman in the cottage must have phoned for an ambulance by now. How long before they arrived?

She let her gaze move away from the boy for a moment to take in the scene around her. The mist was still heavy, but she could make out the shape of a bicycle, lying on its side a few yards away, almost underneath the barrier to the crossing. Perhaps the boy had been cycling and had fallen. A fall could explain the tear in his jeans, but not all the blood. If he'd been cycling at breakneck speed down a steep hill, then perhaps... But at this point on Beach Walk there was nothing to cause him to be thrown from his bike, no stones or other obstacles in his way. Plus, being so close to the railway crossing, surely he would have been slowing at this point.

She looked down at the boy's body again. His eyes remained closed. There was no movement. Perhaps he was unconscious.

As she studied the boy's face she had an idea she had seen him before, here at the beach. He was maybe thirteen or fourteen, angry red pimples on his forehead, dark brown hair cut short around his ears, and what looked like a quiff, now flattened and tangled. She touched his hair, but drew back her hand in horror as she felt the coldness of the blood that now stained her fingers.

If she had arrived moments earlier, she could have done more to help him. Maybe even intervened to prevent the accident - if it was an accident. *If only she had responded sooner to her nephew's pleading.*

Stevie. Thank God he'd paid heed to her for once and had stayed in the car. She was torn between staying with the boy until the ambulance arrived and going to check on her nephew. If Stevie had seen the boy's body, or if he'd seen her running to the cottage, he would know something was wrong. He would be scared.

She ran back to the car and got into the back beside Stevie, pulling him towards her and holding him close. He wriggled free of her and pointed down at his feet. 'My sandal's come off and I can't get it back on again.'

She started to laugh and then within moments the laughter turned to sobbing. It was the shock, but now she was scaring Stevie, whose bottom lip was trembling.

'What's the matter, Auntie? Have you hurt yourself?'

She stared at the blood that stained her right hand, the blood of someone who may have lost his life. She pulled Stevie close again, and as she did she heard the screeching sound of a train braking. Then moments later an ambulance sped past her, pulling up beside the body, the sirens blaring, followed by a police car. There were voices.

'Can we go and see the police car, Auntie?' Stevie's expression was hopeful. Here was the opportunity for adventure.

Christina shook her head, holding tight to Stevie's hand. She peered through the front windscreen and realised that within the last few minutes the sea mist was beginning to lift. She could see the train, stationary at the railway crossing.

She watched the ambulancemen move the boy's body to a stretcher. Two uniformed policemen spoke to the driver of the ambulance before waving him off. Then one of the policemen approached her car, signalling to her to step out.

'Are you alright, madam?' he said.

'Is he dead?' It was all she could think of, all she feared.

'He's on his way to hospital. Did you see what happened?'

She shook her head.

'We will need a statement from you as soon as ...' He stopped speaking, and it was only then she realised he hadn't given her an answer. She didn't know if the boy was alive or dead.

He moved away from her car, back to join his colleague, and she watched while they both paced the ground, inspecting the scene.

She got back into the car, this time into the driver's seat. Moments later another man was beside the car, tapping on the side window.

'Christina. Are you alright?'

For a moment she thought she was imagining things, the shock playing tricks with her mind. The face at the window was familiar. She'd seen photos and remembered his visit years earlier.

'Who's that?' Stevie said, trying to open the car door. Instead, the man opened the door and lifted Stevie into his arms.

'And you must be Stevie.' His voice was thick with an accent, an accent Christina was familiar with, although her father had almost lost his completely.

'*Zio* Giuseppe,' she said, feeling again that she wanted to cry, but aware her nephew was watching her every expression. 'I don't understand. What are you doing here?'

'I was on the train. I saw the...' He stopped speaking, conscious the child was listening. 'The guard asked us to stay on the train, but I decided to investigate.'

The beginnings of a smile crossed his face, and Christina's breathing returned to normal. It was only then she realised she'd been clenching her teeth so tightly her jaw ached.

'How do you know my name?' Stevie said, happy to be in the arms of this foreign giant who looked a little like his Granddad Mario.

'*Andiamo a casa.* We must get you home,' Giuseppe said, putting Stevie down and coaxing him back into the car.

'I don't think I can drive.' Christina looked down at her hands. It was as if they no longer belonged to her.

'I will drive,' Giuseppe said, ushering Christina into the passenger seat. He tried to push the driver's seat back as far as possible to give his legs more room, but still his knees almost touched the steering wheel.

'Are you sure?' Christina watched as he tried to squash his tall frame into her Mini, the top of his head brushing against the roof of the car.

'I will drive and you tell me left and right. It will be your roundabouts that will confuse me.'

'I know the way,' Stevie announced from the back seat.

Giuseppe reversed the car and began to pull away, when

one of the policeman appeared at the window. 'Don't forget we'll need your statements, sir, madam.'

'My niece has had a shock. She will give you your statement later. Tomorrow.'

He didn't wait for a response, but drove away. On one occasion during the journey home Giuseppe forgot which side of the road he should be driving on. Several times drivers blasted their car horns at him. He ignored them all.

The adults travelled in silence, accompanied by Stevie's humming. Then, as Giuseppe pulled up in front of the café, Christina remembered what was missing. 'Your luggage. Where is it?'

'On the train. I will fetch it later from the station. Or tomorrow perhaps. Tonight I will wear your *papà's* pyjamas.'

Giuseppe pulled up outside the café and Christina watched her dad come out to greet his cousin, while she remained motionless inside the car. It was as if she was frozen to the seat, her hands clammy, her lips dry. She was barely aware of her mum coming out to take Stevie inside, of the explanation Giuseppe must have given to her parents about the events of the last hour. It was Giuseppe who opened the car door and encouraged her to move. The café had closed at 5pm, so there were no customers to avoid, no false smiles to conjure up. All Christina wanted to do was to escape to her bedroom, close her eyes and try to blot out the image of the teenage boy, lying crumpled on the ground.

Instead, she sat at the table in the back kitchen and let her mum push a cup of hot, sweet tea into her hand. Stevie had been told to play in the garden for a while.

Giuseppe took the lead, explaining what was known and what was yet to be confirmed. All the while Christina struggled to force her hands to stop shaking for long enough to take a sip of tea.

'Do you think the train driver saw anything?' Mario was trying to grasp the details. 'He will have been going slow there, heading into Norman's Bay. And what about the other passengers? Giuseppe, you can't have been the only one to get off the train?'

'The guard told everyone to stay on the train,' Giuseppe said. 'People do not like to get involved. They want to get home to their family.'

'Do we know the boy?' Anne asked Christina.

'I think I've seen him, but I can't be certain. It was difficult to see his face properly...' Christina covered her face with her hands. 'Oh, God, his poor family. Imagine if it had been Stevie.'

Giuseppe stood and put his hand on her shoulder. 'The police will take care of everything. You must not worry.'

'Did no one help you? There must have been someone nearby. Isn't there a cottage there near the crossing?' Mario said.

Christina heard the anxiety in his voice, anger almost, that his daughter had had to cope with such a dreadful event on her own.

'She called the police. I banged on her door and told her.'

'Isn't she the one you mentioned before? The one who tried to give Stevie a sweet that time?' Mario said.

'She's probably just lonely, poor woman,' Anne said. There was an undercurrent, something unpleasant that no one was voicing. 'Try not to think about it now. It's best we get Stevie in and give him his tea.'

CHAPTER 6
Monday, 6th July
Morning

A strange bed, muddled thoughts, and an insufficient number of blankets, all led to a broken night for Giuseppe. Mario's alarm started its repetitive buzzing at 5.30am, reverberating through the walls into Giuseppe's room. He heard Anne pad through to the bathroom, and minutes later he listened to her slippered feet moving through to the kitchen, while Mario took over the bathroom for shaving and washing.

By the time the kettle was whistling, alerting the Rossi household to the start of the day, the movements in the room across the corridor from Giuseppe confirmed that Stevie was awake. He'd been given strict instructions the previous evening that he should not disturb his Uncle Giuseppe, and for that Giuseppe was grateful. After everything that had happened the day before; a tiring journey ending with the discovery of a dead body, Giuseppe's sleep had been fitful.

In the early hours he'd heard a vehicle passing in front of the café. It moved slowly, stopping for a few minutes before moving on. There was a sound of rattling, the clink of glass on glass. At first he thought of the rubbish lorries that passed in front of his flat in Rome. Lorries that provided his alarm call every morning, followed by the road sweeper who washed and swept the road. But Giuseppe was in Bexhill, not Rome. Here the milk was delivered in bottles, and with a busy day ahead for the café it was likely a crate of milk had been deposited on the front doorstep.

Giuseppe dozed for a while after the milk delivery, only to wake again when his cousin's alarm sounded. There was no rush for Giuseppe to rise, yet each time he closed his eyes they sprung open again. The images of the boy's body were on a repeat loop, merging in his mind with the image of another dead boy, another place, another time. A case left unsolved. But this wasn't a new case, not for him. He was retired; he was in England and the responsibility to find the killer was not his. In the end it was a relief to throw back the bedcovers and get up. He never spent long in the bathroom, he'd always considered it an annoying necessity of life that one had to wash and shave every morning. Once he'd tried to do a rough calculation of the number of hours in a lifetime spent brushing teeth and bathing. He'd abandoned the idea before reaching a definite figure, but he was certain it ran to hundreds of days.

It was his decision to retire and yet losing the daily work routine left him empty. The edges of his world that created structure had been erased. Everything was floating, untethered. In truth, those feelings hadn't only started when he retired. It was when Rosalia left that his life began to unravel.

From the first days of their marriage she prepared breakfast for him. Warm milk, with enough coffee to give it the colour of honeycomb. She laid out *biscotti*, which he dunked into the milky liquid. As soon as the end of the little, oval-shaped biscuit softened, the sweet smell of pine nuts and almonds floated up towards him, smells he associated with home, with family. Then he lifted the starched white napkin to his lips and wiped around his mouth and chin, before refolding it and laying it back down onto the tablecloth.

Early morning routines were what Giuseppe tried to hold on to when Rosalia walked away from their marriage. With his wife gone he feared he would tumble into an abyss. If things were still in place then nothing had changed, even though everything had altered in such a significant way, at times it made him double up with the pain of it. Within days he realised he needed to establish a new routine, only then could he take the first steps towards a different life. The new pattern of his morning was to wash, shave, dress and walk to the small bar on the corner of his road, two blocks away from home. The moment he appeared in the doorway, the bar owner, Franco, began to prepare an espresso for him, half filling the tiny cup with liquid nectar. This short, sharp start to his day gave Giuseppe an edge. The comfort of warm milk and *biscotti* belonged to a different part of his life, one he must leave behind and forget.

Now, sitting in the kitchen, above his cousin's café, gazing out onto a drab English sky, he wondered, not for the first time, what the future might hold for him. Glancing across the breakfast table at all that Anne had set out for him did nothing to lift his mood. He'd never been able to tolerate English tea, even without milk. The alternative of instant coffee was no better. Then there was the insipid, white sliced bread, which had as little resemblance to real bread as tins of spaghetti had to Italian pasta.

Odours remaining from the previous night's supper lingered in the air. His cousin had created something resembling lasagne, but nothing tasted as it should. Of course, it was impossible to recreate the vibrant flavour of fresh basil and oregano when using dried herbs. Thankfully, the liberal covering of *parmigiano* that Giuseppe had brought from Roma added much-needed authenticity. He wished now he had brought a larger piece, enough to last him for... *how long?*

He pushed his unused tea plate away and moved to the sink to pour himself a glass of water. As he let the cold water run through his fingers, he shook his head.

'Even the water,' he said aloud to an empty room. For a few moments he was seized by a longing for the icy spring water that trickled down from the Seven Hills of Rome, feeding into the many drinking water fountains that appeared on every street corner.

It was less than twenty-four hours since his arrival in Bexhill and already he wished he had never come.

He could hear the early morning customers in the café below; Anne's quiet tones, welcoming each of them and Mario's occasional laughter as a joke was exchanged.

His cousin had opened *Bella Café* some eighteen years earlier, shortly after travelling to England with his wife and their two daughters. There was no doubt in Giuseppe's mind that since then his cousin had become more English than Italian, leaving behind his roots, transferring his allegiances. It rankled with Giuseppe, perhaps more than it should. After all, he was not his cousin's keeper.

The four-bedroomed flat above the café was home to the Rossi family. The shop and flat combined had been converted from a large Edwardian house, centrally positioned on Bexhill seafront. To the left of the café was a newsagent's, to the right a cobblers. Beyond the row of shops was a double-fronted house run as a bed-and-breakfast during the summer months. The exterior of all the buildings was drab, with little to distinguish the café and shops from the bed-and-breakfast, except for the large picture windows and the painted signs above each of the front doors. But once inside the café Giuseppe could see that Mario had poured all his energies into creating a warm, inviting space for his customers. Red and white checked plastic cloths covered the tables, leafy green spider plants hung from baskets either side of the door. To reinforce the Italian theme of red, white, and green, a string of miniature Italian flags hung above the counter and framed prints covered the walls, brightly coloured scenes of beaches and landscapes.

By contrast, the flat above was dull, almost soulless, with little by way of colour among the furnishings and decoration.

34

Although the sitting room was large enough to include a family-sized dining table, it appeared to be used more as an office. There were a couple of box files sat on the table, next to a tall metal spike, half filled with a stack of invoices. Above the dining table was a serving hatch leading onto the kitchen. Giuseppe remembered from his previous visit that the family spent little time in the flat, and rarely used the kitchen, with many of their meals grabbed in haste in the downstairs back kitchen.

Giuseppe cleared away his few breakfast things and went downstairs to join Mario and Anne in the café. Anne was serving an elderly man who was more intent in chatting to another customer at a neighbouring table, than in deciding what he wanted for breakfast.

'How is Christina this morning?' Giuseppe asked.

'She's already gone to work. I tried to stop her. I don't think she's slept at all, poor lass. She'll be propping her eyes open with matchsticks before the day is out.'

Anne turned back to face the elderly man who was pointing at a plate of teacakes.

'One of those, Mr Selmon? And a pot of tea? You sit down and I'll bring it over for you.'

Mr Selmon seemed content enough, moving away from the counter, sitting next to his friend to continue their conversation.

'Were you able to sleep, Giuseppe? I thought you'd have a bit more space in Flavia's old room, but it's at the front so it can be noisier, especially early mornings.' Anne said. 'Stevie sleeps in the little box room you were in last time you came and to be honest I couldn't face the thought of moving all his toys and whatnot.'

'Anne, please don't worry. *Sto bene*, I am fine. I just need to speak to Mario for a moment.'

'He was so looking forward to your arrival. We both were.' She wiped her hands down her apron and then brushed away a loose curl that had fallen forward onto the side of her face, but in doing so she smudged her cheek with a few crumbs from the tea cake she had just served.

'There will be time for us to talk together. When you are not so busy with the café and when I have done what I can.'

'If you mean to do with that poor boy, I don't think there's anything anyone can do. Christina phoned the hospital before she went to work but they told her nothing, which is right, of course. It's not like she's related to the lad.'

Giuseppe studied Anne's face. Should he tell her what he was certain of? When the ambulance left Beach Walk on Sunday evening, there were no sirens. There was no rush to reach the hospital, to try to save a life. The life had already been lost.

'I don't think the news will be good,' he said, dipping his head as a sign of reverence.

Mario was happy to lend Giuseppe his car, on the promise he would drive cautiously.

'This is not Roma. People drive more slowly, they consider others,' Mario said.

'Your car will be returned unharmed,' The merest smile crossed Giuseppe's face. 'I am a policeman. I know the rules of the road.'

'You are a retired detective and you are Italian. Two things certain to make you more of a liability than an asset in circumstances such as these,' were Mario's closing remarks.

Mario gave him directions to Eastbourne station, where he had a brief exchange with the railwayman looking after the left luggage depot, resulting in several minutes of confusion.

'You left your luggage with us, sir? Then you should have a

ticket.'

'I have no ticket. My luggage was on the train. I got off. My luggage did not.'

Eventually, the railwayman called a colleague to assist and between them the luggage was tracked down and returned to its owner, leaving Giuseppe free to retrace his route to Beach Walk.

It was a little after 10am by the time he left Eastbourne Station, so the worst of the Monday morning traffic had abated. There was no need for speed, nevertheless Mario's car felt sluggish. Giuseppe tried to recall the car his cousin had ten years earlier, on his last visit to Bexhill. Surely not the same car? But the same model perhaps. A Hillman Imp. A poor comparison with Giuseppe's bright red Lancia, left parked outside his Rome flat.

Before he could stop it, the image of that scene, in the road below his flat, pressed itself uncomfortably into his mind. A boy's body lying on the road below his balcony. *His balcony.* An 'accident' was the official word from the coroner. Despite the verdict, he asked one of his colleagues to look into it - because he couldn't. Too close to home, on so many counts. But nothing of use emerged, meaning he'd walked away from an unsolved case. The only one he'd never brought to a successful conclusion. There were times back then when he didn't think he could continue. It wasn't just his life as a policeman he doubted, it was everything. The whole sorry mess was the reason he chose to retire. He was only fifty-five. His life as a detective could have continued, but no. For months, when he closed his eyes at night, all he saw was the blood-stained road, the boy's body being carried away. Now, when he closed his eyes, he would have the image of another boy's body pressing into his brain. He'd come to England to escape his demons, to take a fresh look at life. Instead he was going to be dogged by the same view – of death.

He tried to shake away the negative thoughts as he regained his focus. *Return to the scene of the crime, again and again, until it gives up its hidden clues.* That had been his mantra throughout his working life. He drove slowly towards a temporary barrier mounted across the turning to Beach Walk.

POLICE - ACCIDENT - ROAD CLOSED

He pulled the car up onto the grass verge that separated the main road from the beginning of the single track road. This morning the beach was deserted, either because of the police signs, or the blustery weather, or both. There were no voices, no traffic, just the crashing of the waves stirred up by the wind and the call of the seagulls overhead as they swooped and dived.

The walk from where he'd parked the car to within sight of the railway crossing was a little over fifteen minutes. Time to think. He pulled his jacket collar up, wishing he'd added a pullover over his shirt. He would need time to acclimatise to the weather. If he was home now, it would be six or seven degrees warmer, maybe more. The summers in Rome lasted well into October, with even winter days offering blue skies and temperatures warm enough to sit outside his favourite bar and enjoy a glass of wine.

The first part of the walk took him past several beach huts, then there was a clear stretch with wooden groynes dividing the shingle that shelved quite steeply in places, down towards the shoreline.

As he reached the unmanned railway crossing, he saw another sign nailed to a post on one side of the road.

ACCIDENT - SUNDAY 5TH JULY
WILL ANYONE WITH INFORMATION PLEASE
CONTACT
EASTBOURNE POLICE ON 777555

Coincidences. Giuseppe didn't believe in them. And yet... he had been on the train that pulled to a standstill within yards of the boy's body. Then, when he left the train with its fretting passengers, he had found Christina sitting in her car, shocked and shaking. Now he was back at the scene he could gain a clearer picture of what may have occurred. He tried to remember what he'd been able to see from the train window, annoyingly it was very little. He'd been in the last carriage of a twelve-car train.

The walk from the car to the site of the incident had been easy, but as he stood near to the railway crossing, he found himself a little breathless. He would put it down to the English climate. Even on warm days, the skies pressed down on him. He took a notebook from his jacket pocket and drew a plan of the scene. A sudden shout startled him, making him drop his pencil.

'You can't be here, you'll need to move along. This is a crime scene.' A young police officer ran over; his face flushed as he spoke. 'Didn't you see the signs? There's been an accident. The road is closed.'

'To cars. I am on foot, as you can see.' Giuseppe was used to taking charge. People deferred to him without him having to say or do very much to ensure it happened. 'I'm assisting my colleague, she is with the *Eastbourne Herald*, helping with your enquiries.' It was a truth of sorts.

'I suppose if you're with the newspaper then it should be fine. But maybe I'd better radio it in, just to check.'

'No need. I am going now. *Grazie.*'

'Well, be careful where you walk.'

Looking ahead of him Giuseppe remembered Christina's detailed description of the position of the boy's body, his head and upper body lying on the road, his legs just on the edge of the shingle, almost as if his teenage form had been chopped in two.

She had mentioned seeing a bicycle lying within a couple of feet of the boy's body, close to the edge of the railway track and the crossing. The police would have removed it, along with any other evidence. Evidence that Giuseppe would not be permitted to see because he was not involved.

This isn't my case. This would have to be his new mantra. No more cases for him. His expertise as a detective was no longer required. Nevertheless, his gaze skirted the ground around his feet. He'd developed a forensic eye in his thirty years with the police force, twenty-five as a detective. Hundreds of cases, thousands of visits to scenes of crimes, looking again and again, willing the surroundings to give him answers, or at least offer him possibilities.

On the tarmac a dark patch signalled where the boy's head had laid, the dried blood discolouring the grey road surface. Clouds had shaded the sun since his arrival, but now a few rays appeared, sufficient to throw light onto something on the ground, in among the pebbles. At first Giuseppe thought it was nothing but a reflection, a broken seashell perhaps. He grumbled as he crouched down low, his body stiffening. He knew enough not to touch before he had looked. Touch affected evidence, creating conflicting fingerprints, losing the accurate positioning of clues that might reveal useful information about the sequence of events. He couldn't kneel, the discomfort of the stones would be unbearable, but in a squat position he was close enough to see it wasn't seashells that caught the sunlight, but coloured glass. *No, not glass, coloured plastic.* He took a handkerchief from his pocket and picked up one of the plastic pieces to study it more closely. The red plastic piece had ridges running across it. Glancing around the immediate area he noticed other smaller pieces of the same red plastic, fragments, all lying within a few inches of the jagged piece he'd picked up. He wrapped it in his handkerchief and slipped into his jacket pocket.

Easing himself to standing, he moved from the edge of the shingle. Despite the sea fret that had moved in during the previous afternoon, the evening and night had been dry. He knew moisture could affect a crime scene. Rain, even drizzle or early morning dew could hamper attempts to gather evidence. But also it could be helpful. A wet footprint could provide valuable information. The type and size of shoe, the location of the print in relation to the victim. Now, as Giuseppe looked around the immediate area, he could see no footprints, at least none that appeared significant. Policemen would have walked across the area, ambulancemen too, when they moved the boy's body. There was no indication as to who might have been with the boy moments before his death. For now, all he could focus on was the piece of red plastic in his pocket. Perhaps in time it would offer up its story.

CHAPTER 7
Monday, 6th July
Afternoon

The clock on the Queen Victoria Memorial chimed 12 noon while Giuseppe stood on the pavement in front of the café, watching. Passers-by may have thought he was undertaking a traffic survey, or some kind of population census. His eyes rested briefly on each person, each car. His physical presence was there on Bexhill seafront, but his thoughts were elsewhere. Not static like his body, but constantly flitting, testing out theories he'd been working through since the night before, unravelling each one before mentally tossing it aside. If Giuseppe was still a policeman, working his usual patch in central Rome, supported by his team, he would be certain of his next steps. At this stage of an investigation everyone was a potential suspect, no one could be ruled out; friends, neighbours, even family. Vital too to consider every possible motive. Although it was difficult to imagine what reason anyone could have for killing a fourteen-year-old boy.

He shook away the dark thoughts, looking across the road to see Christina parking a few yards away.

'Your editor has sent you home?' he asked.

She approached him before replying and when she spoke her voice was monotone, as if she was too tired to form the words.

'I'm in the wrong job,' she said.

Giuseppe didn't reply. He guessed the problem without her needing to explain. An investigative journalist is expected to investigate, gather the back story, ferret out the juicy details that will entice readers to buy the paper. Less than twenty-four hours earlier, Christina had seen a dead body. Probably her first dead body. She would have no appetite for what must come next.

'Your editor wants you to visit the family?'

She nodded. 'I got into the office this morning and was greeted with a hand-clapping of congratulations. All Charles could say was how brilliant it was that I was "*on the spot*". And he doesn't just want the story, he wants it now. "*Get what you can, but I need it in good time for this week's edition.*" How can he even think about deadlines when a boy is dead? I tell you, it turns my stomach.'

'I will come with you.' Giuseppe nodded towards the car, an implicit instruction that they should go immediately. He could see the conflicting emotions flit across her face. She was a professional, she knew what was expected of her, but she was young and fearful. He'd been young and fearful once. It seemed like a lifetime ago.

'The last time I was here you were just thirteen, your hair was long, always tied in a ponytail. Now you have your own style, the word is *chic*, I think. You have discovered your voice, your confidence.'

'You're right, I wasn't certain of anything back then. But with all that's happened in the last ten years I'm not sure I'm confident, even now.'

'Your sister?'

'Do you remember how she was? She hasn't really changed in ten years, it's more that her misdemeanours have become more dramatic.'

'Misdemeanours?' Giuseppe struggled to pronounce the word.

'Behaviour, criminal behaviour mostly.'

Giuseppe looked askance at Christina, trying to grasp the underlying meaning of her words.

'Not the kind of crimes that might get you locked up,' she continued. 'Although maybe now...' her voice tailed off and she switched on the engine.

'And now there is Stevie,' Giuseppe said.

'Yes, now there's Stevie.'

They travelled in silence for a while until they reached Little Common, a village barely two miles away. Set back from the sea, Little Common had become an extension to Bexhill, rather than a separate village. The central village green of past centuries was now a roundabout, with Sea Road leading from the roundabout directly south, past the golf course and several spacious country houses, and on towards the beach.

'You have found your voice now though,' Giuseppe said, breaking the silence.

'Perhaps.'

'A journalist is in a good place to make themselves heard.'

'Not if you're a junior and a woman at that. My boss thinks being on hand at the Women's Institute cake competition is about the extent of my reporting ability.'

'But you will prove him wrong.' Giuseppe said it as a statement rather than a question.

'I've been drafting an article. Charles says he'll print it if it's good enough. Although that probably means only if he agrees with it, so the chance of it ever being read by the population of Eastbourne is zero.'

'Something you are passionate about?'

'Yes. I'm looking at the way life is changing for women, or rather, how it needs to change. I've been interviewing local women of all ages over the last few months and I've got some brilliant quotes. The more argumentative interviewees among them are happy to put their name to their opinions, but most want to remain anonymous. There are too many women scared to speak out, to say how they really feel about work, married life, motherhood. So much for freedom of speech. What's the point if the people are frightened into silence?'

As she spoke, Giuseppe was reminded of the passion he felt when he first joined the police force. Passion that had never dissipated.

'I would like to read it.'

'I'd love you to read it.' Christina was about to say more when she stopped, her face flushing.

'Are you alright?'

'It's just ... I was so busy with that article, I kept putting Stevie off. If we'd come to the beach earlier, who knows...'

'Stop the car.' Giuseppe's tone was authoritative, but not sharp.

Christina pulled over to the side of the road, switched off the engine and turned to face Giuseppe.

'You were present at the place where a boy lost his life. But you are not responsible. Remember that. Use it.'

'What do you mean?'

'Use it for good. Not to punish yourself for what you did or did not do, but to uncover the truth. That is how you will help the family, the people who are left behind.'

As he spoke, Giuseppe's thoughts were about another death, the one he walked away from, but continued to punish himself for.

Christina turned to Giuseppe. 'I'm so pleased you are here.'

He shifted in his seat and then to defuse the slight awkwardness that had developed between them, he said, 'And when you are a senior reporter, please buy a bigger car.'

'Ha,' Christina laughed, started the engine and pulled away. 'It's taken me a year to save up for this old heap of rust. So, don't hold your breath.'

For a while they travelled in silence, with Giuseppe occasionally tapping on the dashboard of the car, as if he was tapping out a tune.

Then he asked, 'Do you know the family?'

'The boy's identity has been confirmed, his name is George Leigh. Let's just say my editor has a mutually supportive relationship with the local police.'

'Mr and Mrs Leigh have two sons.' Giuseppe watched as Christina brushed one hand across her face, which had flushed, her cheeks a fiery red. She paused before continuing. 'They *had* two sons. George and Paul. It's George who...'

Giuseppe could see she was struggling to continue.

'And you've seen the boys before?'

'When Stevie and I have been to the beach. Weekends mostly. I've never spoken to them though.'

She took a left turn off Sea Road, then right into a cul-de-sac, pulling up in front of a semi-detached brick-built house, set back from the road.

'This is it,' she said, turning off the engine, remaining in the driver's seat, staring out towards the house. Giuseppe was reminded again about the contrasts between his homeland and the place his cousin had chosen, contrasts between the way people lived. In Rome everyone he knew lived in a flat, some squeezing large families into tiny places with only one bedroom. Others with the luxury of grand and spacious apartments, like his own. His policeman's salary had provided him with a comfortable life, or at least a life where material possessions were easily bought. But he'd experienced enough in his life to know the qualities that made living worthwhile couldn't be bought. And the contrasts between the way people lived – the way they formed communities - was not just about houses or flats.

Several men gathered in front of the house, some with cameras.

'Turns out it's not only the *Eastbourne Herald* who has the ear of the local constabulary.' Christina said.

'Reporters?'

'I know some of them by sight, but let's say we're not exactly pals.'

'I will lead,' Giuseppe said. 'Don't speak, just listen. And watch. You may notice something I do not.'

He went to get out of the car before adding, 'And take notes. We will forget. We think we will remember, but there will be a small detail we will forget. *Una piccola cosa.* That will be the important detail, the one to give us answers to questions we had not even thought of.'

Christina locked the car, following Giuseppe towards the house, pushing past the other reporters. One man tried to grab at her arm. 'Hey, we were here first, don't think you can barge your way through.'

She pulled her arm free of him and stood behind Giuseppe as he pressed the doorbell.

'What makes you think they'll even open the door to us? I wouldn't if I was in their shoes,' Christina said.

Within seconds the door was opened by a man in his early forties. He was unshaven, with sandy-coloured hair, and was as broad as Giuseppe was tall.

'*Signor* Leigh?' Giuseppe held out a hand by way of greeting, but the man did not reciprocate, choosing instead to put both hands in his trouser pockets.

'We're not talking to the press.' It was a statement of defiance.

'We are very sorry for your loss,' Giuseppe said. 'I am Giuseppe Bianchi and this is Christina Rossi, the daughter of my cousin. She found your son's body.'

The statement sounded harsh, but Giuseppe knew it would act as a permit to enter.

The man stepped back, waving them into the narrow hallway, and then through to the back of the house to the sitting room, which was north-facing and chilled. The room was simply furnished with an assortment of hard-backed chairs and armchairs, none of them matching, and a two-seater settee that looked like it had seen better days.

As they entered the room, a woman came through behind them, the scent of lavender filling the air. *Not perfume, surely? When your son has died you do not think of such things, do you?* She was shorter than Christina, slim and almost mouse-like in her features and colouring. She didn't speak, looking at her husband as if she was waiting for an introduction.

'My wife, Patricia. I'm Robert.' He pointed to the settee, and Christina and Giuseppe sat, while Mr and Mrs Leigh remained standing.

'I've been to see him,' Robert Leigh said. 'It's not something a parent should ever have to do. Seeing their child like that.' He clenched his fists and looked away towards the window.

His wife looked across at him as he spoke, but her face was blank, her eyes fixed. Then she moved towards one of the armchairs and sat, but her movements were slow, almost laboured. The top button of her cardigan was missing, a strand of cotton marking its place. Her tweed skirt was crumpled, as if she had grabbed it from the ironing pile without a thought.

Giuseppe waited for the questions he felt sure were inevitable. Christina had been there, on Beach Walk, perhaps moments after their son had died. She provided a connection, however elusive. *Surely there were details they would want to know.*

'You've got ten minutes, then I want you to leave,' Robert Leigh said, ignoring his wife's questioning look.

Giuseppe glanced at the wooden clock that stood in the centre of the mantelpiece. It was shaped like a star, six sharp points surrounding the clock face, which showed 12.25. He watched it for a few moments to see if the clock hands moved.

Then Robert Leigh spoke again. 'Do they know how it

happened? It was you who called 999? The police have barely told us anything.' Robert Leigh looked at Christina as she looked away. Her shoulder bag was on the floor beside her and now she dipped her hand inside and pulled out a shorthand notebook and pencil. Giuseppe had asked her to take notes, hoping it might act as a distraction, to reduce the tension he was certain she would be feeling, the devastation of seeing a dead body. The helplessness, the anger and futility at the loss of a young life.

'The police are still discovering. It is too soon to know.' Giuseppe said. 'Christina found your son, but she is also a reporter with the *Eastbourne Herald*. The police have asked for help from the local press. That is why we are here.' He left the statement hanging. It was a white lie, but not so far from the truth.

'It doesn't make any sense.' Patricia Leigh spoke now, her voice flat.

'We haven't slept,' Robert Leigh said. 'We spent the night sitting here, thinking about George.'

Giuseppe stood and moved to the tiled mantelpiece, picking up one of the two framed photos that stood either side of the clock. The photos showed the boys dressed in school uniform, navy blazers, blue and white striped ties. They were both staring directly at the camera.

'*Gemelli*. Twins. That is very special,' he said. *It would compound the pain, wouldn't it? Suddenly half your family gone.*

'They're not twins.' There was a note of defiance in Patricia Leigh's tone.

'But they look identical,' Christina said.

'They were born twelve months apart, to the day. Paul first, then George. Paul won't remember a time when he didn't have his brother.' It was Robert who spoke this time.

As his name was mentioned, so George's brother appeared.

49

The framed photo showed a boy of around eleven or twelve, but Giuseppe guessed Paul was now nearer to fifteen. If he'd had a teenage growth spurt, it had not raised his height beyond that of his parents. There were dark shadows around his chin. Soon he would be experimenting with a razor for the first time. Perhaps he'd already made an abortive attempt, as on the right side of his cheek Giuseppe noticed a scratch, a small area of dried blood.

Paul's shoulders were hunched forward, his head bowed. He didn't look at Giuseppe or Christina, moving past his father who was still standing in front of the fireplace. He went to sit on the arm of his mother's chair, but she nudged him away with her elbow. It seemed to Giuseppe an unnecessarily harsh thing to do and he could sense Christina's discomfort.

Paul pulled over a footstool and squatted down onto it, still avoiding eye contact with anyone in the room.

'Hello Paul.' Christina said with the gentlest of tones. Giuseppe guessed she would be seeing nothing but the image of his brother lying on the ground. He wondered if she would do anything with the pencil that was hovering over a blank page of her notebook. As a detective, one member of his team always accompanied him when questioning the family of a victim, to take notes. But this was not his case, he was not here as a policeman and, despite the instructions from her editor, Christina was not here as a journalist.

'You were out with your brother on Sunday, Paul?' Giuseppe said.

Before Paul answered, Giuseppe noticed Mr Leigh turn to glance at the clock once more. Five minutes gone, five minutes remaining.

'We always cycle along Beach Walk at the weekend. If it's not raining.' Paul said.

'And when you and George cycled along Beach Walk

together, did you ever speak to anyone?'

'You mean the bloke who lives in the caravan?' Paul said, scuffing his heel against the rug.

'What man in a caravan?' Robert Leigh raised his voice.

'It was a few days ago. This fella shouted at us, then the man who lives in the caravan came out - the one that's parked up on the beach.' Paul was looking down as he spoke. His voice little more than a whisper.

'What man? Paul, why haven't you told us about this before?' It was Paul's mother who spoke, fear in her voice and something else. *Bewilderment, confusion?*

Paul stood, kicking away the footstool and moving towards the window. As he spoke his gaze shifted between his mother and his father, as if he was waiting for the reprimand he knew would come.

'Me and George were playing down by the shore,' Paul said, 'throwing pebbles, skimming them to see how far they'd go. There was a fella nearby fishing. Anyway, he started shouting at us, really angry he was, telling us to clear off, said we'd disturb the fish.'

'The man was fishing?' Giuseppe asked.

'Yeah. But we were quite a long way away from him when we threw the stones. We weren't doing any harm.'

'And the man from the caravan came out?' Giuseppe said.

Paul fidgeted, moving from one foot to the other. 'Yeah, he shouted back at the fisherman, told him to leave us alone, said we were just kids having fun. But by then we'd been spooked, so we picked up our bikes and rode off.'

'And the man who was fishing, do you remember what he looked like?' Giuseppe could sense an opportunity, information that could lead to something concrete.

Paul looked away, his shoulders hunched.

'You must remember something about him, think lad.' Mr

Leigh said.

'He was sitting on one of those little camping chairs until the shouting started. Then he stood up and waved his fist at us.'

'What did the fisherman look like?' Giuseppe asked. 'Do you remember the colour of his hair or anything about him?'

'Okay, your ten minutes is up. You need to leave us alone now.' Robert Leigh's instruction that the interview was over.

'We are sorry for the intrusion,' Christina said, relief in her voice, as Robert Leigh walked them to the front door.

This time it was Giuseppe who had his hands in his pockets, as he walked down the front path, away from the house. The fingers of his right hand gingerly moving over the broken piece of red plastic he'd found at the scene. Evidence that would bring him back to the Leigh house; he was certain of it, and yet at the same time he hoped he was wrong.

CHAPTER 8
Monday, 6th July
Afternoon

In just twenty-four hours Rose Walker's life had changed. The strategies she'd put in place to make her feel safe had failed. On Sunday morning she'd welcomed the two teenage boys, then, later in the day after all the terrifying sirens had stopped, and the ambulance had driven off, a policewoman presented herself at Rose's front door.

The policewoman had asked her questions. Rose couldn't answer any of them. She left the policewoman standing on the doorstep. She didn't want her in the house. She explained to the policewoman that she'd seen nothing, just the young woman waving her arms around. Then the young woman told her to phone for help. After making the phone call, she'd watched from her front room window. There were flashing lights, police, ambulancemen. Something dreadful had happened, but if she stepped outside she would be involved. There would be questions she would struggle to answer.

When she spoke to the policewoman Rose felt the need to speak slowly as she sorted through the images in her mind. But speaking like that made her sound simple and she'd noticed people took on a look. Pity more than fear, she didn't want that. She'd made mistakes, been so scared that it was as if the world was spinning out of control. But there had been a time when she'd been brave too.

The policewoman made notes in a little pocketbook and when Rose finished speaking she asked, 'You didn't see anything before the woman knocked on your door?'

Rose explained about the sea mist. If the policewoman was local she would know how the weather could suddenly change. Then the policewoman looked past her as though there was something inside Rose's cottage that might help with her investigations. That was when Rose closed the door.

But now, from her front room window she saw the young woman from yesterday - the woman who had found the boy's broken body - approaching her front door, accompanied by a man. She hadn't seen the man before, but the woman seemed to know him. He was tall, several inches taller than the woman beside him. He held himself in such an upright fashion, making him seem taller still. There was something about his clothes, the way he had his hair, that made her think he was foreign. He reminded her of a film star. Cary Grant, maybe, though this man had thick, wavy hair. In the film posters of Cary Grant his hair always looked so smooth, slicked down, with nothing out of place. She'd never been to the cinema, but had often thought how wonderful it would be. She'd treat herself to a choc-ice and watch Cary Grant and Grace Kelly in *To Catch a Thief,* or *Charade* with Audrey Hepburn. Now she thought about it, the young woman outside her front door wasn't that dissimilar to Audrey Hepburn, an elegant look about her, stylish too. Yes, a trip to the cinema would be like the times when she was transported to another place through the pages of a book, only better, because the images would be there on the screen, as large as life.

In an attempt to regain her equilibrium after the events of Sunday afternoon, Rose had been cleaning. She always started her cleaning schedule with the bathroom and toilet, moving on to the kitchen. She'd almost finished mopping the kitchen floor when Tabitha ran in from the back garden, leaving wet paw prints in her wake. Rose shooed her out with the mop and got a fearsome *miaow* in response. She moved on to the bedrooms, leaving the front room until last. Monday was her cleaning day and regardless of the season, she always opened the front room window as wide as she could. Every week there was so much dust and fluff to pick up. Of course, most of it was Tabitha's. But the last pile of dust kept moving away from her each time she bent to sweep it into the dustpan. She realised the air rushing in from the outside was sending her dust pile into a swirl. She would have to close the window, otherwise the dust would continue to fly away and she'd have to start cleaning all over again. It was when she moved towards the front room window that she saw the man and woman walking up her front path.

The man's skin was deeply tanned, suggesting he'd spent a lifetime in the sunshine. She opened the door before they knocked and when he spoke she knew she was right. He was foreign. French perhaps, or Italian.

'I don't know you,' she said.

'My name is Giuseppe Bianchi and this is my cousin's daughter, Christina Rossi. You met Christina yesterday.'

She focused on the way he pronounced his words but wasn't really taking in what he was saying. Now that he stood in front of her she was able to guess his exact height. Rose finally stopped growing when she was fifteen years old, but by then she'd already reached five feet nine inches. This man was at least three or four inches taller than her.

'And you are?' Although his questioning was forthright, his foreign accent made him somehow seem more friendly.

'Mrs Rose Walker.'

'Christina works for the *Eastbourne Herald*. She is helping the police to investigate the accident that happened here yesterday.'

Rose realised the man was speaking again, raising his voice a touch and speaking slowly. Perhaps he thought she was hard of hearing as he was focusing on her face, almost as though he thought she was lip-reading. 'I am helping Christina with her enquiries.'

'You're French or Italian, but I can't decide which.' The words tumbled out and then Rose blushed. She wasn't usually so forthright.

'I'm Italian, from Roma.'

Rose closed her eyes for a moment. Foreign lands had always fascinated her. She'd read about the Holy Roman Empire, the persecution of the Christians. This man would know all about the Colosseum, the amphitheatre where the lions were set against criminals, fighting to their death.

'What's Rome like?'

'*Molto bello.* Very beautiful. Most of the time blue skies. And excellent coffee.' The beginnings of a smile crossed his face.

He had mentioned coffee. The three of them were still standing in the entrance hall. Perhaps Rose should invite them in, offer them a drink. She had been cleaning, which meant she was wearing her housecoat. She looked down at the duster hanging out of one pocket and her rubber gloves stuffed in the other. Perhaps she should apologise. It wasn't the way to receive visitors.

She opened the door to the front room and gestured for them to sit. Tabitha was spread out on the settee.

'Off with you, Tabitha.' Rose shooed the cat off the settee and then realised the cushions were covered with ginger hairs. The Italian man was wearing a dark blue jacket, the cat's hairs would stick to it. She was certain he wouldn't want that. Although there were creases in the collar of his shirt and a grey smudge on his cream trousers. Perhaps he was not so concerned about his appearance as she had imagined. The woman wore a black and white sleeveless dress, that stopped short, well above her knees. Rose could imagine the woman strolling down a catwalk, cameras clicking, admiring glances from onlookers. The woman's hair was expertly styled, curling around the sides of her face. Rose had never had her hair styled, she wondered what a hairdresser might suggest, how it would change her appearance.

'You helped Christina yesterday. You dialled 999.' The Italian was speaking again. He'd perched on the edge of the settee, such that if he leaned forward any further Rose feared he'd topple over. 'Sadly, the child was already dead when Christina found him. There was nothing anyone could do.'

Rose covered her face with her hands. 'Oh no, please no,' she whispered. She removed her spectacles, holding them in her hand. For several moments she couldn't speak, the words were stuck deep inside her. She hadn't been outside since it happened. She didn't want to see the spot where a boy had lost his life. She didn't want to know any more about it. And yet she was compelled to ask...

'What was the boy's name?'

'George Leigh.' The woman spoke this time. 'He has a brother, Paul. You may have seen them here at the beach. They often cycle this way at the weekend.'

Now Rose was certain she couldn't breathe. She grabbed the arm of her chair and the Italian man stood and moved to her side.

'I will get you a drink of water' he said. 'It is a shock. Something like this to happen in front of your house.'

She took several deep breaths, regaining enough control to speak.

'He was in here with his brother.' She blurted out the words and instantly knew she had made a mistake. She should say nothing. A question here, a loose word there and it would all unravel.

'They came here? To your cottage?' The Italian was speaking again, she wished he would keep speaking because the sound of his voice was soothing. He returned to the settee, perching again on the edge of the seat.

'They were going to have tea and biscuits.' Rose thought again about the boys' visit. She'd been disappointed they hadn't stayed longer. Now one of them was dead.

'Do they often visit you?' The Italian's tone was non-judgemental and yet any answer Rose gave would only lead to more questions.

Giuseppe stood, easing out his back and moving to the window. She watched as he spent a few moments looking towards the caravan parked on the shingle opposite the cottage, yards from where the boy's body was found. Her breathing was returning to normal, the pounding in her heart settling.

Then the Italian turned and moved to the mantelpiece. 'That's a beautiful clock.'

'It was my father's,' Rose said, a reverence in her voice.

'It keeps good time?'

'I check it against the chimes of Big Ben.' Perhaps the Italian had never heard of Big Ben. She had a fleeting thought they could have a conversation about it. She could tell him what she knew of its history, but then he might think she was showing off. It was a stupid idea.

'You will remember what time the boys were here, for their tea and biscuits.' Giuseppe nodded, as though she'd already given him the answer.

'There's no 11am train on a Sunday, but I like to keep to a routine.'

'They were here in the morning?' Christina asked.

Beside the carriage clock stood a silver-framed photo of a young boy in school uniform.

'Your son?' Giuseppe asked.

Rose moved to stand beside Giuseppe, stepping forward, forcing him to step away. She picked up the photo and ran her finger over the picture, tracing the outline of the boy's face.

'He looks like a happy lad. He's at school now, is he?'

Rose put the photo back onto the mantelpiece and tapped the top of the clock. 'I need you to leave now. I have to get myself ready. The children come out prompt at 3.30.'

CHAPTER 9
Monday, 6th July
Afternoon

As they left Rose Walker's cottage, Giuseppe pointed towards Christina's Mini. 'We must visit the police station.'

'They won't want to tell us anything.'

'No, but we must tell them. You were the first person on the scene. I arrived soon after. We must give our statements.' Christina shrugged, getting into the driver's seat and throwing her shoulder bag onto the back seat.

'Do you know anyone at the police station?' Giuseppe was more than aware of his position. The local police would not want him interfering in their case. He was a foreigner in a foreign land. Nevertheless, he was certain this was a crime and one he could help to solve. He'd always brought even the most complex of cases to a successful completion. Except for that last one, the one that continued to give him nightmares.

'I don't know anyone. I've never even been to the police station and to be honest with you, I'd prefer to keep it that way.'

'That is no way for a journalist to talk. You want to be more than a junior reporter, don't you? Here is your opportunity.'

Giuseppe knew he must tread a fine line. Pushing Christina forward may help, but it could also hinder. His own desire to be involved could easily colour his judgement.

Arriving at the police station, they were shown into an interview room by a young police constable. After a few minutes, an older man entered the room. Giuseppe guessed the man was a similar age to him, in his mid-fifties. His hair was flecked with grey, thinning on top. He wore a scruffy tweed jacket, which was unbuttoned, revealing a paunch. His shirt buttons were just about holding together and his tie looked uncomfortably tight around his thick neck.

'Detective Sergeant Pearce,' the man said. 'And you are?'

'Giuseppe Bianchi and Christina Rossi, the daughter of my cousin.' Giuseppe waited for the sergeant to sit before he did the same, gesturing to Christina to sit beside him.

The room was airless, a lingering smell of sweat and cigarette smoke. In the centre of the room was a small wooden table, with four chairs, two on each side of the table. The only item on the table was a full ashtray, until the sergeant laid down the foolscap pad he'd been carrying.

A single light bulb hung over the table. It had no shade, so it cast a glaring light over the centre of the room, while the corners remained in shadow. Giuseppe looked up at the single window, set high up on the left-hand wall. The window was closed and appeared from the grime and cobwebs around it that it had not been open for many months, even years.

'I found George Leigh's body,' Christina said. 'I need to give you my statement.'

The sergeant took a packet of cigarettes and a small lighter from his jacket pocket. He put the cigarette in his mouth, then took it out again as if he'd had second thoughts.

'Been trying to give up for weeks now,' he said, putting the cigarette back into the packet. 'What about you two? Either of you smoke?'

Giuseppe recognised the sergeant's approach. It was something he'd used many times in the past. Encouraging witnesses to relax by engaging in small talk.

'I was also a smoker,' Giuseppe said. 'It is two months now since I stopped, but every day I long for just one. But then, one will turn into many.' He noticed an acknowledgment in the sergeant's expression, acceptance they were now on an equal footing.

'Giuseppe arrived on Sunday, on the train that was

there...just as it happened.' Christina turned away from the detective as she spoke.

'I am a detective.' Giuseppe stepped into the silence. 'At least I was a detective for many years, in Roma. But now I am retired.'

'And you're here on holiday?'

'*Sì*. But I would like to help if I can.'

Sergeant Pearce appeared to ignore Giuseppe's offer. Instead, he slid the pad of paper towards him, took a pen from his inside jacket pocket and waited.

'So, Miss. Can you tell me everything you remember about the events of Sunday afternoon.'

Christina looked at Giuseppe before speaking. He gave her a nod of encouragement.

'I was taking my nephew to the beach.'

'Your nephew?'

'Yes, my sister's child. I...' Christina hesitated.

'Christina helps to care for her sister's child. His mother is working in the north of England.'

'I see.' Sergeant Pearce made some notes, then nodded to Christina to continue.

'Stevie, my nephew, well, he wanted to go to the beach. But by the time we got there the mist had come down. I was planning to turn the car around and that's when I saw him.'

'George Leigh?'

She nodded, looking down at her hands.

'Tell me exactly what you saw.'

As Christina described the position of George Leigh's body the sergeant kept writing.

'And what time was that?'

'Around 5.30. At least we left home about 5pm, so it must have been nearly 5.30 by the time we reached the beach.'

'Then what happened?'

'I left Stevie in the car and ran to the cottage. I asked the woman in the cottage to ring for an ambulance.'

'*Signora* Rose Walker.' Giuseppe said.

Sergeant Pearce stopped writing and looked at Giuseppe. 'You know her?'

Giuseppe shook his head. 'We visited her earlier today.'

'And why would you do that?'

Giuseppe noticed the sergeant's face flushing.

'We also visited the Leigh family, to pay our respects.' Giuseppe guessed what was going through the sergeant's mind. He would be sensing the danger of interference, not just from a reporter who had an advantage of being first on the scene of a crime, but also from a retired detective who may struggle to remain uninvolved.

'I shouldn't need to tell you that interfering in a police investigation is as frowned on here in England as I am sure it is in your country.' Pearce kept his voice low and controlled.

'Italy,' Giuseppe said.

'Well, you are in England now, sir, and I hope I won't need to remind you again that you should stay away from anyone involved in the case.'

'Is it a case?' Giuseppe asked.

The sergeant ignored the question and picked up his pen again.

'And you were also present at the scene yesterday evening?'

'*Sì*, as Christina explained. I was travelling on the train from Hastings to Eastbourne. The train stopped suddenly. I heard emergency sirens. I thought perhaps I could help.'

'You thought you could help.' Giuseppe didn't miss the sarcasm in the sergeant's tone.

'I left the train and walked along the track towards the sirens. Then I saw Christina and Stevie and took them home.'

'You didn't see the body?'

'The ambulancemen were lifting the body into the ambulance when I arrived.'

'I think I've got everything I need for now. Where can I find you, should I need to get in touch?' Sergeant Pearce stood, pushing his chair back and picking up the pad of paper from the table.

'*Bella Café*, Bexhill seafront,' Christina said.

'Good luck with your investigations,' Giuseppe said, holding out his hand towards the sergeant.

CHAPTER 10
Monday, 6th July
Evening

Christina loved her sister. There was a time when she liked her too. But it was so many years ago she could barely remember how it felt.

When they were little Flavia was amusing, making even the most boring of chores in the café seem like fun. If they were asked to help clear the tables on a busy Saturday morning Flavia put on a swagger, sauntering between the tables, telling customers in her poshest voice, 'Thank you so much for coming. Do visit again.'

The customers laughed, thinking her delightful, complimenting her parents on their charming little daughter. What they didn't see were the faces Flavia pulled as soon as the customers left.

Once Flavia reached her teenage years her behaviour became more daring. On several occasions, when the sisters were out together, Flavia suddenly darted across the road just in front of a car, causing the driver to brake or swerve. She'd reach the other side of the road, stand with her hands on her hips and laugh.

'You'll kill yourself or someone else, is that what you want?' Christina shouted.

'So what,' was all she would get by way of reply.

Shoplifting became a regular thing, with Flavia finding endless ways to avoid being caught. It was the same with her smoking and drinking. Being one year older, Christina was weighed down by the sense of responsibility for her wayward sister, always trying to pull her back into line.

Tales filtered back to Anne and Mario. The local police constable made several visits to the café, helpfully waiting until the place was closed to customers, to stop tongues wagging. Each time he came Flavia sat demurely, listened to his warnings, smiled at the reprimands. The next day she continued as before. Nothing changed. If anything the misdemeanours escalated.

And then there was the trouble with Tony.

Tony wasn't the first boy to ask Christina out. She'd had a few dates with other local lads, nothing serious, but each time pushing the boundaries one step further. Her first kiss at the age of fourteen with a chap from the local Dr Barnardo's home felt daring. Afterwards she'd been so embarrassed she'd run off and then spent the next few weeks trying to avoid him.

Christina tried cigarettes too. Having watched Flavia taking long drags and puffing out perfect circles of smoke, she got to thinking it would be fun. Everyone was smoking, it was the thing to do if she wanted to be accepted by the 'in-crowd'. Trouble was the first puff nearly choked her and the coughing fit that followed made her determined never to try it again. Instead she chewed gum. It was almost as good and gained her approval with a group of lads who hung about outside the café on a Saturday.

They called themselves 'Teddy Boys', in their drainpipe trousers and long jackets, with velvet collars. Some wore fancy waistcoats, trading their school uniform for uniform of another kind. The girls who hung around with them had their own fashion, with swirling skirts and long ponytails that swayed and bobbed whenever they danced to their beloved rock and roll.

There had been news reports of gangs of Teddy Boys being involved in riots in London's Notting Hill. But not Tony. He wasn't a leader or a follower. Yes, he loved the fashion, but most of all he loved the music. Their first date was a trip to the record shop where he asked Christina for her opinion on

'*Jail House Rock*', the latest Elvis song to hit the charts. After that they spent Saturday mornings in the record booth at the *Disc Jockey*, listening to Duane Eddy and Buddy Holly. Tony's record collection filled one side of his bedroom, with LPs and singles filed alphabetically by artist. Every time she tested him, trying to catch him out, he'd prove he didn't only know the name of every album, he could cite the title of every track, and the order they appeared.

He told her his plan was to buy his own jukebox one day. She laughed every time he mentioned it. There was barely enough space left in his bedroom for his record player, let alone a juke box. He even tried to persuade Mario to install a juke box in the café.

He was fun, everything she dreamed of in a boyfriend and nothing was going to stop her from hanging on to him. Until Flavia decided to set herself the challenge.

Late one Saturday, when Christina was coming home from a friend's house, she saw Tony and Flavia in the distance. They were sitting on a bench on the seafront, close to *Bella Café*, and they were kissing. When she confronted her sister, Flavia just laughed, saying, 'It's no big deal'. Christina called her sister selfish and spiteful and they had a blazing row.

The next day Tony appeared genuinely surprised when Christina dumped him. Then a week later Flavia bragged about a '*one-night stand*'. A few months after that Christina listened to her sister in the bathroom, retching every morning. She confronted Flavia.

'You're pregnant, aren't you?'

'What's it to you if I am?'

'You'll have to tell Mum. If you don't, then I will.'

In the end, it was Anne who confirmed it to Christina. 'Your sister has gone and got herself in the family way,' she said. 'But we're family and as a family we stick together.'

Christina wasn't certain if her mum was trying to convince herself more than anyone else.

Christina asked her sister outright if Tony could be Stevie's father, but her sister never confirmed it. Maybe she didn't know, or worse still didn't care. Whatever the truth, Tony turned up at the café from time to time and asked to take Stevie out to the playground, or the beach. Stevie idolised him, but there always an awkward atmosphere when Tony visited. As no one knew for certain who Stevie's father was, it was a situation everyone skirted around.

On Monday evening, in a vain attempt at taking her mind off the tragic events of the night before, Christina was up in her bedroom with her transistor radio tuned to the new pirate station. Since *Radio Caroline* had come on air a few months ago, it was the only station she listened to. *'I can't explain'*, came on and made her smile. Tony had told her ages ago *The Who* would make the big time any day soon and it looked as though he was right. She turned up the volume and sat on the edge of her bed, tapping her feet to the rhythm.

A few minutes later there was a knock on her bedroom door.

'Turn your music down and stop tapping.' Her dad shouted through the closed door. 'It's giving your mother a headache.'

She jumped off her bed and opened the door to see her dad heading back downstairs.

'And Tony's downstairs,' he said without turning. 'He's called in to see Stevie, he heard about what happened.'

'It's nothing to do with him.'

'Well, he's here and wants to speak to Stevie?'

'Can't you just tell him to go?'

'Christina love, don't harbour grudges, it's not worth it. It'll end up making you bitter and twisted.'

Before she had a chance to think about her response, Tony's face appeared at the bedroom door.

'You okay?' He looked as though he'd come straight from work, a streak of grease down one of his cheeks. It was all Christina could do not to walk over to him and wipe it off.

Tony worked in a local garage. He'd stayed in the same job since leaving school and he'd told Christina often enough how much he loved it. As a car mechanic he knew how to tinker with engines. So now most of his wages went on making constant improvements to his beloved Lambretta. He'd fine-tune it to make the best sound, putting RedEx in the tank so that a large stream of grey smoke flowed from the engine exhaust.

He'd traded his Teddy Boy clothes for the 'uniform' that all the Mods were wearing. A US Army Parka, bought from the local second-hand army surplus store, dressed up by wearing highly polished black shoes, flared trousers and a gold pin through his shirt collar. Most weekends he joined his mates, riding along the seafront, from Bexhill through to Hastings. There had been trouble in Hastings over the Easter weekend and then again on the May Bank Holiday. Fights broke out between the Mods and the Rockers, with people calling it the 'Second Battle of Hastings'. But, for all his faults, she couldn't imagine Tony punching anyone. In truth, there were so many times she longed to join him, riding pillion, wrapping her arms around his waist and holding tight. She never admitted those longings to a soul, barely acknowledging them even to herself.

'I thought I'd look in on Stevie, see if he's alright. It must have been scary for him. For both of you.' Tony said.

'It's his bedtime.'

Despite herself she led Tony through to her nephew's bedroom. Any chance of keeping the situation calm was lost, as the next moment Stevie threw the bedcovers back and hurled himself at Tony.

'Auntie Christina saw a dead body and I've got a new uncle and he's Italian.' Stevie's words came out in a rush. Attempts to keep the facts of the incident from the youngest member of the family had clearly failed.

'A new uncle, eh? Well, that's great. Just as long as you don't prefer him to me.' Tony picked Stevie up and the child wrapped his arms and legs around him.

'Have you brought me a present?'

'You want me to buy your favours now? Is that it?'

Christina couldn't argue about the connection between Stevie and Tony, but she wasn't happy about it. Tony could be reckless, especially when he'd had one too many beers. She feared for the examples he set her impressionable six-year-old nephew, that life was all about having fun, with no consideration for the consequences. She worried that once Stevie reached his teenage years he'd fall in with a bad crowd, like his mother had.

'Okay, that's it, time for lights out.'

'Spoilsport,' Tony and Stevie said in unison.

Once Stevie was reluctantly back in bed and they were out on the landing, Tony held a hand out towards Christina. 'How about you, Chrissie? Are you okay?'

'What do you care?' she said, leaving him to follow her downstairs, without giving him a backward glance.

CHAPTER 11
Tuesday, 7th July
Morning

Rose Walker sipped her tea, having decided she couldn't face breakfast. She was just back from the school when the 9.05am London train rattled past.

Another night had passed and she still couldn't sleep. When she closed her eyes she imagined she'd rolled the boy's body over to see his face, but it was Vincent's face staring up at her. The noises outside, noises she was used to, all conspired to keep her awake. She was even tempted to go outside, freeing herself from that feeling of enclosure that often caught at her. Instead, in the early hours of the morning she made a pot of chamomile tea, taking it into the sitting room. She picked up Tabitha and held her so tight the cat hissed and jumped down, scuttling away, leaving Rose alone. In the end she took the photo frame from the mantelpiece and held that on her lap instead.

The police had asked her to attend the station. Everything she told the policewoman on Sunday she would have to repeat. She pictured the route from the cottage to the bus stop. It would mean walking past the very spot where the boy had lain. His twisted young body.

Yesterday the Italian man and the reporter had badgered her and now at the police station she would face more questions. They wouldn't stop. She knew that. On and on until she said, '*yes*', when she meant '*no*', just to get them to be quiet.

She glared at herself in the hall mirror, standing with her hat in one hand, a hat pin in the other. She took her spectacles off and then put them back on again.

'No, Rose,' she said to her reflection. This was not an occasion for hats or hat pins.

She checked the contents of her handbag three times, keys, purse, handkerchief. The strip of blue ribbon was there in the right-hand pocket of her coat, where it had been for two years. Then she pulled the front door closed and walked up the path.

The bus stop was at the far end of Beach Walk, the road being too narrow for buses to pass along beside the shingle. She would have to walk past the caravan and past the police roadblock and on to the junction with the Marsh Road. It was a route she rarely took. The school was in the opposite direction and all her food shopping was done at the village stores, which meant just a short stroll across the fields.

Since the man had arrived in his caravan she hadn't been able to walk down to the shoreline for fear of him speaking to her. It was something she used to treat herself to, the simplest of pleasures, to sit on the shingle just above the tideline, where the pebbles were still dry. She'd learned about the rule of twelfths, how the tide ebbs and flows over each twelve-hour period, slow on the turn and increasingly faster as each hour passes. Even on the wildest of days nature was ordered, patterns repeating over and over.

Today the weather promised much, but had yet to deliver. The sun was shaded by milky clouds, with no breeze to blow them away. Later she'd tidy the flower borders in the back garden. The bedding plants were past their best, but the buds on the dahlias were all opening. The colours were mixed. It wasn't what she'd have chosen, but there it was. Nothing could be done, not for this season anyway. Just a few weeks earlier the standard roses were in full bloom. Each afternoon, as the sun warmed the petals, she opened the back door and breathed in their heady scent. Sweet perfume she could recall even now.

Thinking about the garden helped to relax her. She slowed her pace, but as soon as she was alongside the caravan she increased her speed, wishing she'd worn her hat after all. She could have pulled the wide brim down over her face and felt protected.

The railway cottage had been perfect. No neighbours, very little passing traffic, the reassuring sound of the trains, the raw call of the seagulls, and the briny smell of the sea. Now, whenever she stepped outside her front door, she sensed his gaze. She never looked directly at the caravan, but she was certain he was there, looking out of the window straight at her. She'd never spoken to him and the one time he waved at her, she pretended not to notice.

Just a few minutes after Rose arrived at the bus stop, the bus pulled up. She put her hand out to signal to the driver. She knew that was the protocol, but it felt showy, as though she was drawing attention to herself, saying, '*Look at me, I'm here.*' She took a seat at the back, putting her handbag onto the empty seat beside her, hoping it would deter anyone from sitting next to her.

It was just four stops and then she was there, in front of the police station. She couldn't control her heartbeat, which, in turn, made her head hurt. She remembered the advice she'd been given about breathing.

'Slow, deep breaths.'

She used to try it when she was struggling to sleep, lying for hours staring at the ceiling. She'd take a breath in, counting, five, six, seven, then out again. But all it did was make her head spin. It was as though there wasn't enough air in her lungs. The thumping in her heart was easier to cope with than the airlessness. It was as if she was suffocating.

She took the steps up to the front door of the police station, as slowly and carefully as she could. A policeman rushed past her on his way to a waiting patrol car. He glanced at her, but said nothing.

She was inside now, standing at the front desk, a policeman

asking her name.

'What do you want?' he said.

'I don't want anything,' she said.

He gave a look, which she couldn't read. Perhaps he thought she was being clever, or rude. She'd never been either. 'I was asked to come. A policewoman. WPC Foster.'

'Take a seat, please.' He waved her towards some plastic chairs. They were in assorted colours, as if they'd been gathered from several different places and no longer belonged to anyone. She chose a yellow one and sat, holding tightly to her handbag, tucking her feet below the chair. A neat and tidy pose.

She watched the desk sergeant lift the telephone receiver. He spoke so quietly she couldn't catch all the words, but *'waiting'*, *'accident'*, *'woman'* were a few that drifted towards her, seemingly disconnected.

She looked down at her lap and noticed a brown stain on her coat. It must have been there all along, when she walked to the bus stop, when she sat on the bus. She wondered how many people had seen it, what they might be thinking about her. She moved her handbag to cover the stain, and then she heard her name.

'Mrs Walker.' It was the WPC. 'Thank you for coming in. Follow me, please.'

She found a way of moving that meant she could keep her handbag in one position, still covering the stain on her coat. As soon as she was home she'd deal with it. Talcum powder perhaps. She remembered reading in the *Woman's Realm* that it lifted grease stains; it was worth a try.

The policewoman opened a door and gestured to Rose to enter.

'Take a seat.'

Rose looked at WPC Foster, wondering which side of the

74

desk she should sit, but then the policewoman sat, leaving only one chair empty.

'You told me to come.' Rose said, hoping she'd understood correctly.

'Yes, that's right. There's nothing to worry about, I just need you to go through your statement again, repeating what you told me on Sunday evening. I'll write it all down. Then I will ask you to sign it. Is that okay?'

Rose knew it wasn't okay. It could never be okay.

The police interview room was small and dark, with one window high up, close to the ceiling. The window was closed and the air in the room was stale, a residual smell of smoke lingered, perhaps from a previous interviewee, more likely from the ashtray that sat to one side of the desk. Several cigarette stubs remained in the ashtray. Rose wished she could empty it into the waste basket and then give the table a wipe. The surface was covered with sticky rings from spilt drinks. The whole place needed a good clean.

'Can you tell me again what you saw on Sunday evening?' The policewoman had a kind face. Rose wanted to tell her about the nightmares, but if she started to explain she was terrified it could all unravel.

'It was such a shock.'

'Did you hear any sudden noises? Another car perhaps? I know how distressing it must have been. That's why we are so grateful for anything that will help us understand exactly what happened.'

Rose was struggling to swallow, her throat was dry, her tongue seemed to be too large to fit comfortably in her mouth. 'Could I have a glass of water?'

Rose studied the policewoman's face. Why would a pretty young woman choose such a difficult job? She couldn't imagine there were many easy crimes to solve. But watching out for children, making sure they didn't get into trouble, that would be rewarding. Rose would be good at that.

The policewoman left the room, returning moments later with a glass of water. In between sips of water, Rose Walker repeated all she remembered about the events of Sunday evening. The boys had been in her cottage earlier that day, but that wasn't relevant, was it? There was no need to tell the policewoman.

The WPC wrote out the statement, then passed it to Rose. 'If you could read it through and let me know if you want to add anything. Otherwise, if you are happy with it, then you just need to sign it.'

A few moments passed while Rose read both sides of the sheet. Then she asked, 'How did it happen? Did he fall?'

'I'm not at liberty to discuss the case, I'm sure you understand.'

'Do you think someone did it on purpose?'

'As I say, it's not something I can talk about.'

'It could have been an accident. You don't know, you can't know for sure. People make mistakes.' As she said the words aloud she tried to focus on them. The alternative was that someone had murdered a young boy, right there in front of the cottage. Rose could sense a tightness in her chest. She took a deep breath in, then out, closing her eyes for a moment while she concentrated on counting.

'Try not to worry. We have it all in hand.' Foster said, sounding confident. 'Are you happy to sign your statement now?' She placed a pen down onto the table, sliding it towards Rose.

'You don't want to ask me any more questions?'

'Do you have anything else to add?'

'I haven't done anything wrong.'

'Mrs Walker, we are very grateful for your help. You have

nothing to feel guilty about. On the contrary...'

Rose nodded. It appeared the interview was over and soon she could get the bus home. She lifted the pen and began to write her signature.

'Oh,' she said, scribbling through it, then starting again. 'There.' She pushed the signed statement back towards the policewoman. 'Am I free to go now?'

'Of course.'

As Rose Walker out of the police station she slipped her hand into the right-hand pocket of her coat. Touching the slip of blue ribbon gave her small comfort as she walked towards the bus stop and waited for the bus to take her back to the cottage.

CHAPTER 12
Tuesday, 7th July
Morning

A large playing field and two playgrounds divided Downland Junior School from its counterpart Secondary Modern. Being sited about halfway between Bexhill and Little Common, it catered for local families from the surrounding area, stretching almost as far as Norman's Bay. The red brick school buildings were one storey high, spreading out over an extensive area to the north of Bexhill, backed by woodland.

Most mornings Christina drove the five-minute journey to the school, dropped Stevie off and then continued her journey on into the newspaper offices, based in the centre of Eastbourne. On the odd occasion that Anne took to Stevie to school she preferred to walk, although a half-hour stroll for her became almost an hour with Stevie dawdling and chatting as they went.

On Tuesday morning it was Christina who dropped Stevie off at school and as she did, there was a moment when she hesitated in letting go of his hand. As soon as she did, he ran off into the playground, happy to be free.

Everything about her relationship with Stevie left her feeling conflicted. She was nineteen when she took on the responsibility for caring for him. Stevie had just had his second birthday when Flavia left home. At first, Anne and Mario hoped Flavia would regret her decision to leave Stevie behind, that she would settle, find a job and somewhere to live and then return for her son. But Christina knew as soon as her sister departed she had no intention to return. Motherhood didn't sit well with Flavia's chaotic lifestyle.

Although Anne was always there in the background, it was Christina who Stevie turned to every evening for his bedtime story. It was his aunt he sought out to play games with him in the garden, or to teach him his first words. Aunt and nephew formed a tight bond, but four years on Christina felt the weight of that responsibility. After the break-up with Tony and all that followed, Christina shied away from a serious relationship. She'd had a few boyfriends, but none that lasted beyond a couple of months. Often she felt her life was on hold. Mostly she blamed Flavia for that, on occasion she blamed Stevie.

She stood for a while, watching her nephew. He'd joined three other boys who were taking it in turns to kick a ball at a low brick wall that edged the playground. He was short for his age, but what he lacked in height he made up for in confidence. As she watched, she noticed Stevie had taken charge, gesturing to the other boys to form a line, and then clapping his hands when he wanted them to take a shot at the target.

No doubt you are your mother's son, she thought, before turning away from him towards some of the other mothers who were standing around in tight groups, intent on their conversations. Several of the women glanced up at her when she approached. It was difficult to read their expressions, but it was as though finding George Leigh's body had tainted her somehow. Yet when she nodded a greeting to one of the mothers she had spoken to on a few occasions the woman smiled at her. She put a hand on Christina's shoulder, said how terrible it must have been. Moments later Christina was surrounded by the other women. She became the centre of attention and it made her feel uncomfortable. A child had died. Any sympathy should be reserved for his family, not for her. The women asked questions, wanting to know exactly what she'd seen.

'Our children aren't safe, not while there's a killer out there,' said one woman.

Then someone asked, 'And that woman from *Rose Cottage*, she was there?'

'She's odd, a bit of a loner,' another woman added. 'You know she comes to the school sometimes, stands there watching the children playing.'

'Is her son at the school?' Christina asked.

The only reply was a shrug from a couple of the women. Christina didn't understand the antipathy, and yet she had pulled Stevie away from the woman that time. Perhaps she was as judgemental as the rest of them.

The school bell rang. A teacher asked the children to stand in line in pairs. She wanted to give her nephew a final wave, but he didn't give her a backward glance.

The *Eastbourne Herald* newspaper offices were housed in a newly built tower block in Eastbourne town centre. Once a derelict bomb site, the glass and concrete building stood six floors high and imposed itself on the tightly packed area of shops close to the railway station. Despite the relentless bombing suffered all along the south coast, Eastbourne had recovered quicker than some of its neighbouring towns. Tourists now flocked to the resort to enjoy their holidays in the smart hotels that lined the seafront. Throughout the summer the cafés and restaurants were packed, the town centre shops busy. On winter days the town's amenities belonged to the locals again. Some said that being a popular tourist resort was a mixed blessing.

Once in the office Christina probed Charles. Had the police passed on any more information? She told him about her visit to the Leigh family and what little she and Giuseppe had discovered. There was no need to mention their conversation with Rose Walker. She knew the story Charles wanted and it wouldn't include a lonely woman who had seen nothing and appeared frightened of her own shadow.

'I asked you to get the back story, stuff about the boy to fill out an article.' Charles said.

'I can't do it,' she told him. 'It's not right. I'm intruding on a family's grief.'

'Information is what we need. You're in a prime position, you were there, you found the body. We can stay ahead of the pack. Let's not blow it, eh? Go back, see if you can't get the boy's mother to open up. A mother will know all there is to know about her son, trust me.'

She thought about Flavia, a mother who knew nothing about her only child and seemed happy not knowing. But perhaps her editor was right. After all, she had a job to do, and perhaps Mrs Leigh would appreciate the chance to talk about George, to share her memories.

The day had started bright and looked set to continue in much the same way. When she pulled up at the Leigh house Mrs Leigh was in the front garden. She didn't appear to have a reason for being there, no garden tools or lawnmower in evidence. She was looking down at a solitary hydrangea bush that was yet to flower.

'Hello.' Christina's greeting caused Mrs Leigh to turn, her mouth dropped open as if she'd been woken from a reverie.

'You're the reporter.'

'Yes.' Christina wanted to apologise for being there, for being a journalist, for being the person who had found George, but was unable to save him.

'My husband says we're not to talk to the papers.'

'I understand, really I do. I just thought, perhaps you might like a chance to share some of your memories about George. I'm happy to listen and it can be off the record if you'd prefer it that way.'

'Would you like to see George's room?'

Perhaps no apology was needed.

Christina followed her into the house. Mr Leigh was not in

evidence, nor was Paul. She wondered whether Paul had felt able to go to school, or whether he was holed up somewhere, finding his own way of coping with the tragedy.

Mrs Leigh led her upstairs to a wide landing. The third door on the left was closed, a handwritten sign on the door stating boldly, *George says keep out.*

'He was always so tidy, you see,' she said, pushing the door open to reveal a sunny room, the walls covered with *Dr Who* posters. The bed was neatly made, a chair alongside the window, stacked with newly laundered tee-shirts.

'It's a lovely room,' Christina said, wondering if she should say anything at all. Perhaps all that was needed was for someone to listen.

'Paul has the box room. You can barely move in there it's such a tip. I told him he can't expect me to sort out his mess, he'll have to do his own tidying.'

She walked around the room slowly, her movements awkward, stilted, as though she was recovering from an operation or dreadful illness. On top of the chest of drawers were an assortment of models - Daleks, Dr Who's Tardis. Mrs Leigh picked up each one, ran her fingers over it and placed it down in an almost reverent way.

'Robert says we should let Paul have this room now. But it's not right. George was my baby, my youngest. He was a sensitive lad and I think he'd know.'

Christina was feeling out of her depth. She wished Giuseppe was with her, leading the conversation, making sense of it all.

'How is Paul managing? Has he gone into school today?'

'I'm a good mother.' Mrs Leigh spoke with emphasis, as though there were those who would wish to contradict her.

'It wasn't your fault.' Christina's response was automatic and yet as she spoke she realised how odd it sounded. Of course it wasn't the poor woman's fault, how could it be.

'They like going out on their bikes. It's normal for boys that age to want to explore, isn't it? But I've always told Paul to look out for his brother. They may look alike, but inside they're as different as can be. I don't know who Paul takes after, but George, well he was just like me when I was a girl.'

Christina wished they could go downstairs. Being in George's bedroom felt oppressive, the weight of emotion being compounded by the sight of the boy's prized possessions.

'Shall we go downstairs?' She was tempted to suggest she made them both a drink, but that would just delay her escape.

'I haven't offered you anything. A cup of tea or coffee. I'm sorry, you must think me rude.' Mrs Leigh's manner had suddenly changed. She had become the hospitable host, welcoming a stranger.

Christina followed Mrs Leigh downstairs and into the kitchen. The kitchen window looked out onto the back garden. There was a timber shed at the far end, ivy growing up one side and over the asphalt roof. The deep flower borders displayed a colourful show of delicate cottage garden flowers. Despite the day being so still, the phlox and aquilegia moved gently to and fro, as bees buzzed around them.

'When I was here yesterday with my uncle, Paul mentioned a man who had shouted at them. The man who was on the beach fishing?'

'His father was furious with him. It's a long time since I've seen him so angry, I thought he was going to hit him.'

This wasn't what Christina wanted to hear. It sounded like an extreme reaction to a relatively harmless admission.

'It turns out it wasn't just that fella in the caravan they've been talking to. They went into that woman's house. The cottage by the railway crossing.'

'George and Paul?' This confirmed what Rose had said.

'Just a few hours before it happened, they were in there together.' Mrs Leigh's voice was shaky, her arms tightly wrapped around her chest, as though she was trying to hold herself together.

'I'm sure there was no harm done. I've spoken to Mrs Walker, she seems very nice. A little shy, perhaps.'

Mrs Leigh stared at Christina, then spoke slowly as if she were trying to explain the simplest thing to someone who had no grasp of English. 'She's odd, everyone says it. Paul says she kept staring at them. Then Paul tells us he's been inside the caravan too, but the fella told him not to say. It's not right. A man like that, on his own, asking young boys in. And why keep it a secret, eh?'

CHAPTER 13
Tuesday, 7th July
Morning

Paul Leigh knew there would be an argument when he appeared at the breakfast table in his school uniform. His mum would tell him it was too soon, his dad would agree he should go if he wanted to, then they would shout at each other and he would wait it out. Regardless of the outcome, he was going to school. Better to be out of the house and let them get with on their disagreements.

Arriving in the playground he tried to appear nonchalant, but he was like the pied piper, friends swarming around him, wanting to hear what he had to say. The boys sought the gruesome details. *Was there much blood? Did he see his brother in the mortuary?* The girls wanted to touch his arm, his hand, offering comfort. *How terrible it must be for you. Do you want to talk about it?*

He wanted to shout at them. Tell them they were all hypocrites. Now that George was gone, they had time for him. Before it was only his brother's company they sought.

'There's nothing to tell,' he announced, pushing his way through the group that seemed reticent to leave his side. 'I wasn't there.'

'Are the police going to arrest someone? Was it murder?' One of the girls saw her chance to attract a little attention. Shock tactics, using words others shied away from.

Then the deputy head appeared, but instead of ringing the school bell as usual, he came across to Paul and his classmates. Boys and girls stood aside, creating a pathway.

'Paul Leigh, with me please.' His tone was sharp, a tone that usually preceded the announcement of a detention, or worse.

Mr Winston led Paul into the school, and the group of boys

drifted off.

The only time Paul had been inside the deputy head's office was when he was in trouble for cheating. The history homework had been impossible. George excelled at history and Paul persuaded George to do the history homework for him, in return for two weeks' pocket money. George had been saving up for the latest model Dalek. He just needed another shilling, so the incentive sealed the deal. George wrote out the answers, all relating to the Tudor reign over England, who married whom, dates, names. Paul copied it down in his neatest handwriting. Trouble was, he copied the words exactly, so the phrasing used in both boys' essays proved to be Paul's undoing. He thought of suggesting it was George who had been the cheat, copying his older brother's words. But he knew he'd never get away with it. All the teachers knew George was the brightest of the Leigh brothers. It wasn't only history he was good at, George always came top in maths and English. He'd been chosen for the school football team and regularly won prizes for swimming. He was everything his brother was not.

Mr Winston waved at Paul to sit. Last time he was in the office he stood to attention, glancing around at the shelves of books that lined the room, the desk with its inlaid leather top, the master's chair that squeaked when Mr Winston sat back in it. On that occasion he was wondering whether his punishment would be a detention, or the cane, or both. As it was, Mr Winston had given him a sermon about how liars and cheats would always be found out in the end. On and on he went. At one point Paul wanted to laugh, but he knew that would really rile the master. Instead he'd kept his head bowed, saying meekly, 'Yes sir, sorry sir,' at appropriate points.

This time though Paul was able to ease himself back into the leather armchair and watch his feet dangling off the floor.

His thoughts went briefly to the woman in the cottage, how tall she was, how long her legs were, compared to his stumpy limbs. Being absorbed in his thoughts he realised he'd missed what the deputy head had said.

'Sorry, sir, what was that?'

'I'm surprised to see you here, Paul. There's no need for you to come to school for the time being. Given the circumstances.'

Choosing his words was clearly an effort for the teacher.

'I want to be here, sir.'

'But shouldn't you be with your family? Your mother will need your support, I'm sure of it.'

Paul held the gaze of the teacher. He wanted to say that his parents had never looked to him for support and he was doubtful they would now. On the contrary, him being around was a reminder that he was alive and George was not. There was a lot he wanted to say, but he was certain the master wouldn't understand any of it.

'During dinner break there is to be a visit from the detective sergeant who is in charge of your brother's case.'

Again, Mr Winston's tone was emotionless, as though he was speaking about nothing more dramatic than the loss of a purse or a wallet.

'Is he coming to see me?'

'No, he's planning to address the whole school.'

'I see. Thank you, sir.'

'If you'd rather not attend the talk, you can be outside in the playground, or even go home if you prefer.'

With that, Paul was dismissed. He stood, briefly aware there would now be even more intrigue for his classmates to enquire about.

The morning's lessons passed without event. Double maths, followed by English. Both teachers did their best to avoid eye contact with Paul. It was clear they would prefer him not to be in the class. His presence served as a reminder of an event that was associated with such raw emotion. The violent death of a boy who a few days earlier had sat in front of them, always shooting his hand up to answer their questions. A teenager who appeared genuinely interested in his studies, who was well liked and had a bright future.

Paul chose not to go home during the dinner break and rather than lingering in the playground, he lined up with the others as they filed into the school hall. The headmaster stood in the centre of the stage, the policeman to his left, the deputy head to his right. The policeman was introduced as Detective Sergeant Pearce. Paul hadn't seen him before. It was a policewoman who had come round to the house on Sunday evening.

The detective sergeant walked to the front of the stage. The school hall fell silent, bar a few boys who were whispering and pointing at Paul.

'Boys and girls,' the detective sergeant began. 'You will all know the very sad news that one of your school friends died on Sunday evening. He was riding his bicycle along Beach Walk.' He paused and looked across the sea of faces, all fixed on him, anticipating what he might say next.

'We are working hard to piece together any information that might help us to understand how and why George Leigh died.'

He let each statement sink in before continuing.

'If anyone thinks they know anything at all, however insignificant it might appear, then you must come forward. It doesn't matter if you weren't at the beach on Sunday evening. Perhaps you were there on another occasion and you saw something out of the ordinary. We will be putting up notices around the town, asking people to come forward with information.'

Several of the children turned to look at Paul. He saw them out of his peripheral vision, while keeping his own gaze firmly forward, focused on the detective sergeant.

'And that brings me to the other reason I am here. Please remember that if any stranger tries to speak to you when you are out on your own - man or woman - then you should walk away. If you feel you need to say something so as not to appear rude, then you should say, *I'm not allowed to speak to strangers*, and walk straight on.'

One of the boys shot his hand up. 'Excuse me, sergeant, but a police constable stopped me the other day when I was coming out of Gage's newsagents. He tried to speak to me and when I ran off he shouted after me that I deserved a hiding. But I did the right thing, didn't I, Detective Sergeant?'

Several boys started sniggering. The boy was Pip, in the year above Paul, described by pupils and teachers alike as a *'mouthy clever clogs'*.

'We don't need any clever remarks from you, Philip Southward. Now I'd like you all to offer a brief round of applause by way of thanks to Detective Sergeant Pearce for giving us his time today.' The headmaster gestured to the pupils to stand. But before the applause could begin, Pip had more to add.

'What about if we've seen something at the beach, sir? We'll need time off from lessons so we can go to the police station, won't we, sir?'

Pip received a fearsome stare from the headmaster, while Pearce said, 'If anyone has information they'd like to share, then please come into the police station. Make sure one of your parents comes with you and, of course, this should be after school hours.'

The pupils were dismissed. All opportunities for skiving

lost.

Pearce's speech had offered nothing unexpected, although Paul hadn't really known what he was expecting. The nonchalance or bravado, or whatever it was that had seen him through until the sergeant had finished speaking had vanished, leaving him with a sinking feeling in the pit of his stomach. He had a choice - he could sit through the afternoon's science and history lessons, or he could take Mr Winston up on his suggestion that he didn't need to be at school at all.

Half an hour later he was at the beach, tapping lightly on the caravan door, hoping Sean Murphy was at home. When he was with Sean he could forget about the bad stuff. They talked about fishing, about the sea and how the tides worked. Sean told him stories about the time he used to captain a huge trawler, bringing in tons of fish every day.

'What did you have to do?' he asked him the last time they met.

'Everything. You can't be a captain and expect everyone else to do the work. I started off as a youngster, learning the ropes.'

'Yeah, but what did you have to learn at school? I mean, what did you have to write down on your application form?'

Sean laughed and told him he'd been thrown out of school aged fourteen, joined a fishing fleet and never looked back.

'But it's a hard life, lad. The sea can be cruel. You think you're in charge when you're a skipper, but you come to learn that it's nature that has the power.'

Since that conversation Paul had made a decision to do the same thing and with each day that passed his plan grew more definite in his mind. He was certain Sean would understand. There was even an outside chance Sean would let him share the caravan for a while, just until he'd got a place on a boat and then it was goodbye to Bexhill forever.

CHAPTER 14
Tuesday, 7th July
Morning

Giuseppe came down into the café on Tuesday morning to find Mario standing at the door, a cotton pullover slung around his shoulders and car keys in his hand.

'Anne is insisting I take a couple of hours off. She's right, of course, we've waited ten years to see you, after all.'

Giuseppe gave a half-hearted smile. Spending time with his cousin was fine if this was a normal visit. It had been his plan to embrace everything that was different about life in England as a way of blanking out all that was wrong with his life in Rome. But there had been little normality since his arrival. Now he was more intent on interviewing potential witnesses to George Leigh's death than on taking a walk with his cousin.

There was also the problem of the cigarettes. Each time Mario lit up, Giuseppe was reminded how much he missed the hit of the nicotine, the smell, even the feel of the cigarette in his hand.

'No point both of us being stuck inside on a day like this,' Mario said. 'We'll drive to Hastings, take a stroll along the promenade, work up an appetite for lunch.'

Anne had yet to find a meal Giuseppe enjoyed. He poked and prodded at the food on his plate, took a few mouthfuls, then apologised; he was full up, he had eaten too many biscuits at breakfast. Soon he would run out of excuses and would have to admit English food did not suit his stomach.

Giuseppe got into the passenger seat of the Hillman Imp, stretching his legs into the footwell, kicking aside some sweet wrappers.

'*Caramelle*. You always loved your sweets,' he said. 'It is no surprise you decided to run a café. Cakes every day, eh?'

Mario lit a cigarette, before pulling out into the traffic. He didn't offer a reply until they had left Bexhill and were approaching the putting green that backed on to the start of the seafront. West Marina Gardens separated the road from the promenade. The swathe of neatly mown grass offered a bowls green and putting course, as well as formal flower beds.

Whenever Giuseppe thought of his cousin, he pictured him surrounded by green spaces. It was the one aspect of England that might have persuaded Giuseppe to make the same choices Mario had made years earlier.

Despite the bright sunshine there was no one playing bowls, but as they continued Giuseppe glanced across to see several people walking along the seafront, which ran from the putting green all the way to Hastings Old Town.

'That area beside the putting green, they call it Bo Peep,' Mario said, breaking the silence.

Giuseppe didn't reply.

'The nursery rhyme, Bo Peep,' Mario said.

'You will have to explain.'

'There's an English nursery rhyme about Little Bo Peep. They say that centuries ago West St Leonards was popular with smugglers.'

'I do not know English nursery rhymes.' He felt unaccountably irritated. He put it down to the smell of Mario's cigarette.

'Smugglers. Hide and seek. Bo Peep. I suppose it makes sense,' Mario continued, oblivious to the frown on Giuseppe's face.

'You learned the English nursery rhymes when Christina and Flavia were small?'

Mario shook his head. 'It was only when Stevie came along. There was no chance to be a good father in the middle of a world war.'

'Of course. And for Anne, giving birth in a foreign country. *Difficile.* Very difficult.'

They continued the journey in silence, but then Mario said. 'Sometimes I let Stevie sit in the front seat, that's the reason for the sweet wrappers. Anyway, I recall you were the one with the sweet tooth.'

'He is full of spirit.'

'Stevie?'

'*Si.* It must have been a difficult time for you all. When Flavia and Christina were teenagers.'

'Anne is an amazing mother, and grandmother.'

'And wife?'

'Of course. She's all that keeps me sane on my worst days.'

'You still have bad days?' Giuseppe asked.

'Don't we all?'

They lapsed into silence until they reached Hastings Pier.

Mario pulled into the small car park that bordered the beach and grabbed a rain jacket from the back seat.

'Let's walk from here,' Mario said.

Just after they passed the Pier the sky darkened and within seconds the rain was falling heavily, enough to cause them to run for cover. Mario pointed to one of the wooden shelters and once there they both needed to catch their breath before speaking. Giuseppe brushed the rain from his jacket, but as he did so drops ran from his hair down the back of his neck, wetting his shirt collar.

'Your wonderful English summer,' Giuseppe said. 'Next time we go out I will borrow an umbrella.'

'Don't tell me it never rains in Roma. I was born there, remember?'

'But England is your home now.'

Mario paused before replying. 'My life is here, the café, my family.'

'And your family in Italy? They no longer count?'

It was ten years since Giuseppe had spoken face-to-face with his cousin, able to watch his reactions, rather than guessing at them from the other end of the telephone.

'Please don't start on that again. It's all too long ago. Events that can't be undone and memories best forgotten.'

'You were just a boy. There was nothing you could have done and still you blame yourself.'

Mario attempted to brush a mark away from the bottom of his trousers, avoiding his cousin's gaze. He took out his packet of cigarettes, offering it to Giuseppe.

'You should give up,' Giuseppe said. 'Like I have.'

'And be forever tapping my fingers to keep them busy?'

'It helps me to think.'

'And cigarettes help me relax.' Mario took a few deep drags on his cigarette. 'And you and Rosalia? I was sorry to read your letter with that news. Although the last time you were here, you suggested that perhaps...'

'It was my fault. I did not pay her enough attention and without attention a flower will fade and die.'

Now it was Giuseppe's turn to look away, scuffing his heel against some small pebbles that had blown up into the shelter in the last storm.

'So we both blame ourselves for matters beyond our control,' Mario said. 'And what about this case - the death of George Leigh? I don't think you have taken well to retirement. Getting involved with this case when you've come here for a holiday.'

'You will see how hard it is when you have to give up the café. One day you are doing what you have done for years and the next you wake up and wonder what is the point of waking. I am *in pensione,* retired. I am not paid as a detective. But it does not stop me from being a detective. It is in my blood. Perhaps like the café is in yours?'

'It's hardly the same thing.'

Giuseppe shook his finger in disagreement. 'I have watched you with your customers. They are your friends, you are at the centre of a community.'

'I don't see it like that. We just provide a service. And a listening ear when time permits.'

'Detectives too. We also provide a service, to protect the public. And we must make time to listen, because it is when we listen that we hear what we do not expect.'

Mario stood, folding his wet jacket over his arm. 'Come on, let's continue our walk now that it's stopped raining.'

They fell in step with each other, reverting to silence until they reached the end of the seafront and the beginning of Hastings Old Town.

'It is good to have time to walk and think.' Giuseppe said.

'You were always a thinker, even as a boy.'

'A lifetime ago, eh?'

'Have you been able to get a grip on the case? Any thoughts at all about how the lad might have met his death?'

'Many thoughts, very few facts. There is a long way to go before we reach the end. But I am hopeful.'

'Well, I'd say we've reached the end of our walk, or at least the half-way point. Let's turn around and head back and keep our fingers crossed for no more rain.'

'I don't think we came here last time, did we?' Giuseppe said.

Mario came to a stop in front of some tall wooden structures, with no windows, but shutters high up. Painted black, they rose up towards the sky, reminding Giuseppe of a photograph he'd seen in a school history book. The image depicted three English men from Victorian times, wearing hats that were tall and thin, making them look so strange.

'The fishermen use them to hang their nets,' Mario said. 'They date back to the 1800s, I think they are specific to Hastings, at least that's what I've been told.'

It was late morning now. The rain had abated. Most of the fishing boats were already out, leaving the beach looking desolate. They stood for a while, breathing in the sea air, listening to the screech of the seagulls. A man ran down the beach a little way from where they were standing. Then a boat came close to the shoreline, the fisherman jumped out of the boat, waist high in the water, grabbed a rope, threw one end to the man on the beach and between them they pulled the boat onto the pebbles.

Giuseppe could smell the fish, he could almost taste the sharp saltiness of freshly cooked white flesh. It took him back to days in Anzio, when he'd sit at one of the fish restaurants that lined the harbour and savour a freshly caught seabass, lightly tossed in a pan with a little olive oil, served with nothing but a generous squeeze of lemon.

The work of the fishermen here wasn't so different from Anzio. But here the holidaymakers and locals enjoyed their fish covered in batter, eaten from a sheet of newspaper. He thought of Rosalia and what she might make of the English ways.

'You have also had bad days,' Mario said, breaking into Giuseppe's thoughts.

'The miscarriage. It changed everything.'

'You had your work.'

'*Sì.*'

Giuseppe recalled the arguments, how Rosalia used to tell him that police work was all he thought about, that he'd be good for nothing else. Now she would be proved right. Although when he compared his life with his cousin's, Giuseppe felt stultified. Mario and Anne lived a small life, one that existed within a tight community. There was little that happened day-to-day to upset their routine. Already after just two days Giuseppe was restless, grateful for the chance to focus on the familiar, solving a crime.

From the brief time he'd spent with Christina he could sense she had the vibrancy and energy that reminded him of his own younger days, when he first joined the police and had so much to learn. He had such a thirst for knowledge back then. Each experience only increased his desire for more. Every case, every individual, taught him something new. He made no assumptions and over the years he came to realise that although there were certain patterns of behaviour among criminals, there were also many who fitted no pattern, who were unique in their motivation. The most frightening individuals were those who appeared to have no conscience and no respect for authority. For them there could be no deterrent.

Rather than retracing their steps along the seafront, the cousins made their way inland along the cobbled streets of Hastings Old Town. The rain clouds had passed, the warm sun returning, enticing people out. As they made their way up the High Street, Mario pointed to a queue gathered at a van selling ice-cream, satisfied smiles on the faces of children and adults alike as they walked away with their cornets and wafers.

'To pander to our sweet tooth?' Mario said, smiling.

Nothing could come close to the taste of Italian ice-cream for Giuseppe, but there was no harm in trying a few pence worth of a *Mr Whippy* vanilla ice-cream. At least it would give him a genuine excuse if he couldn't face Anne's lunchtime offerings.

Despite their conversation pulling him back into the past, the walk had given Giuseppe time to think about the case. He smiled to himself as he realised he was still thinking like a detective. Retirement was just a word, after all.

CHAPTER 15
Tuesday, 7th July
Afternoon

It was a little after midday by the time Giuseppe and Mario returned to the café. Christina was sitting on a high stool up at the counter, chatting with Anne, who kept being distracted by customers. As the cousins approached, Anne turned her attention to her husband.

'Caught up with all the news?'

'Made a start,' Mario replied. 'You take a seat out back, have a rest. I can see to things for a while.'

'Shall I make you both a sandwich?' Anne said, wiping her hands on her apron, before pushing a strand of hair away from her face.

'We have had ice-cream,' Giuseppe said, the pleasure of the summer treat evident from his voice.

'Lucky you,' Christina said. She gestured to Giuseppe to follow her to one of the outside tables. 'Can we talk?'

The population of Bexhill and the surrounding area had grown in number over the years. At one time Bexhill-on-Sea was little more than a rural village. Then, like many other places, once the railway arrived, so did the people. Then culture and entertainment came, courtesy of various generations of the De La Warr family, culminating in the De La Warr Pavilion, an expression of art deco architecture standing prominently in the centre of the seafront. Luckily the Pavilion escaped the bomb damage suffered by many of the surrounding buildings. But Bexhill saw a decline in day trippers after the war, so the Rossi family built their café trade by making themselves a central part of the local community. It was their regulars who kept them going.

There was just enough space on the pavement for *Bella Cafè* to offer sixteen of their customers a chance to sit outside; four tables with four chairs at each. The tables were only in use on warm, dry days as Mario had never quite got around to organising a canopy to keep any rain off, despite his wife's constant reminders.

'I've been back to speak to Mrs Leigh,' Christina said, keeping her voice low.

The other three tables were occupied. An elderly couple were sharing a cheese sandwich between them. At another table, a middle-aged woman kept dropping crisps to the floor, each crumb swept up immediately by her Scottish terrier. The third table was taken by a young woman who was more intent on jiggling the pram that sat alongside her, than in drinking her coffee, which looked destined to remain undrunk. It was apparent no one was interested in the conversation between Christina and Giuseppe.

'Anything useful?' Giuseppe asked.

'Just confirmation of some tension within the family. Seems as though Mr Leigh has a temper.'

'It is easy to be angry when we are pushed to our limit.'

'Charles seems happy for me to do what needs to be done to follow up on the case. Do you think there is a case? I mean do you think someone intended to kill George?'

'It is not good for us to think this or that. We must concentrate on collecting facts and talking to everyone who might know more than we know.'

'The owner of the caravan?'

'*Preciso.* Exactly.'

Half an hour later and they were at Beach Walk. The door to the caravan was closed as they approached. It wasn't easy to see whether anyone was inside without peering through the glass. Giuseppe knocked on the door, which was opened immediately to reveal a middle-aged man, with a black, bushy beard and untidy hair, framing a ruddy face.

'Yes?'

'*Buon giorno*, sir,' Giuseppe said, 'May we enter your caravan?'

'A long time since I've been called sir.' The man stood back and beckoned them in.

Christina extended a hand. 'We're with the *Eastbourne Herald*, just trying to gather a bit of background.' She paused, hoping for a response before realising she hadn't asked a question. 'The accident. You would have seen it. I expect it was quite a shock.'

She looked around, taking in her surroundings in as subtle a way as possible. At one end of the caravan was a sofa arrangement with a couple of threadbare cushions stuffed in one corner. She guessed the sofa must double as a bed. In front of the sofa was a small table, the type that folded flat when not in use. But right now it was in use; covered with a half-finished jigsaw puzzle. Immediately in front of the door was what seemed to be the kitchen area, a flat surface with a small washing-up bowl, filled with dirty crockery and a half-empty bottle of whisky standing on the two-ring gas burner. Underneath was what appeared to be a makeshift cupboard, with a piece of ragged material pulled across the front.

'Picked it up at the local tip.' The man, who spoke with a strong Irish brogue, had been watching Christina taking in the surroundings. 'Amazing what people will throw away, isn't it?' He picked up a pipe that had been lying on top of the jigsaw. Giuseppe watched as Sean took a packet of tobacco from his trouser pocket, filled the pipe, and then made several attempts to light it. The rich odour of pipe tobacco quickly filled the caravan as the Irishman puffed on his pipe. Minutes passed when no one spoke.

'You'll see I'm kind of tight for space in here, so I'll not offer you a seat and there's no chance of tea, I'm afraid.'

Giuseppe stepped forward so that Christina could stand behind him. 'Sunday afternoon. The boy who died.'

'Sorry,' Christina added. 'We should introduce ourselves. I'm Christina Rossi and this is my uncle, Giuseppe Bianchi.'

'Sean Murphy. Nothing original about the name, or the man.' He winked and then said, 'Local press taking foreigners on now, are they?'

They didn't have a chance to reply as a sudden thud on the side of the caravan startled the three of them. Sean Murphy stepped past his visitors, easing them out of the way so he could stand on the caravan step.

'Clear off. I've told you before.' Sean followed his shout with action, running off down the beach towards a couple of young lads.

'Pretty weird bloke,' Christina whispered, despite the Irishman being well away from the caravan.

'He is not English. His accent?'

'Irish. Maybe from the north, I'm not certain. Perhaps we should look around while he's out of the way.'

Giuseppe raised an eyebrow. There were protocols in police work, but it seemed that journalists did not follow the same rules. 'What are you hoping to find?'

'It's okay, I'm not going to disturb anything.'

She opened the inner door, which revealed a bathroom of sorts; a portaloo and a bowl balanced on a tea-chest. Returning to the main living area, she pointed to the jigsaw.

'Looks like our friend enjoys a puzzle or two.'

She pulled aside the ragged curtain below the gas burner, revealing a stock of tinned and packet food.

'You think he is on 'oliday?' Giuseppe remained standing close to the door, watching Christina who was still ferreting around.

'Holiday,' she said, with emphasis. 'I doubt it. Looks to me like this is his permanent residence.'

'Still here then?' Sean appeared at the caravan door, flushed from running, or from temper. 'Pesky kids. If it's not stones, it's a football. You'd have thought they'd be home having their tea or doing their homework. When I was their age I'd get a clip round the ear if I was out of line. They're not bad lads, but I'm pretty sure their parents don't know where they are half the time.'

Christina caught sight of two young lads walking back up the beach, one of them sticking his tongue out as he passed the caravan. 'The children irritate you?'

'No, not a bit of it. There's no harm in them, high spirits that's all.'

'Don't you feel cramped in here?' Christina said.

'I've got all the space I need out there.' He gestured towards the beach. 'More than I can handle sometimes.'

'It must get lonely? No-one to talk to. No neighbours.'

'There's her.' Sean nodded towards the cottage. 'Although we've never exchanged a single word in all the time I've been here.'

'How long have you been here?'

'Look, I've already told the police what I know about the accident, which is precisely nothing. I was busy with this at the time.' He pointed to the jigsaw.

'They've questioned you.' A statement from Giuseppe, rather than a question.

'Of course. I'm yards from where it happened. Trouble with the police is they like to ask questions but aren't so keen on hearing the answers.'

Giuseppe felt something brush past him and looked down to see a ginger cat, which had positioned itself at the feet of the Irishman.

'Hungry again, are we?'

The cat mewed in response, winding itself around Sean Murphy's legs, its tail swishing back and forth.

'If you budge over a bit, I'll grab some food for this mite. She's not mine, but she treats the place like her own.'

'Her name may be Tabitha,' Giuseppe said, receiving a quizzical look from the Irishman.

Sean pulled the tattered curtain aside and took out an open tin of cat food. He took a saucer from the washing-up bowl, emptied some food onto it and put it on the floor. The cat seemed able to continue meowing while eating, unperturbed at being the focus of attention.

'We thought you might have seen something, heard something,' Christina said. 'We are trying to support the family, to help them by finding out what happened to their son. I'm sure you'll want to help as much as possible.'

'Like I said, I was focused on my jigsaw. It's a devil of a thing. One of the toughest I've done. But it helps me relax. You should try it some time.'

'You know the boy. At least you've spoken to him and his brother.' Giuseppe said.

'Yes, I've spoken to them. Chatty pair, at least one of them liked to chat, the other not so much.' During the time they'd been in the caravan the Irishman had yet to make eye contact with either of them. He bent down and picked up the cat, who'd finished eating and was making a show of cleaning itself, licking its fur and purring.

'Christina, we must go.' Giuseppe took Christina's arm, guiding her towards the door. When Christina turned to say goodbye Sean was already sitting, with the cat on his lap, his focus on the uncompleted jigsaw.

CHAPTER 16
Tuesday, 7th July
Afternoon

As they walked away from the caravan Giuseppe nodded towards *Rose Cottage*.

'Now we are here...' he said, walking towards the cottage, without waiting for Christina's reply. As he approached, he spotted a side path leading to the back garden. Rose was in the garden, pegging out the laundry.

'*Buon giorno.*'

Rose stood motionless, with a peg in her right hand and a pillowcase in her left. It was as if she was frozen to the spot, her eyes wide with fear.

'Sorry, I didn't mean to startle you.'

'What are you doing in my garden?'

She turned her back on him, her shoulders hunching forward, her hands clasped in front of her.

'You are very lucky living here in England. So much green, so many pretty gardens. You must work hard every day to keep it so perfect.' Giuseppe said.

'Why are you back here? I've already told you what I know.' Rose turned to face Giuseppe. She wore her hair pinned back into a tight bun, but today the wind caught at it, strands escaping and softening her face.

'Please, continue to put out your washing. It is a good day for it. Perhaps it is always windy here by the sea?' He looked down at the items in the washing basket, each piece neatly folded. Every item hung on the line had been arranged with precision, pegs evenly spaced, larger items alternating with smaller ones.

'In Roma we don't have gardens, only flats,' he continued. 'I have a small balcony, but each time I try to grow a flower it dies.' His attempt at small talk brought back the image he'd tried to blank out so many times. Standing on his balcony, looking down at the crowd that gathered, moments after it happened.

'The watering is important to get right,' Rose said, her tone easing a little. 'Too much and you drown it, too little and it will shrivel up and die.'

'May we come inside, just a few moments of your time?' Giuseppe said.

'I told you yesterday. I didn't see anything.' Rose picked up the laundry basket, appearing uncertain as to her next move. And then she said, 'I suppose I could brew a pot of tea,' as if she needed to mull over the idea before deciding.

Giuseppe and Christina waited. Then, as Rose walked towards the back door of her cottage, they followed her.

Once inside, Giuseppe noticed again how ordered and neat the cottage was. The back door led straight into the kitchen. Rose took slippers from a small shoe rack, exchanging them for her outdoor shoes. Giuseppe stood on the door mat, with Christina hovering behind him. He wondered if he should take his shoes off. It was as though there was a protocol to be followed.

A smell of bleach emanated from the wide work surfaces and the enamel sink set under the window, all scrubbed clean. The kettle was already set on the gas cooker. Rose filled it from the kitchen tap and put it back on the stove, lighting the gas with a match. On the other side of the kitchen was a small table, covered by a plastic tablecloth, with a vase of freshly cut flowers in the centre.

Giuseppe watched as Rose set out cups and saucers, poured milk into a matching jug, then opened the door to the pantry. Over Rose's shoulder he could see the shelves, each one filled with home-made preserves, packets and tins of food, enough provisions for a family and yet there was only one change of footwear on the shoe rack.

Rose opened a packet of pink wafer biscuits, setting them on the plate in a criss-cross pattern, such that Giuseppe was loath to take one for upsetting the neatness.

He was concerned about the tea. It was a drink he'd never been able to stomach. He could just about manage it with a slice of lemon, but with milk he found it unbearable.

In his peripheral vision he saw Christina reach into her shoulder bag. He guessed she was going to pull out her notebook. He gave an imperceptible shake of his head, indicating this was not the time for note-taking. It was clear to him Rose Walker was a delicate soul who needed a careful approach.

The tea was poured, Giuseppe asking for his to remain black. Rose sipped hers, looking up now and then, as though waiting for Giuseppe to start the conversation.

'You don't have many neighbours. It must be very peaceful living here.'

'Just the trains.'

'Of course, the trains. Have you lived here long?'

Rose frowned. 'My father liked trains,' she said.

'He worked for the railways?' She shook her head.

'And the man in the caravan? You have met him?' Giuseppe gestured vaguely towards the window.

'I don't know who he is. I know nothing about him.' The words came out in a rush.

Observation was a skill Giuseppe had perfected. He estimated the woman's age at late thirties. Younger than his cousin's wife, but more worn somehow. Anne managed to juggle her responsibilities: the café, running a home, being a wife, a mother, even a grandmother, while always remaining calm and fresh-faced. Rose, on the other hand, was pale, her hair pulled tightly back from her face, making her look drawn and tired. Each time she lifted the cup to her lips it was a precise movement, as though she had learned to control her behaviour in the smallest aspects of her life.

'This is a very pretty cottage, so neat and tidy.'

She nodded and smiled, her shoulders relaxing a little.

'It can't be easy with a young lad at home. Boys can be very messy, can't they?'

Her smile faded, her shoulders tensed again. He noticed her breathing, slow and controlled, as though she was counting.

'I've seen the boys go into his caravan,' she said, the words rushing out of her mouth in-between breaths.

'The Leigh brothers?'

'You haven't had a biscuit.' Rose pushed the plate towards him.

'They often visit the caravan?' Giuseppe asked.

'I've seen them a few times, they cycle this way. Nice lads...' she paused.

Giuseppe was aware of Christina fidgeting in her seat.

'We must depart. We have taken enough of your time,' Giuseppe said. 'Thank you for the tea and biscuits.'

'Yes, thank you,' Christina said, as Rose showed them into the hallway. 'It must be a difficult time for you with all that is happening right outside your front door.'

Rose opened the door without replying. Then, as they were half-way down the front path, she added. 'I'd rather you didn't come back.'

Leaving the cottage behind, Christina turned to walk back to the car, but was stopped by Giuseppe, who put a hand on her arm.

'Look,' he gestured towards a uniformed policeman who was removing the notice they had seen the day before, replacing it with another. 'Wait a moment until he has gone.'

She gave him a quizzical look before following his gaze. A few minutes later the policeman got into the Panda car and pulled away.

'Come,' Giuseppe said, walking towards the new sign without waiting to see if Christina was following him.

A FATAL INCIDENT OCCURRED AT THIS SPOT ON SUNDAY 5TH JULY. EASTBOURNE POLICE ARE APPEALING FOR WITNESSES. PLEASE PHONE 777555

Christina read the words aloud.

'They are confirming it was fatal and no longer an accident', Giuseppe said.

'There are no witnesses, at least none who want to speak.'

Before Giuseppe could answer he was aware of a distant sound and a gentle tremor beneath his feet. Then, a few moments later, a train came into view. Its approach was slow. Giuseppe stood yards from the crossing, from the track, and from the place where the boy's body had been found. As the carriages crept past he was close enough to see the passengers. To prove a point he lifted his hand in greeting and a girl who had her face pressed up against the train window immediately waved back.

'*Bravo* Giuseppe,' he said aloud, 'You are a genius.'

'You've had an idea?'

'*Sì*, I have had an idea. Come, we will take a walk.'

CHAPTER 17
Tuesday, 7th July
Afternoon

Giuseppe waited for the train to pass along the track, leaving the crossing clear. Then, gesturing for Christina to follow him, they crossed to the other side of the railway line, following the path of the train. The track swerved away from the coastline, inland, towards Norman's Bay, the station closest to Beach Walk, along the route to Eastbourne. Christina helped Giuseppe to climb over a stile, put in place to keep a small group of sheep from escaping their field. After half an hour or so they arrived at the station. The ticket office was on the far side of the track, reached by a footbridge.

Giuseppe noticed Christina give a brief shiver as they moved from the warm sunshine to the dull interior of the ticket office. She was wearing a sleeveless cotton shift dress and he wondered briefly if he should offer her his jacket.

The ticket office clerk was deep in conversation with an elderly man. The two men appeared to know each other, as their chatter seemed to have nothing to do with the purchasing of tickets. When the two men had exhausted their conversation, the elderly man moved away, leaving Giuseppe to step forward. Christina stood to one side, but Giuseppe noticed the way the clerk's gaze kept going towards her.

'*Buon giorno,*' he said.

The ticket office clerk didn't respond, continuing to look at Christina.

'I hope you can help me,' Giuseppe continued.

'Destination? Single or return?'

'I don't want a ticket.'

The railway man glared at Giuseppe and then looked beyond him, as though hoping a more lucrative customer was waiting in line behind him.

'Does she want a ticket?' the clerk pointed at Christina.

'We would like to ask you some questions about the incident that happened beside the railway crossing, near to Beach Walk. On Sunday.'

The man's glare was now replaced with an impassive expression.

'A young boy died. Perhaps the police have been to speak to you?' Giuseppe said.

'I don't mean to be rude, sir. If you want to buy a ticket, then I'm your man. Otherwise I'm afraid I can't help you.'

During his walk alongside the railway track Giuseppe had been imagining ways in which a criminal could escape a crime scene.

Paul Leigh had spoken about a man who had been fishing down by the shore. The man had shouted at them. What if the man had done more than just shout? Perhaps he had threatened George for some reason, resulting in the boy's death. If that was the case, the man would need to escape the scene. What better way than to climb onto the train while it was stationary on the crossing. It would provide him with a chance to merge with other passengers, to alight unnoticed when the train was finally allowed to proceed to the station. Then all he needed to do was to buy a ticket for onward travel.

The ticket office clerk stood and moved away from the counter.

'I'm about to have my lunch. Cold beef sandwiches today. It's usually cheese and jam, so beef is a bit of a rare treat. And if I know my missus she'll have added a spread of English mustard.'

The clerk made a point of putting his lunch box on the counter, removed a sandwich from it and took a bite.

'We do not want to disturb your lunch. Perhaps you weren't

working on Sunday,' Giuseppe said.

The thought of a sandwich made with cheese and jam distracted Giuseppe for a moment. He was certain he'd never get used to English tastes.

'I work every afternoon,' the clerk said, before taking another bite.

'No days off?'

'I work my rest days and if it's a Sunday, then it's time and a half. Every penny counts, you know.'

Giuseppe nodded. 'If there is nothing you can tell us, we will leave you to enjoy your sandwich.'

It had been a wasted visit. Giuseppe turned and took a few steps away, then stopped as the clerk said, 'There was a man bought a single to London,' almost as though he was talking to himself.

'That would not be unusual?'

'I thought it a bit odd, because he still had his shorts on, looked like he'd come straight off the beach.'

'People on holiday, wearing shorts to the beach. This is not unusual?'

The clerk tutted. 'No, that's right enough. But you don't usually see grown men wearing their shorts on the train. Although nowadays I suppose anything goes. But it wasn't the shorts that bothered me, it was his attitude.'

'Go on.'

'He came right up close to the grille, staring right at me. Quite gave me the shivers, it did.'

'Do you remember much about him? Was he tall or short?'

'Shorter than you. A weasel of a man, thin features, a look about him as though he hated the world and everyone in it. And he had a tooth missing, just here.' The clerk pointed at his own front teeth. 'I wouldn't be surprised if someone hadn't landed him a punch, knocked the tooth clear out of his mouth.

I asked him if he was down on holiday, if he'd had a nice time and he nearly snapped my head off. Downright rude he was. When all I was doing was taking a friendly interest. Told me it was none of my business what he was doing.'

'And you have never seen him before? He is not someone who usually catches the train at this station?'

'Never seen him before in my life. Can't say I want to see him again either.'

And with that the clerk held his newspaper up, indicating the conversation was over. It was time for him to finish his last beef sandwich.

If the death of George Leigh had been reported in the national newspapers Giuseppe hadn't seen it. The sudden death of a teenage boy in a small seaside town was 'news' by any standards. If the same incident had happened in Anzio, the seaside haunt for many Romans, then it would make the front page. But here it seemed they took a different approach. Of course, the weekly edition of the *Hastings Observer* and the *Eastbourne Herald* would all feature George Leigh as their front page lead, but Christina explained that these papers were only printed weekly, on a Thursday. She also told Giuseppe that her editor had been pressing her for more background on the Leigh family so he could publish an exclusive from the '*first person on the scene*'. Charles had given her until Wednesday lunchtime and told her not to come into the office until she had something worthy of a double-page spread.

As Giuseppe and Christina walked back alongside the railway line and along Beach Walk to her car, Christina was quiet.

After a while, Giuseppe said, 'You are thinking?'

'I am worrying. Well, not worrying exactly. I just feel so conflicted.'

Giuseppe waited for her to explain.

'I only ever wanted to be a journalist. Right through my teens, when Flavia was doing all those crazy things. All I could think about was how much was wrong with the way we live.'

'Your family?'

'No,' she said, with emphasis, her face relaxing into a smile. 'Mum and Dad are sound, they run the café, care for me, for Stevie...'

'And each other?'

'Of course. No, I'm talking about the rest of it, the prejudice, poverty, war. I could go on.'

'And being a journalist gives you a voice?'

'Exactly.'

'What is your conflict?'

'There are things I want the chance to say. That article for example, the one I'm working on, about social injustice. Now I have a chance to say something meaningful, but it's wrapped up with such dreadful circumstances. I feel as though I'm taking advantage of a family's grief just to grab my first proper byline.'

'Byline?'

'My name against the article.'

They had reached the car and Giuseppe stood beside it, facing the sea, his back to Christina.

'There are two things we must do tomorrow,' he said quietly, as though he was talking to himself. 'First, we must ring the detective in charge of this case.'

'Pearce?'

'*Si*. We will tell him we have more information for him. We will ask him to meet us somewhere outside the police station.'

'Why outside?'

'Inside is his territory, outside we can be more like equals. We have information, but he will also have information. The

114

police have had forty-eight hours to investigate. They must have discovered something.'

'If there's anything to discover.' Christina sounded defeated.

'Of course, if they have not yet solved the crime, then the information we have will be even more important,' Giuseppe said with emphasis. 'But before we meet Detective Sergeant Pearce, I will visit our Irish friend again, if your father will lend me his car once more.'

'You don't want me to come with you?'

'Take some time to look at your article again. Once your first *byline* appears, there will be demand for more from Christina Rossi.'

'Hardly,' she said, laughing.

CHAPTER 18
Wednesday, 8th July
Morning

Breakfast for the Rossi family usually took place in the back kitchen of the café. Giuseppe opted for an early morning stroll along the seafront, avoiding breakfast altogether, except for a glass of orange juice. Christina rarely sat down to eat her breakfast, persisting instead to move around the kitchen with a bowl of cereal in her hands. Mario found the constant movement so disconcerting he opted to do the early shift in the café, complaining that his daughter's fidgeting made him feel seasick. Anne was keeping an eye on Stevie, buttering a second slice of toast and slipping it onto Stevie's plate, just at the moment he'd finished his first slice.

Christina's thoughts were elsewhere. 'Stevie, hurry up and finish your toast. We've got to go or we'll be late.' She realised her tone was unnecessarily sharp when Anne gave her a warning glance.

She nodded to her mother, acknowledging the gentle reprimand, and put her half-eaten bowl of cornflakes on the draining board. The midday deadline Charles had set her was fast approaching. Giuseppe had suggested a plan to gather more information, both from Detective Sergeant Pearce, and the Irishman who lived in the caravan. Perhaps it would be enough. Even so, she'd prefer not to be put in the position of grabbing an opportunity to push her career forward at the expense of a family's grief. Although she knew what Charles would say. *Do you want to be a journalist, or not?* Or something along those lines. And he was probably right. She needed to toughen up.

As a useful distraction, she turned her mind to dogs. The *'dog discussion'* had taken place around the Rossi family table many times over the past months. Stevie pleaded, Anne placated, Christina listed all the reasons why it couldn't happen and Mario tried his best to keep out of it. None of the adults were prepared to admit they wanted a dog as much as Stevie did, but the practicalities of work and the demands of the café continued to be a deterrent.

Nevertheless, in the aftermath of recent events, Christina was coming around to the idea that bringing a dog into the Rossi family would be a perfect diversion for Stevie. On a couple of occasions since Sunday evening Stevie had woken screaming. Christina had gone into him, reassuring him it was just a bad dream. The first time it happened Stevie clung to her, his tears dampening her cotton nightie.

'Hey, what's all this?' she said, holding him tight and gently rocking him back and forth.

'There was a man. He was tall, like a giant, and he had a really loud voice. He kept shouting at me to get off the beach.'

'Well,' she said, putting on a serious voice, 'I can tell you no giant is going to keep us off the beach. How dare he? And I think if there was a giant he'd want to be in the sea splashing around with us, like this.' She started to tickle Stevie and soon they were both giggling, with dark thoughts forgotten.

But again on the drive into school on Wednesday morning Stevie made it clear his fears hadn't gone away.

'Auntie, Richard put his hand up in class yesterday and asked Miss if George Leigh had really been murdered. Then Miss told us all we mustn't talk to anyone we don't know and we mustn't go out to play on our own without a grown-up. But I can go into the garden, can't I?'

Christina tried to keep the emotion she was feeling from showing on her face. It was terrifying to imagine there could be a murderer, here among the local community. Someone who could inflict such brutal injuries on a teenage boy, leaving him to die. Her instincts were to wrap her arms around Stevie, hold him close to her and never let him out of her sight. But that would scare him even more. The conversation made her determined to speak to the mother of Stevie's friend, William Selmon, about their Beagle, Max. She had spoken to Mrs Selmon a few weeks earlier when Christina noticed William scratching at his arms. Christina recognised the red, scabby sores as eczema, a condition Flavia had when she was young. Mrs Selmon had explained her son's condition had worsened since they got Max.

'William's been on and on at me to get him a dog. I never dreamed it would make his eczema so bad,' Mrs Selmon told Christina. 'It doesn't help that he's cuddling up with him at night, despite me telling him not to.'

Christina sympathised, but the seed was planted in her mind. If Mrs Selmon was looking to rehome the dog, then it could be the perfect solution for both families.

Having waved Stevie into school, Christina spotted Mrs Selmon and waved to her. Max was pulling at his lead, attempting to jump up as Christina approached.

'Max, get down,' Mrs Selmon said, without enthusiasm. 'Oh, this dog is fair wearing me out. He's got too much energy for me. What with that and all the mess he makes shedding his hair all over the house, and William's eczema just getting worse and worse. Most days I'm ready for my bed by ten o'clock in the morning.' She wiped a hand across her forehead, pushing back her fringe.

'Have you ever thought of rehoming Max?' Christina said, bending to pat the dog, who was now much calmer.

'I think about it every day.' Mrs Selmon said, her breathing laboured. Christina noticed a slight wheeze.

'It's just that we've been promising Stevie a dog. But I'm sure you won't want to part with Max. William would be heartbroken.'

'Heartbroken or not, we can't go on like this. I'll speak to him tonight. He's a good boy, I'm sure he'll understand. Maybe I'll get him a budgerigar. It'll be a whole lot easier to cope with. Besides, he and Stevie are good pals. There's no reason why William can't carry on seeing Max now and then.' She paused, taking a deep breath before continuing. 'At least that's what I'll tell William,' she said with a wink.

CHAPTER 19
Wednesday, 8th July
Morning

While Christina was discussing possible dog ownership with Mrs Selmon, Giuseppe had left the café early, making his way to Beach Walk, as planned. He found Sean Murphy sitting on the steps, a pile of fishing line trailing from his hands.

'*Buon giorno.*'

Sean Murphy didn't look up, remaining focused on the line.

'Can I help you with that? Although you look as though you know what you are doing.'

This time the Irishman did look up, dropping the line onto a tarpaulin laid out at the foot of the caravan steps.

'Come back to do a bit more snooping?'

Giuseppe crouched down and picked up a length of fishing line, making a show of examining the tangle of small knots at one end of it. 'You have chosen a very peaceful place to live.'

'I can think of worst places to hide out.' Sean picked up his pipe that had been lying beside him on the caravan step. He lit it, puffing smoke towards Giuseppe, who was grateful for the chance to breathe it in.

'You are not hiding though, are you.' Giuseppe said. It was a statement, rather than a question.

'Clear view of the horizon.'

Giuseppe waited for the Irishman to explain.

'That's why I chose this spot. Nothing between me and the edge of the world.'

'Sometimes a small boy kicking a football?'

Sean looked up at Giuseppe. 'I don't mind the youngsters.'

'And you have family nearby? Or friends?'

Sean ignored the question, continuing to unravel the fishing line.

'The boys like to talk to you. Paul Leigh said you chased away a man who was shouting at him and his brother.'

'I bet the beaches are a whole lot nicer where you come from,' Sean said, making it clear he chose to deflect the conversation.

'You made friends with the brothers and yet you choose not to help solve the murder of one of them – right here, beside your caravan.'

'Murder? You're sure about that, are you?'

Giuseppe shrugged and waited, hoping he might have triggered a sense of responsibility in the Irishman to tell him what he must have seen that day.

'People like to think the worst of outsiders,' Sean said.

'Are you an outsider?'

'You and me both. You'll find folk round here won't welcome a foreigner interfering.'

Giuseppe went to crouch down to sit on the shingle before realising his limbs wouldn't allow him. He tutted before standing straight again.

'Age, eh?' The Irishman said. 'It comes to all of us. At least it does if we last that long.'

The man was starting to irritate Giuseppe. His manner was offhand, his jokes in poor taste.

'Take that woman in the cottage,' Sean continued. 'You don't see many locals extending a hand of friendship in her direction. Town like this, people close ranks. I've seen it before.'

'You have not extended your hand?'

'From what I can see she likes to keep herself to herself. Can't say I blame her.' Sean dropped the fishing line, stood up and looked directly at Giuseppe.

'I may return.' Giuseppe said.

'You can return as often as you like. There's nothing more

I can tell you.'

Giuseppe turned and walked back along the road to where he had parked his cousin's car, sensing the glare of the Irishman and wondering what it was he was so keen to hide.

A couple of hours later, the grumbles were muted as Giuseppe squeezed into the passenger seat of Christina's Mini, trying in vain to find a comfortable position. He received no sympathy from Christina who was entirely focused on the drive across the busy Marsh Road towards Eastbourne and their meeting with Detective Sergeant Pearce.

When Giuseppe had telephoned the police station earlier in the day he was put through to Pearce. Giuseppe could hear the caution in the detective sergeant's voice. There were unspoken questions, pauses in Pearce's responses. *He will want to know what it is about this case that is driving me to get involved.*

Pearce had agreed to a meeting, albeit reluctantly, suggesting they meet at the far end of Eastbourne seafront. With Pearce leading the way, the three of them began a slow walk up over the headland to Beachy Head. As they climbed up over the hill the wind picked up, to a force that Giuseppe would call freezing, while his cousin's description would more than likely be 'fresh'. Giuseppe pulled the collar of his jacket up, turning to see Christina take a cotton scarf from her shoulder bag, which she wrapped around her shoulders.

'Enjoying your holiday?' Pearce said, half turning towards Giuseppe.

'I have put my holiday to one side for now.'

The detective sergeant mumbled something under his breath.

The only other people to choose Beachy Head on such a blustery day were dog walkers. Giuseppe watched one couple in the distance. The dogs - a Labrador and a Scottie - were paying little attention to their owners, who were taking it in turns to call for them.

'This is a dangerous spot, they should keep them away from the edge,' Pearce said.

'The English and their dogs. I think you like your pets more than you like people.'

'You might be right there.' Pearce pointed to a sign that was less than fifty yards from the cliff edge. 'They warn of "*Danger*" and yet it's the danger that draws people here.'

'What do you mean?'

'It's a suicide spot.' Pearce gestured towards the cliff edge. 'Turns out it's more popular than the Golden Gate Bridge.' The three of them peered over, looking at the sheer drop and the waves crashing over the rocks below. 'I've dealt with a few over the years. I expect you've seen your fair share.'

'In all my time as a policeman I have learned little about the minds of men.'

'But you've solved plenty of crimes, so you'll know all about the minds of criminals.' Pearce said.

'What makes a bad man? Is it someone who wants something they can't have, but they decide to have it nevertheless?'

'Robbery?'

'Yes, also crimes of passion, crimes with envy, jealousy or greed at the centre of them.'

They moved away from the cliff edge, retreating to a bench positioned to the side of the footpath.

'And then there are the men who are not criminals and yet struggle so much with life they choose to end it, like your suicides,' Giuseppe continued.

'Not my suicides. I have no more understanding than you.'

'Can we concentrate on the reason we are here?' Christina's tone was sharp. 'It's bad enough we are having to discuss one

123

tragedy, without contemplating a host of others.'

The three of them sat in silence for a while, watching the dog owners, who had now retrieved their wayward pets, clipped on their leads and were making their way back towards the car park.

'What do you have for me then? Any luck getting people to talk?' Pearce directed his question at Christina, but it was Giuseppe who responded.

'You are treating George Leigh's death as murder?' Giuseppe asked.

'We now know for certain it wasn't an accident. The post-mortem confirmed the injuries are highly unlikely to have been caused by the boy just falling from his bicycle. It seems there were two distinct blows to the head. It was the second one that caused a bleed to his brain, and ultimately his death.

'Could a vehicle have been involved?'

'We can't be sure,' Pearce said. 'There were no tyre tracks or skid marks, but we are keeping an open mind.' He turned to Christina. 'You definitely didn't see a car?'

She shook her head and then, 'We have spoken to an interesting man who likes to do puzzles.'

The detective sergeant nodded. 'Sean Murphy, the Irishman in the caravan. I've had a chat with him too, for what good it did me.'

'I have met many strange people in Italy,' Giuseppe continued, 'but a man who lives in a caravan and likes to do jigsaw puzzles. I think this is a new experience for me.'

'You said you spoke to the Leigh family?' Pearce asked.

'They are broken.' Giuseppe said.

'Well, of course, they would be. Losing a child, it's a parent's worst nightmare.'

'But I think they are also broken in another way.' Giuseppe studied his fingers as he spoke. 'The mother is grieving, the father is angry and the boy...'

'Remember they're English.' Christina had their attention. 'We're still living in the shadow of Victorian attitudes in this country, with the crazy notion that boys shouldn't cry or show any emotion. It's supposed to show weakness. I think it's unhealthy, shutting down all those feelings. Better to do what the Italians do, wail and scream.'

The detective sergeant muttered something, which neither of them heard.

'I have never wailed or screamed.' Giuseppe said. 'Perhaps I am not as Italian as I thought.'

'And Mrs Rose Walker? What do you make of her?' Pearce tried to refocus. 'From what I've heard about her she sounds as vague as the sea mist that surrounds this case.'

'You think she is vague? I say she is scared.'

Pearce looked askance at Giuseppe, who then continued. 'I see it in her eyes, her manner. She is haunted by something, by someone.'

'I haven't spoken to the woman. My WPC interviewed her on Sunday, soon after the ambulance took the lad away, and then again when Mrs Walker came into the station.'

'She is holding herself tight together. Attempting to control her fears by controlling all that is around her. Her house is so neat, her garden too.'

'You're reading a lot into someone who likes to keep a tidy house. I wonder what you might think if you came round to mine.' Pearce gave a rough laugh, triggering a cough. Giuseppe watched as the detective sergeant put his hand into his jacket pocket, only to remove it seconds later. It was Giuseppe's guess that Pearce was about to take out a packet of cigarettes, before remembering he was supposed to be giving up.

'It could be she's guilty of something. Not telling us the full story perhaps?' Pearce stood, indicating it was time to go. 'Shall we walk back down?'

'You have a plan for your investigation?' Giuseppe said, guessing that whatever the plan was Pearce was unlikely to share it with a stranger, a foreign stranger at that.

'We are pursuing enquiries.'

'Of course. The violent death in a small community. Many people will be scared until you find the person responsible. It is the motive that interests me. It is the key that opens many doors. Find the motive and you are a long way to understand the crime and the criminal.'

'Please don't tell me how to do my job, Mr Bianchi. I've been a detective probably for as long as you.'

The three of them walked for a while in silence as they made their way down towards the car park. Either side of the footpath were alternating areas of grass, interspersed with gorse bushes, a paradise for rabbits given the piles of droppings underfoot. The view from the headland took in Selsey Bill, a coastal peninsula some fifty or so miles to the west. Turning to the east the visibility was such that they could just make out the Dungeness Lighthouse, fifty miles in the other direction.

The summer sun had turned much of the grass yellow, with bare patches here and there, worn away with constant footfall. Giuseppe slowed his pace, falling back behind the other two, giving him a moment to reflect on the sharp mismatch of such beauty and such tragedy. A place where it was possible to see the best of what life has to offer and yet also a location for those who feel nothing but despair.

Finally, Giuseppe broke the silence. 'Has your team visited the railway station?' He kept his tone as level as possible, knowing the detective sergeant would be irritated if he felt the Italian was trying to score points.

'Norman's Bay?'

126

'*Sì*. We have spoken to the ticket clerk. He told us about a man who bought a ticket to London.'

'Not unusual, a man buying a train ticket at a ticket office?' Pearce didn't hide the sarcasm in his voice.

'We only want to help. We're not trying to interfere.' Christina said.

'What about the man then? You think there's something in it?' Pearce said.

'The clerk said the man was not a regular, but also that his manner was aggressive. Perhaps more questions need to be asked?' Giuseppe said.

Pearce nodded by way of acknowledgement. 'I'll send a constable to interview the clerk. See if we can't get a clearer statement from him.'

They reached the car park and Giuseppe extended his hand towards the detective sergeant. 'I hope you have success with your investigation.'

It wasn't a race to the finish line, but Giuseppe was certain he still wanted to compete, even though he could no longer compete on an equal footing.

CHAPTER 20
Wednesday, 8th July
Afternoon

It was mid-afternoon by the time Christina returned to the café, having been into the office to type up the article for Charles. She slammed it down on his desk and left the office before he had time to read it. *'Local boy in fatal incident'* was the headline she'd chosen, although Charles was just as likely to change it. She knew the piece she'd written was good, which in itself was a reminder to herself that she could write well. There were enough demons chasing around in her brain, so if she could shed the one that undermined her confidence, perhaps she could start to move forward.

In writing the piece she'd stuck to the facts, giving the briefest of details about her own involvement and a bare mention of the Leigh family. It was her way of trying to protect them from further invasion into their privacy once the national press got hold of the story. She was surprised they hadn't already run a piece. After all, any violent death usually sparked a flurry of mildly political features, whether the police were doing all they should to keep the streets safe, that kind of thing. If she'd given any hint about the undercurrents that both she and Giuseppe sensed when they'd visited the Leighs, it would give the less scrupulous among her fellow journalists too much ammunition to pry. All too often she'd seen headlines in some of the more scurrilous nationals that she was certain had little or no basis in truth. She might be ambitious, but she was determined to make her mark without stooping to such depths.

For the last few evenings she'd taken to watching the late night news. No one else had watched the television since its arrival. It was perched on the sideboard in the sitting room and looked so out of place, like an unwelcome intruder. Investigations into the assassination of President Kennedy were still ongoing. President Johnson had set up a commission to elicit the facts and it was due to report soon. The news presenter spoke about the repercussions of such a dreadful act, then went on to talk about the plane crash that had taken place last month where Edward Kennedy was seriously injured. It seemed that the family were blighted. Closer to home, the news focused on the three hundred or so people who had been injured when the Beatles returned home to Liverpool after their sell-out American tour. Christina adored Beatles music, but she couldn't imagine screaming and crying and pulling her hair out just to be close to them. There was so much about the world and the people in it that confused her.

Giuseppe was sitting outside the front of the café when she arrived. After feeling a little chilled during their earlier walk across Beachy Head, Christina was now too hot. The wind had eased during the afternoon, and the wispy clouds provided little respite from the sun. She smiled as she approached, noticing Giuseppe still had his jacket on.

'Still not hot enough for you?' she said, pulling up a spare chair and sitting beside him.

Giuseppe had his eyes closed, his hands folded in his lap. She wondered for a moment if he was asleep. Then he opened his eyes and looked across at her, having to squint in the sunshine.

'I left my sunglasses indoors,' he said. 'Your father should put up a shade. In Roma many of the cafés have them.'

'Mum's been telling him the same thing for years. Maybe you'll have more luck.'

'Is Charles happy now?'

'I doubt it. I left the article on his desk and scarpered. He's got the facts, so it's up to him if he prints it.'

'He will print it. I am sure of it. He has an exclusive. An *Eastbourne Herald* reporter, the first person on the scene. That will certainly sell his newspapers.'

Christina sighed. 'I hate the way that makes me feel. On so many levels.'

'Think no more about it. We need to focus.' He leaned forward and started drumming his fingers against the edge of the table.

'*We?* Have you enrolled me onto your investigation team?' she said, smiling.

'A murderer, perhaps somewhere here among us. It is not a cause for smiling.'

'You're right. And I'm worried about Stevie.'

'Your mother has gone to fetch him home from school. You know he will be safe. The police will solve the crime.'

'Is there really nothing more we can do?'

Giuseppe closed his eyes again, a sign that the conversation was over, at least for the moment.

Christina went inside and minutes later Anne arrived with Stevie, who was carrying his school tie, twirling it around like a lasso.

'Stevie, go and get changed out of your uniform, then ask Granddad to get you some milk and biscuits. I need to talk to your Uncle Giuseppe.' Anne said, following her grandson upstairs.

Moments later she returned, gesturing to Christina to follow her back outside.

'What's that?' Christina said, pointing to the letter her mother was holding.

'It came in this morning's post. I thought I'd show it to Giuseppe, see what he makes of it.'

'I'll get us a drink,' Christina said, going inside and returning seconds later with three glasses of lemonade.

Giuseppe was reading through the letter, then he set it down on the table and took a drink.

'Who's it from, Mum?'

Anne took up the letter and read it aloud.

Dear Anne

I hope you don't mind my getting in touch. I know it's been a long time since we shared any news.

It's about my sister, Barbara. Three months ago she walked out of the flat we'd been sharing and I haven't seen or heard from her since.

I kept waiting for a phone call or a letter, even a postcard. Then, as the time went on, with no news, I wondered if she'd had an accident. I told the police, but they just told me to check the hospitals. Seems that if you're an adult you can walk out of one life into another and there's nothing your loved ones can do about it.

You're probably wondering why I've chosen now to write to you.

We had some good times together, didn't we? You were always so kind to us both. Your mother too. And I know you had to bear the sadness of losing her soon after the war ended. So sad, she was a special lady.

I feel I'm in a kind of limbo until I know what has really happened to Barbara.

I got to thinking about the happier times the three of us had together and I wondered if you could spare an afternoon to come up to London? We could meet in a café close to the station, maybe just for an hour or so?

Please say you'll come.

Yours

Matthew Harding

'Who on earth is Matthew Harding?' Christina asked.

'Matthew and his sister, Barbara, they lived with us for a while. During the war.'

'Evacuees?'

Anne nodded. 'It was just days before war was declared.

Trainloads turned up here in Bexhill and Hastings. Thousands of children. The Government called it Operation Pied Piper. The news bulletins were full of it. They said that in London alone, trains were leaving the main stations every nine minutes, crammed full of children and expectant mothers.'

'I can't imagine it.' Christina was trying to imagine Stevie, sent off on a train to some unknown destination, with no certainty when he might return. 'It makes me feel ill to think about it.'

'I remember the little ones looked as though they'd landed on a strange planet, their eyes wide, their hands grasping tight to their bag. A luggage label was pinned to each coat with their name, it was as if they were parcels being shipped from one town to another, not someone's beloved daughter or son. They all had a little bag with them, some had satchels and a few paltry belongings; not much more than a change of clothes, their toothbrush and a pat of soap.'

'And you were there when they arrived?'

'Mum took me to the station to greet the train as it arrived. I'd already told her I didn't intend to share my bedroom with a stranger.'

'What did your mum say?'

'*You'll do whatever is necessary. We all will.*' Anne recounted, the hint of a smile on her lips.

As mother and daughter were talking Giuseppe listened, but said nothing.

'And your mum chose Matthew and Barbara?' Christina asked.

'I remember the two of them standing on the platform, their hands linked tightly together, their heads down, trying not to look at anyone. They were probably hoping they wouldn't be chosen by a new family, so they could get straight back on the train and go back home.' Anne smiled, then continued. 'Anyway, Mum gathered the pair up and we took them home. Suddenly, I had to share everything, my bedroom, my books.'

'There was rationing, wasn't there? How did you manage for food?'

'Some mealtimes there was little more than a few slices of bread and some home-made jam.'

'Crikey, Mum, it must have been such a difficult time. How long did they live with you?'

'A little short of two years and when they finally returned to London, it was to a bombed-out city.'

'But you stayed in touch?'

'At first Matthew wrote quite often.' Anne's expression was wistful. 'I can still picture his face. He was a few years younger than me and to be honest with you I think he had a bit of a crush on me.' Christina noticed her mum's face colouring up.

'He told us they were waiting to be rehoused, along with so many other families. But then the correspondence fell off, except for an exchange of Christmas and birthday cards.'

'I remember now. We used to send them Christmas cards,' Christina said. 'You made us sign our names. One year I drew some holly beside my name and you let me colour the berries with a felt-tip pen and the whole thing smudged when I closed the card too quickly. And Matthew was younger than you?'

'I was fourteen and Matthew was twelve when they first came to us, Barbara just ten. By the end of the war I'd joined the Military Nursing Service. Matthew was too young to join up, he didn't have his eighteenth birthday until war was almost over. Then, of course, I went to Italy to work in the army hospital. I wrote when your dad and I got married and when you and Flavia were born. Once we settled back here in Bexhill with the café, I asked them to come and visit. But their lives had moved on. I understood that.

'And now his sister is missing?'

'From the letter, it seems she moved out months ago and he's not heard from her since.'

'Why does he think you can help?'

'I should have written more often. I get the sense their lives haven't been easy. Barbara was such a funny little thing, a bit of a dreamer, always making up stories. She'd say all sorts about her parents, made out they lived in a grand house with servants. Matthew was forever trying to bring her down to earth.'

'And now suddenly Matthew is writing to you?' Giuseppe had been looking over the letter again.

'I don't know what I think about it,' Anne said. 'What do you make of it?'

'Perhaps it is time I began to enjoy my holiday. A visit to London, a day out.'

Christina looked at Giuseppe, wondering what was behind his sudden change of heart.

'You'd go to London? Visit Matthew for me?' Anne said.

Giuseppe gave the merest of nods, as if he was still considering the matter.

'You'd certainly know the right questions to ask. And if Christina went with you, you could enjoy a spot of sightseeing while you're there.'

'I live in Roma. I know about city life.'

'But you could see Buckingham Palace, the Houses of Parliament, the Tower of London...'

'When we have the Colosseum and St Peter's Basilica and two thousand years of history?' Giuseppe kept a stern face for a moment, then broke into a smile, taking Anne's hand in his. 'I am joking with you. Of course I will go. Christina can look after me and make sure I do not get lost. And together we can see what we can do to help your friend.'

Later that evening, Christina waited for everyone to be in bed before slipping through to the sitting room and closing the door. She switched on the television and for a few moments there was no picture, just a buzzing sound and black and white lines flickering across the screen. She turned the sound low and waited. Then a picture emerged, a newsreader sat at a desk, formally dressed in a suit and tie. She turned the sound up and heard the presenter talk of the war in Vietnam. There'd been more killing and yet more young American soldiers were to be sent to fight. Christina tried to imagine what it might be like for the young men, arriving in such a place and found that she couldn't imagine any of it. It was too far from everything she knew. Perhaps to become a good reporter, she had to put herself not just into the shoes of others whose lives were so different from hers, but into their minds too, to try to imagine their emotions, their fears.

She continued to sit with the sound turned off, until the test card came onto the screen. Programmes were finished for the day. It was time for bed.

CHAPTER 21
Thursday, 9th July
Morning

The next morning Giuseppe was ready at the front door of the café, clutching an umbrella he'd borrowed from Mario. Christina emerged from the bathroom and sauntered down the stairs to meet him. She was wearing an outfit Giuseppe hadn't seen before. A pink cotton tunic worn over a pinstriped shirt, over her arm a pale blue raincoat that had a shine to it.

'You are dressed for the city,' Giuseppe said.

'Closest I'm likely to get to King's Road, Chelsea.'

He raised an eyebrow.

'Mary Quant. Bazaar. *The* place for fashion. Not that I can afford any of it.'

'Ah,' he said.

'But I'd better warn you, I'm not good with early mornings,' Christina said. 'I'm fine without breakfast, but you'll have to put up with me putting my face on when we're on the train. Otherwise I will scare the natives.'

'Your face?'

'My make-up.'

Once on the train Christina grabbed the window seat, pulled a mirror from her handbag and proceeded to apply her makeup. Giuseppe glanced at the items she took from her bag of cosmetics.

'If there are smudges I'll have to sort them out when we get there, in the station toilets.' Christina said, more to herself than to Giuseppe. There was little or no chance for conversation during the train journey as Giuseppe had his eyes closed for most of it.

On their arrival at Victoria, Christina pointed towards the station exit.

'Shall we do Mum's visit first, get it out of the way, before we go sightseeing?'

'We are here to see if we can help your mother's friend. It is not something to "*get out of the way*".'

'You're right, sorry.'

'You know the way to this man's house?'

She waved an A-Z of London at him, flicking through it to the page showing their destination.

'We'll need to get the Victoria Line and change at Oxford Circus. Are you okay with the Underground?'

'The English do not have a monopoly on underground trains.'

'Sorry - again. Are you okay? You sound annoyed.'

'My mind is elsewhere.'

'Back at Beach Walk?'

'Perhaps.'

'Try to leave that behind for a few hours. Let's battle our way through this lot and buy a ticket.'

With underground tickets purchased, Christina and Giuseppe made their way to the platform, which was packed with travellers. They stood as far back from the edge as possible.

'I hate the underground.' Christina was gripping Giuseppe's arm a little too tightly. 'You know that whoosh of hot air that comes through the tunnel just as the train arrives? It's like a ferocious beast, sucking all the oxygen from us. I almost expect it to be breathing fire.'

'The train?' Giuseppe wasn't certain he'd understood.

'Ignore me. I might as well forget about Fleet Street, I'll never be a city girl.'

As the train arrived, there was a great push forward as almost everyone on the platform moved at the same time. Christina and Giuseppe squeezed inside the carriage just before the doors slid closed.

Giuseppe had a theory that the inside of an underground train was the perfect place to study humanity. He'd never voiced his theory, but enjoyed any opportunity to put it to the test. Here was a concentration of people in a crowded place, providing scope for observation. On each occasion he'd caught an underground train he noticed most people chose to do anything possible to avoid eye contact with a stranger. They might stare at a newspaper, look out of the window at the inside of a tunnel, or keep their gaze down at the floor. As he looked around he noticed how the outfits of other young women mirrored what Christina was wearing. It was as if there was a common theme. So too, the make-up she had applied so expertly this morning, the white lipstick, thick black eyeliner, and mascara. Even her hairstyle. He guessed the young women were modelling themselves on some pop star or film star. He hadn't noticed anything similar among the Italian women, not the dress style, or the make-up. But then he had so rarely looked.

While Giuseppe was musing on such things, Christina was focused on the Underground map displayed on the side of the carriage.

'Ours is the next stop,' she said, pulling on Giuseppe's arm.

The tube train came to a halt and they pushed their way through the group of people who were clustered around the door.

'Come on, this way.' She pointed to a sign indicating the passageway they needed to take to connect with the Bakerloo line.

Ten minutes later and they emerged into the fresh air, albeit it was raining heavily.

'Welcome to London,' Christina said, as Giuseppe opened his umbrella and almost poked a passer-by in the eye.

'Watch out mate,' the man said, before rushing past.

'English weather - why do you put up with it?' Giuseppe said, the man turning back to discover if the question was aimed at him.

'It's not like we have a choice,' Christina replied.

'There is always a choice.'

They attempted to walk alongside each other, with Giuseppe trying to hold the umbrella over both of them. Several times one or other of them had to move out of the way of oncoming pedestrians.

'This is it. Just as well I memorised the route.' The rain was falling heavily now, the A-Z safely tucked away in the pocket of her mac.

They stopped in front of a doorway to a three-storey building, a haberdasher's on the ground floor, with two flats above. To the side of the shop was a narrow entrance, with a door set back, providing a little protection from the rain. To one side of the entrance a handwritten sign displayed two names, a bell push beside each one. She pressed the buzzer against the name of Harding and waited.

'He doesn't know we're coming?' Giuseppe asked.

'No. There was no phone number, just an address.'

'Then he will probably be out.'

'Yes, probably. But I think we deserve a bit of luck, don't you?'

They stood, looking up at the flats above.

'Shall I go into the shop? Ask if they've seen him, if he's at home?' Christina said. Then one of the upstairs windows opened, a man leaned out.

'Hang on a minute, I'm coming down.'

'Hello there,' Christina called back. 'I'm Christina Rossi and I'm here with my Uncle Giuseppe. My mother received your letter.'

She heard the window close, then a few moments later there was a click and the door opened, revealing a thin-faced man in his late thirties, wearing a checked shirt, open at the neck, and workman's jeans.

'Come on in,' he said, standing back as they stepped into the gloomy entrance hall. Giuseppe looked down at the floor, as the rain dripped off his jacket and umbrella, and Christina held a wet hand out towards the man.

'Matthew Harding?'

'That's me. Come on up, there's no lift, I'm afraid.'

'We will make everything wet,' Giuseppe said, looking at the trail of footsteps he was leaving behind him.

'It's not a problem,' Matthew said, waving a hand at them to follow.

He trudged ahead of them up three flights of stairs, until they reached a small landing. He pointed at a door at one end of the landing. 'The bathroom, if you need it. I share it with Moira, but she's out all day. Hairdresser, nice woman.'

He turned towards a dark green door, put the key in the lock and gave it a shove. 'Always sticks in the damp weather.'

They stepped forward into a narrow hallway, which led into a larger room, set out with a settee at one end and a kitchenette at the other. The room was dark, with one window at shoulder height, looking out onto neighbouring flats. A two-bar electric fire was the only apparent source of warmth for colder days. A folded table was pushed up against the wall beneath the window.

'You'll have tea?'

Giuseppe shook his head to decline and Christina spoke for both of them. 'No, we're fine really, thanks anyway.'

'How is your mum? Keeping well, I hope. You're just like her, as I remember her anyway.' His tone was apologetic, as though he'd said more than he meant to.

He waved his visitors towards the settee, plumping himself down on one of the wooden chairs next to the table. 'Sorry, it's not that comfy. Lost its springs - a bit like me.' He attempted a smile, but all it did was make him look sad.

'Mum showed me your letter. She was sorry she couldn't come, but she needs to be there for the café, it's pretty busy most of the time.'

'The café, of course.' Matthew looked at the floor as though momentarily overwhelmed by emotion. Then he took a deep breath and said, 'Lucky you didn't come any earlier. I've just finished my shift.'

'You had an early start?'

'I'm a postman. Early mornings, but all done by lunchtime.'

'You and your sister lived with Mum during the war, is that right?' Christina couldn't decide whether it was something about Matthew Harding that was making her feel uncomfortable, or if it was the damp smell pervading the flat.

'Your gran was very kind to us. I was very sorry to hear she'd passed over.'

Giuseppe watched the man as he spoke, focusing on his expression and body language, rather than the words, some of which he was struggling to understand.

'And your sister? Mum explained you are worried about her.'

'Silly idea, really, to write to your mum.' Matthew leaned over in his chair, his hands covering his face. 'It's just that it's been three months now and I've heard nothing, no letter, no postcard.' Some of the tension in his body relaxed as he spoke about his sister.

'I think I will have that cup of tea now, if that's okay.' Christina said.

Matthew filled the kettle and set it on the gas. While he stood with his back to them Christina spent a few moments taking in their surroundings. The room was sparsely furnished; a small sideboard with a dark brown wireless set at one end, which looked as if it belonged to the nineteenth century. Beside it was a bowl of apples. There were no pictures on the walls and no ornaments. The geometric wallpaper design was yellowed in places, patches of mildew around the skirting. To one side of the room was an old wooden clothes airer. Two shirts, a few pairs of socks and a tea towel were draped across it, looking as though they'd been there for days. A man's home, one with no trace of a woman's influence.

'Did your sister used to live here with you?'

The kettle boiled at that moment, a loud whistle piercing the quiet. For the next few minutes Matthew busied himself, filling a tea pot, laying a tray. By the time he went to pour, it was as though he'd forgotten Christina's question.

Then he said, 'My sister loved Bexhill. The first time she saw the sea she ran in, shoes and socks still on her feet. Your gran shouted at her, but nothing was going to stop her.'

Then, suddenly, he began to sob, taking great gulps of air. He remained standing as though the grief was taking away his ability to move. Christina stood beside him, patting his back, while Giuseppe wondered about all of it; the man, the sister and how anyone could have fond memories of walking into the cold English Channel.

They stayed another half an hour, by which time Matthew had rallied a little. The remaining conversation centred around little more than small talk. All the while Giuseppe was wondering why Anne had ever thought they could be of any help.

As they were leaving, Christina said, 'I don't suppose you have a photo of your sister you could spare?'

Matthew left the room, returning with a small black-and-white photo which he handed to Christina.

142

'Thanks, it might help, you never know.'

'Give my best to your mum,' was his parting remark.

A little later that afternoon they'd taken shelter from the persistent rain, in a steamy back street café. 'The photo is useless,' Giuseppe said. 'It's from years ago, when she was just a girl.'

'There'll be some resemblance, won't there? Granted, she might have changed her hairstyle, even the colour, but the shape of her face won't have changed. Maybe a few lines here and there. Her face is familiar somehow. I think Mum must have shown me photos of the three of them when they were living together in Bexhill. What I don't get is why she'd disappear and not contact her brother? He says they were close - good friends. If it's true, then why walk out and abandon him?'

'He told us very little about his sister. It was as if he did not want to talk about her and yet the letter to your mother suggested the opposite. Perhaps he has killed her and buried her in the garden.'

'You're not serious, are you? That's such a grim thought. Anyway, he doesn't have a garden. And if he has done away with her, why would he be asking us to help him find her?'

'Double bluff.'

'I'm impressed.' Christina clapped her hands together, causing the people at a neighbouring table to look over at her.

'My experience as a detective?'

'No, your English. Double bluff isn't a common phrase, is it? Come on, let's brave the weather. I promised you some sightseeing.'

Giuseppe looked out at the grey sky, interspersed with black clouds, still heavy with rain.

'It's okay, I promise we won't take an open-top bus.'

CHAPTER 22
Thursday, 9th July
Afternoon

It wasn't an open-top bus, but a crowded one that took them to Charing Cross. They were lucky to get two seats together, as soon after they caught the bus the conductor was calling out, '*Standing room only*,' at each bus stop along the rest of the route.

It was impossible to tell whether Giuseppe was quiet because of the '*dreadful English weather*', or if he was considering the conversation they'd had with Matthew Harding. At least during the bus journey he didn't close his eyes - or not so she noticed. Instead, he seemed to be studying the passengers with such intensity that she was just waiting for someone to object.

Despite the rain, which was now more of a summer shower, Christina assured Giuseppe the best way to see Buckingham Palace was to approach it by walking up The Mall.

'We can pretend we're royalty,' she teased, trying to break the silence. With Charing Cross station in sight, she grabbed Giuseppe's arm and pulled him out of his seat. 'This is our stop.'

Although the rain had stopped, the tree-lined avenue of The Mall resulted in them getting a soaking from overhead branches.

'Maybe put the umbrella back up?' Christina said, after raindrops from a particularly large branch showered down on her.

'What do you think? Impressive, eh?' She pointed towards the Palace.

'Your Queen lives there?'

'Some of the time. When she's at home they hoist a different flag, not the Union Jack. So today it looks as though she's out. Pity, I was hoping to be invited in for tea.' She nudged Giuseppe in the ribs and was rewarded with a smile.

'Where do we go next?'

'Anywhere you like. We could walk up to Hyde Park Corner and then down to Piccadilly. How does that sound?'

He nodded and increased his pace.

'There's no rush, we've got the rest of the day.'

'I don't like to walk slowly.'

A while later and they had reached Piccadilly Circus.

'Shall we grab a coffee before we go any further?' she said, pointing to a café displaying a sign for *Real Italian coffee*. 'That's the broadest smile I've seen since you arrived.'

Once inside and coffees ordered, they chose a corner table. Italian music was playing and Giuseppe started to hum along with it, tapping the tune out with his fingers against the edge of the table.

'You know this song?'

'My mother used to sing it to us when she was trying to get us to sleep.'

'Your mum and dad's mum, they were sisters, weren't they? Dad never talks much about any of it. She was my grandmother, but I know virtually nothing about her, or my grandfather.'

'They were good people. Hardworking, kind.'

'When Flavia and I were little, we used to plead with Dad to take us to Italy. Every summer we'd ask him and every summer he'd say the same thing. "*Too much money. Save your pocket money and you can go yourself one day, when you're older.*"'

Giuseppe looked down at the half-empty coffee cup. 'Flavia has created many problems for your family, for you.'

'All families have problems.'

'But you feel the responsibility for Stevie? That must be very hard for you.'

'You have no idea.' For a moment Christina felt ready to share some of the dark thoughts she'd had about her sister, the way she felt when Flavia had 'stolen' Tony from her. Instead, she looked away from Giuseppe and was quiet.

'Stevie loves you very much.' Giuseppe said.

'It's confusing for him. I'm his aunt, but sometimes he forgets that's all I am. You know the other day he called me Mum.'

'What did Anne say?'

'I haven't told her. I'd rather you didn't mention it to be honest. She'd probably say I need to change the way I am with Stevie, but he's six years old, for goodness' sake. He's bound to be confused when his own mother wants little or nothing to do with him. Anyway, let's change the subject.' She drained her cup, pushing it away from her. 'How about we talk about Dad? All those years away from his family. He must have missed them. You must have missed seeing him. You were close as boys, weren't you?'

'We had good times together. Days out at Santa Marinella - one of the beaches near Roma - swimming, picking sea urchins from the rock pools.' He sat back in his chair and gave a little chuckle. 'One time he slipped on a rock and fell. He was five or six years old. He started screaming and crying, making a fuss. Shock, I think. I stood and laughed at him. That made him angry, so he reached out to punch me and fell in again.'

They both laughed, then Christina squeezed Giuseppe's arm. 'Do you think you'll persuade him to go back with you, for a while?'

'There is the café to think of.'

'I know, but I could take a couple of weeks off to look after things. It would be brilliant for Mum and Dad to have a proper holiday.'

'A visit to Italy would not be a holiday for your father.'

'Because he was born there?'

'Because of things that happened a long time ago. Before you were born.'

'What things? He met Mum there. That must have been good?'

'Yes, of course. That was good.'

'And Rosalia?'

Giuseppe pushed his cup away with force, upsetting the sugar bowl from the centre of the table, and sending tiny white crystals scattering in all directions.

'Do you ever hear from her?'

When Rosalia left Giuseppe he wrote a long letter to his cousin, defending his wife, saying that to be the wife of a policeman was difficult. He worked long hours, was never at home and even when he was at home his mind was always on an ongoing investigation. The story was *'it wasn't her fault'*.

In subsequent letters more detail emerged, although much of it had to be established by reading between the lines. Rosalia had come from a wealthy family, she was used to fine things. An Italian policeman was well paid, but not enough to buy her the furs and jewellery and the beachside villa she craved. She chose to go and live with a 'friend' whose property included a private mooring. There was no suggestion of impropriety, no mention of the friend's name, but Christina was convinced it was a 'romantic liaison'. She'd seen the photos of their wedding. Rosalia was a real beauty and Christina could imagine her lying on a yacht, soaking up the sun, being waited on by some gorgeous Italian Romeo.

Christina was brought back to the present when the waitress brushed past in her haste to collect the empty cups and wipe the table.

'How about another coffee? Now we've found the real thing, best make the most of it.' Christina didn't wait for a reply. She took her purse up to the counter and ordered, this time adding two pastries to the order.

'I guess you'd rather not talk about Rosalia. Sorry, I shouldn't have brought it up,' she said, returning to her seat.

'We are not in touch. She lives her life, I live mine. I hope she is happy.'

'Will you ever divorce?' Christina was certain if Mario was sitting beside her right now he'd have been tempted to give her a clip round the ear for her impertinence.

'Marriage vows are blessed by God. You can't undo them, just because you change your mind.'

The waitress arrived with the coffee and pastries and for a while the two of them sat in silence.

'Another subject now, I think. Let us pretend you are the detective,' Giuseppe said, having finished his pastry in two bites.

'You can pretend away. I wouldn't have the first clue where to start.'

'We have already started. Imagine you are writing a report on the case for Detective Sergeant Pearce. A summary.'

'There'd be little or nothing in it.' Christina looked away, towards a mother and child sitting at a nearby table. The child was persisting in sticking her finger into the sugar bowl, but each time the girl got close her mother smacked her hand away.

'Rose Walker. Sean Murphy,' Christina said, with more certainty than her expression suggested. 'Both know more than they are saying.'

'*Si. Altro?* Anything else?'

'There was broken glass at the scene. I nearly put my hand on it when I crouched down beside George. Maybe worth exploring what kind of glass?'

'*Forse.* Perhaps.'

'Not much to go on though, is it?'

'We are just at the beginning. But remember, as we continue, you are a reporter who needs to think like a detective. Question everything.'

'My turn now,' Christina said. 'You wanted to come to London to distance yourself from the investigation, didn't you?'

'It is not my case. It can never be my case. I am a retired Italian detective.'

'You say that as though you are still trying to convince yourself.'

'Perhaps I am.'

'Is there another reason you want to be involved?'

'You see. You would make a good detective.' Giuseppe gave the briefest of smiles. 'Intuition.'

'Do you want to talk about it?'

'A child died. I couldn't investigate the incident because it happened where I live, just there on the road below my flat. In fact, there was no incident. The coroner decided it was an accident.'

'And you think otherwise?'

'*Sì.*'

'Okay, that's the serious conversation over for now. Time for more sightseeing. Come on.' Christina pushed her cup away and wiped the pastry crumbs away from her mouth. 'This time I guarantee you'll love it.'

Watching Giuseppe's evident enjoyment as he sipped his Italian coffee had given Christina an idea. She'd heard her mum mention a part of London people called '*Little Italy*'. Anne explained that after the war many Italian families had settled there, creating an enclave, populating the area with Italian ice-cream parlours and family-run shops, where it was possible to buy every Italian delicacy, the best olive oil, all types of salami and every shape of pasta.

'Okay, now we need to catch the number 38 bus,' Christina said. 'And I guarantee this shopping experience will bring a smile to your face.'

'Plenty of space up top,' the conductor called out as they jumped on the bus.

Christina chose a window seat, pressing her nose against the rain-spattered glass, which still provided her with a clear view of the street below. All her life the café had been her mum and dad's first priority. There were very few times when they managed a day out together as a family. School holidays usually meant the girls amusing themselves, spending days at the beach, or in the woods. Later, once they were in their teens, they often passed the day lying out on the terraces of the Bathing Pool, hoping one of the boys would notice them. Usually the boys were too busy showing off their diving skills to notice a couple of giggly girls. Although one summer Flavia was chatted up by two boys at the same time. She'd played them along until she got bored and told them to get lost.

'You can be cruel when you choose, you know,' Christina told her sister after watching the forlorn faces of both boys.

'Toughen up. Life's cruel, get used to it,' was all she said, making sure her laugh was loud enough for the boys to hear.

The bus driver jammed his brakes on as a cyclist sped in front of him, causing Christina to bang her head against the window.

'Are you okay? Maybe do not sit so close to the glass?'

'No harm done,' Christina said, rubbing her forehead. 'Italian ice-cream, that's what I'm going to have when we get there.'

She was remembering a day when the four of them had come to London for a rare family day out. She must have been ten or eleven, Flavia a couple of years younger. She couldn't recall if her parents had closed the café for the day or if someone had looked after it for them. But she did recall the excitement of them all being together. They caught the train at Bexhill and Mario told the girls they could have the biggest knickerbocker glory they could find.

'With a cherry on top?' she'd asked, her mouth watering at the thought.

Once they'd had their fill of ice-cream, they went to Trafalgar Square. Flavia was desperate to climb up onto one of the lion statues and her mum told her not to be so silly, at which point Flavia had a tantrum and her dad promised them a cream tea in an attempt to soothe the mood.

With the memories sharp in her mind, she continued looking out of the bus window, but wasn't seeing anything.

'We will not miss our stop?' Giuseppe's question brought her back to the present.

'Ring the bell, quick. The next one is ours.'

Walking through the busy streets towards the Italian delicatessen shop, Christina's thoughts were once again back in Sussex, specifically at Beach Walk.

'Giuseppe, what about if you hadn't retired? The child who died near to your flat. Could you have persuaded them to reopen the case?'

'It was time to walk away.'

'Well, we're not going to walk away this time. I think that once we're back, we should take up the reins again.'

'Reins?'

'Continue to be involved, whatever Detective Sergeant Pearce says. Don't we have as much of a responsibility to the community we live in as the police do? There will be people too scared to let their children out of their sight for fear the same will happen to them?'

'Today I am on holiday. Tomorrow...'

Giuseppe pushed the door open to the delicatessen.

Christina watched him survey the shelves, crammed full of pasta, risotto rice, jars of peperoni, bottles of deep green olive oil, and rich red sauces. Stacked in piles across the floor of the shop were packets of *grissini* breadsticks and amaretti biscuits.

Christina moved over to one of the shelves and picked up a packet of *Lavazza* ground coffee.

'I think we have the answer to your prayers,' she said, handing it to Giuseppe.

He turned towards the shop counter where there was a display of Italian coffee machines. 'And one of these, I think,' he said, smiling.

'I'd say that right now our problem is not what to buy, but how much we can carry.'

Two hours later they were back at Victoria Station, their arms weighed down with bags of Italian food.

'Enough to keep you going until you go home?' Christina said as they pushed forward to get on the train.

'*Forse*. Perhaps.'

CHAPTER 23
Thursday, 9th July
Evening

While Anne waited for Christina and Giuseppe to return from London, she kept revisiting the words in Matthew's letter. It had taken her by surprise to hear from him, and the news about Barbara's disappearance was more than unsettling. She'd felt guilty asking Giuseppe to make the journey on her behalf, and yet, she couldn't face the thought of making a trip to London. She'd always hated big cities, so many people, so much noise. On the rare occasions they'd gone for a day out as a family, she couldn't wait to get back to the relative tranquility of Bexhill.

The day-to-day routine of the café suited her best. Mornings were for customers and fried breakfasts. Over the years countless rashers of bacon had been fried and trayloads of eggs cooked in every possible way - fried, scrambled, poached, on occasion even omelettes. It was fascinating to see the fuss people made about their eggs. Sometimes Anne joked with Mario, challenging him to remember which of their regulars liked eggs runny, which well done, and all options in-between. It was joking she kept for Mario's black days.

Since Giuseppe's arrival, Anne had been reminded about those early days after she first met her husband. Back then, Mario's black days were frequent. Anne would say goodbye to him at the end of a date and he'd be full of smiles. Then, the next time they met, it was as though he'd taken on another persona. She'd replay their conversations, anxious she might have said something to upset him. Then the mood passed and he was her Mario again. She never asked him about it, even after they married. They moved to England and the children came along and life took over. Her dad was the only person she confided in about Mario's moods. He reminded her the war changed people. Mario would have seen comrades blown to pieces. Anne didn't need reminding. She had seen the dreadful results of conflict in the military hospital. Young men who had lost limbs, who screamed out every night, not from the pain, but from nightmares they couldn't escape.

Over the years she became so used to her husband's moods that now she barely noticed them. But in recent days, seeing the cousins standing side by side, Anne felt a stab of discomfort. Perhaps her husband still carried the weight of his past more than she realised. Giuseppe was older by two years and yet he looked younger. He was broad-shouldered, muscular and stood tall, while Mario had developed a slight stoop. Both men had thick dark hair, both showing a smattering of grey, but the pallor of her husband's skin, the sadness around his eyes, made him look jaded. It was only now she realised how many of these changes had gone unnoticed during the years the girls were growing up. In their own way, each of her daughters gave her worries. But it was Flavia who had given her the most heartache.

By the time Flavia reached an age to have her own opinion, she seemed intent on making it known on every occasion. Most mealtimes ended with an argument. When Flavia eventually announced she was leaving home, Anne's only thought was relief.

And then there was Stevie. It was clear to her Christina had become more like a mother to him than an aunt. Anne couldn't decide how she felt about that, or even if there was much she could do to change it.

As she closed up the café, clearing the tables and sweeping up, she settled on an idea. She would prepare a special tea for Giuseppe and Christina on their return from London. Until now there had been virtually no English food that could tempt

Giuseppe to clear his plate. But she knew he had a sweet tooth, so decided on a spread with scones and jam, as well as some hastily made shortbread.

The downstairs kitchen at the back of the café had always been the centre of the home, even when the girls were small. But this evening she decided to lay the dining table in the upstairs flat. She cleared away the papers and files and spread out a tablecloth, arranging the scones and shortbread over the three-tiered cake stand she hadn't used since Christmas Day.

There were footsteps on the stairs and Mario's voice. 'You've been busy for tomorrow? I can smell baking.'

'Come on up and you'll see.'

'Best tablecloth, eh? Well, you'll have no problem tempting him with those fruit scones, they look delicious.' Mario went to pick up a piece of shortbread, but Anne tapped his hand.

'Oh no you don't.'

'How do you think they got on, meeting Matthew?'

'I still feel bad that I didn't go myself.'

'You shouldn't feel bad. It's given Giuseppe a chance to clear his head, get him thinking about something other than poor George Leigh.'

'Maybe if you spent more time with your cousin...'

'Don't start, Anne.'

'I'm just saying...'

'I know what you're saying. You just have to let me handle things in my own way. I'm not a talker, never have been. You of all people should know that. We've been married long enough for you to know all there is about me.'

'I don't though, do I?' Anne said, taking his hand in hers.

'Not now, Anne.' He pulled his hand away, then touched her shoulder by way of apology. 'Stevie's still playing in the garden. I'll call him in and give him his bath and I'll get him a spot of tea. Leave you to finish getting things ready for when they get back.'

A little after 6pm, Anne heard the front door open and Christina's voice.

'We come bearing gifts.' Christina placed two shopping bags down by Anne's feet. Giuseppe followed behind with another bag and a parcel.

'I can smell Italy without even opening a single packet,' Anne said, lifting a packet of *amaretti* biscuits from one of the bags.

Giuseppe took out the packet of coffee and then unwrapped the coffee machine.

'Okay, I can take a hint.' Anne took the coffee machine through to the kitchen, taking the pieces apart and rinsing them under the tap. 'I'm guessing you won't want a home-made scone now you've got all this lovely Italian food to enjoy?'

'A real cup of coffee and an English scone. *Perfetto*. I can think of nothing better,' Giuseppe said, smiling.

'Mario is just reading a bedtime story to Stevie. I thought it best not to give Stevie something else to worry about so he had his tea earlier.'

A little later, once plates were filled with scones and cakes and cups were filled with freshly brewed coffee, Anne turned to Christina. 'Before you tell me about your day, I want to ask you about Stevie. He's been having nightmares, hasn't he?'

'You've heard him, then? I've tried to reassure him, but he's convinced some bogey man is out to get him. I'm not sure what they're telling the kids at school, but whatever it is, I'm not sure it's helping.'

Giuseppe picked at the remaining crumbs on his plate, prompting Anne to push the cake stand towards him.

'I've been thinking about the perfect way to take his mind off it all.' Christina continued. 'Although I'm not sure I'll be very popular when I tell you what it is.'

Mario eased his chair back from the table, took a cigarette from the packet lying beside his plate and lit it. 'You'd better tell us, before we end up guessing the worst.'

'A dog.' Christina recounted her conversation with Mrs Selmon and how she'd ended up agreeing to have Max on a *'trial basis'*.

'Oh, Christina,' Anne said. 'Haven't we got enough to be worrying about without a boisterous dog into the bargain.'

'He's not boisterous, just lively. He's young still, I'm sure he'll settle down.' She paused, allowing her words to settle, then continued. 'There are all sorts of bits and pieces we'll need to get. One of the first things will be some kind of gate, so he doesn't go into the café every time we open the door to the back kitchen.'

'I suppose I could dig out some of those old blankets we put up in the loft,' Anne said, appearing to warm to the idea. 'They'll do to cover the settee and the car seat if you take him any distance.' She collected the empty plates, putting them onto the serving hatch. 'Anyway, we've time to think about the dog and make proper plans. For now, I'd like to hear how you both got on with Matthew.'

'I'm still not sure why he wrote to you, Mum,' Christina said. 'Perhaps he needed to reach out to someone and you came into his mind.'

'Perhaps he still holds a torch for you,' Mario said, with a sideways glance at his wife.

'Now you're just being silly,' Anne said, flushing a little. 'Do you think there's anything we can do to help him? Did he tell you much more about Barbara? Did he say why she left?'

'He gave us this,' Christina said, handing her mum the photo of Barbara.

'Oh, now that takes me back. You can see from this photo

what a timid lass she was. The fear in her eyes never really went away all the time she was with us. The only time I ever heard her laugh was when we took her down to the beach. The first time she ran straight in, never even took her shoes and socks off.' Anne's expression was wistful.

'Matthew said the same thing,' Giuseppe said.

Their conversation was interrupted by a knock on the front door, taking everyone by surprise. Mario went downstairs, returning moments later with Mrs Selmon and one very excitable Max, straining at the lead. It seemed Mrs Selmon had seized on the opportunity of William being at cubs and decided to visit the café, laden with Max's possessions.

'We've started his training, but he hasn't really got the hang of it as yet,' Mrs Selmon explained. 'He loves his toys though. He's happy to spend hours running and fetching a ball.'

Christina could guess what her mother was thinking. No one had the time to spend hours throwing a ball for Max to catch.

'I hope you're not thinking Giuseppe will help out with Max,' Anne said, once Mrs Selmon had left. 'I don't know if he even likes dogs.'

'It's just a trial, remember,' Christina said.

'And who's on trial? Max or us?' Mario said, ruffling the dog's ears.

Christina pulled the dog towards her. 'Well, I know one six-year-old boy who will think tomorrow is Christmas Day when he wakes up and meets you.'

CHAPTER 24
Friday, 10th July
Morning

The next morning it was clear that having a dog to worry about during an already hectic morning schedule was not helping anyone. With only half an hour to go before they had to leave the house, Stevie was still in his pyjamas, more intent on rolling around the floor with Max than on getting dressed. Voices were raised and tempers frayed by the time Christina managed to get Stevie into his school uniform. She hadn't had a chance to watch over him while he ate his breakfast, but she was fairly certain he'd fed most of his cornflakes to Max.

At last, they were ready.

'I want to hold his lead,' Stevie announced. Without waiting for a response, he clipped the lead onto Max's collar and let the dog tug him towards the back door.

'He can't come to school with you, Stevie. He'll have to stay here.'

The temper tantrum that Christina was expecting was neatly averted by Giuseppe's arrival and his helpful suggestion. 'I will come with you. Then Christina, you can go to work, Stevie can go to school and I will walk Max back here.'

Getting an excitable Beagle onto the back seat of the Mini, alongside an even more excitable Stevie, almost proved too much for Christina.

'You need to get Max to sit still, Stevie, otherwise we'll end up having an accident.'

With Giuseppe grumbling again about there being no space, Christina tried to ignore her passengers and focus on the short drive to the school.

Pulling up alongside the playground, she breathed a sigh of relief. Once out of the car Stevie was way ahead within moments, with Max straining at the lead.

'I'm sure I saw Rose Walker at the school yesterday,' Christina said to Giuseppe.

'Do you think her son attends the school? Do we think she even has a son?'

'I can't quite make her out.'

Before Giuseppe could respond Christina tapped him on the arm and pointed.

'It looks as though Detective Sergeant Pearce took your advice.' She gestured towards a new poster that had been pinned on one of the posts close to the entrance to the school playground. The poster was a photofit image of a thin-faced man, his mouth slightly open, showing a missing front tooth. 'It's based on the description the ticket office clerk gave us.'

Giuseppe nodded. 'The clerk must have spoken to the police and they have decided it is worth exploring.' He kept his voice low as several other mothers had gathered beside him, each wanting to get close enough to the poster to get a good look.

Below the image were the words:

HAVE YOU SEEN THIS MAN?

The women glanced at the poster, then seemed more intent on staring at Giuseppe. Having a handsome Italian in their midst was clearly proving a topic for fascination. Christina listened to the chatter among the women within earshot. Then one of the mothers said, 'I don't think we should let our children go to school. Not until the police have found this man. Who knows what he might do next?'

Giuseppe stepped forward. '*Signore, per favore*, ask yourselves, have you seen this man? Have your children seen this man? Here at Beach Walk, perhaps fishing?'

'You mean he's been lurking among us, just waiting to murder one of us?' one woman exclaimed.

'What are the police doing about it? That's what I want to know,' said another.

Christina pulled Giuseppe to one side, away from the crowd of women who were now nudging each other and looking increasingly perturbed.

'Look, it's Paul Leigh, over there by the crossing.'

Christina lifted a hand to wave, but Paul was looking in the opposite direction.

'Let us speak to him before he goes into school,' Giuseppe said.

While they'd been talking Christina was keeping an eye on Stevie, who was trying his best to encourage Max to walk to heel by tugging the dog back each time he strained on the lead. She moved forward as they reached the entrance to the playground.

'Well done, Stevie. Let me take Max now and you run in and join your friends.'

'Will Max be here this afternoon, when school finishes?'

'We'll see,' was the best Christina could offer. She took hold of Max's lead, then looked up to see William Selmon standing to one side of the playground. He glanced over a few times, but it was only when Stevie let go of Max's lead that he waved back.

'Remember, William might not want to talk about Max. He might feel sad about letting him go.'

'Am I 'lergic, Auntie?'

'*Allergic*. No, Stevie, you're not. But that doesn't mean you can have Max in your bed with you. He has his own bed.'

Stevie gave her a brief questioning look, then ran off into the playground.

As they turned to leave, Paul Leigh was approaching them.

'Hello there, how are you?' As soon as Christina had spoken she wished she hadn't, or at least that she had chosen her words more carefully. Paul shrugged his shoulders and went to walk past.

'Paul, a moment please.' The authority in Giuseppe's voice made the boy stop walking. 'We hope you can help us.'

'I need to get to my class.'

'This poster.' Giuseppe pointed towards the photofit image.

'Yeah, what about it?'

'Does he look like the man you saw at the beach that day? The one who was fishing and who shouted at you and your brother?'

'Maybe,' Paul said, not looking at the poster, instead looking away from Giuseppe and towards the playground. 'I need to go in now.'

'You have many friends here at school,' Giuseppe continued.

Paul shrugged again, avoiding any eye contact with either Giuseppe or Christina.

'Is that why you and George visited Mrs Walker? Because you are friends with her son?'

It seemed Paul was not in a mood to communicate. He edged past them on his way towards the playground entrance.

'I haven't done anything wrong.' His words came out as more of a mumble, making it hard for Giuseppe to catch what he was saying.

'You're not in any trouble,' Christina added.

'Dad said I wasn't to speak to the bloke in the caravan again. I don't know why, 'cos he's okay. He was a ship's captain, you know.'

'Who was?'

'The Irishman. His name's Sean. He knows all about the sea and the tides, tells us which shells to look out for. He's promised to tell me about the different kinds of bait. You need different sorts for sea fishing, you know.'

The sound of the school bell signalled the end of their conversation. They'd gained little or nothing more from Paul. Perhaps they should leave it to the police. After all, they were the experts.

CHAPTER 25
Friday, 10th July
Morning

Detective Sergeant Pearce's day had started off badly. His wife had arranged a supper date with their next-door neighbours and was convinced he hadn't told her he might have to work late. As a result, by the time he left for work they weren't speaking and he'd left his lunchbox on the kitchen table. There was no time to go home and he refused to buy sandwiches, so all he could do was work his way through a packet of digestives he kept in his desk drawer. They weren't even chocolate digestives.

He looked out from his office, through the glass screen partition. He wished he could describe the scene as a flurry of activity. Instead it was more like looking at a handful of spectators who had arrived early for a performance at the Bandstand and didn't know what to do with themselves. Bailey was yawning, staring blankly out of the window, Albright was moving pieces of paper across his desk as though they were chess pieces and the youngest member of the team had been stirring his tea for so long he could have made a hole in the bottom of his cup. Only WPC Foster looked focused, leafing through several manilla folders laid out on her desk.

Five days had passed and the incident board was still sparse with details. The team had dealt with several calls since the article in the *Herald*. Some of the callers had been on the train, but had little to add to existing knowledge. One caller wanted to know what the police were doing about speeding. There was an assumption the boy had been knocked down by a car, even though there had been no mention of a car at the scene.

WPC Foster dealt with several of the callers, her attempts to calm those who railed at her falling on deaf ears.

'You're supposed to control law and order, aren't you? If folk can go tearing around with no thought for anyone but themselves, then they should be locked up,' announced one irate caller.

'When we find the culprit that's exactly what we will do, madam,' she said, keeping her tone polite and objective.

Foster gathered a list of the calls and passed the details to DS Pearce.

'What's this?' he demanded, calling her into his office. 'You were told to report anything relevant to the incident.'

'Yes sir.'

'What part of *"relevant"* is confusing you?'

'I'm not confused, sir.'

'I'm not interested in busybodies who think it's our job to sort all the problems in the town.'

'No sir, sorry sir.'

Pearce couldn't quite figure Foster out. She was quick thinking, intelligent, but sometimes he caught a look from her that made him think her subservience was all part of an act. The story was she'd always wanted to join the police force, following her father into the uniformed ranks. Being the Chief Constable, he'd probably pulled a few strings to get her in, or maybe she'd done it on her own merit. But whichever it was, Pearce was determined she wasn't going to make a fool of him.

'Right you lot.' The booming voice, together with the loud bang as he thumped his fist on one of the empty desks, shocked them all to attention. 'Why does this incident board still have questions and no answers? Eh? Tell me that.'

The three constables stared at him, wondering whether to respond.

'Albright. You first. What have you got for me?'

Albright stood, pulled his notebook from the pocket of his uniform, turned over a page, hoping to gain confidence by reading the words exactly as they were said to him. 'Two interviews, sir. Both with train passengers.'

'And?'

'Er, nothing, sir. They didn't see anything.'

'I'd call that convenient. They'd soon have their eyes open when they want to stick their nose into other people's business.' He thumped his fist once more on the table. 'Foster. Tell me something I don't already know.'

'We've created the photofit, sir. From our interview with the ticket office clerk. We've put posters up near to the school, plus several around Eastbourne, Pevensey Bay, and at Beach Walk.'

'Okay, well, that's something, I suppose. And what about the fellow from the caravan?'

'Sean Murphy hasn't been in yet, sir. Should I make another visit? Remind him to come into the station?'

Before Pearce could reply, the internal phone rang and Foster answered it. The rest of the team waited until she ended the call.

'Well?' Pearce said.

'There's a Mr Bianchi at the front desk, sir. Says you will want to see him regarding information relevant to the enquiry.'

'Give me strength.'

'Wasn't he the man who suggested we interview the ticket office clerk, sir?'

Pearce didn't respond, but gestured to her. 'Think you're so smart, then you'd better come with me. Make yourself useful by taking notes. And you two.' Pearce pointed at the two remaining constables. 'Get Sean Murphy in here.'

'Yes, sir,' they said, in unison.

As Pearce entered the interview room the Italian was sitting, his back to the door, one hand resting on the table, his fingers appeared to be tapping out a tune.

'You told the desk officer you have information for me.' Pearce said.

Pearce sat, while Foster remained standing. She took a notebook from the pocket of her uniform and stood with her pencil poised.

'What do you have to tell me then? Anything new since we met the other day? You didn't need to come into the station, you could have telephoned.' Pearce's tone was sharp.

'Your team has spoken to the ticket office clerk. I saw the new poster at the school this morning. I hope it will bring you more information.'

'You haven't come here to congratulate my police artist, have you?' Pearce didn't hide his irritation.

'I wondered if you have spoken again with the Irishman who lives in the caravan?' Giuseppe continued.

'Not yet, but I visited the school on Tuesday and the next day we had a couple of youngsters ringing the station. At least their parents did.'

'They had useful information?

'Seems Sean Murphy likes to chat to the kids. Overly friendly maybe?'

'There is no harm in being friendly.'

'Maybe not.'

The brief encounter Pearce had with Sean Murphy on Sunday evening provided little or nothing. He wouldn't be at all surprised if he had something to hide, but whether it was to do with the death of the Leigh lad, he still wasn't certain. The Irishman was the kind of fella who thought it was clever to mess with authority.

'We know the Irishman has spoken to the Leigh boys on

several occasions.' Giuseppe said in a measured tone.

Pearce stood, pushing the chair from behind him, such that it tipped over. Foster bent to pick it up as the same time as Pearce and they almost clashed heads.

'When you talk about "*we*" I hope you are not assuming you have been seconded onto the Eastbourne Police force, Mr Bianchi. We are grateful for your help, but you need to remember at all times that first and foremost this is a police enquiry.'

'Of course, detective sergeant. I speak about myself and Miss Christina Rossi, the reporter working for the *Eastbourne Herald*. She has a particular interest as she was the first on the scene.'

The Italian was playing with him, Pearce was certain of it, he was trying to prove a point. Well, he'd be damned if he was going to get the better of him.

'And the children who contacted the station. They say they have also met the stranger?' Giuseppe asked. 'The subject of your new poster?'

'Not yet they haven't. But, as you know, the photofit only went up today. So, there's a chance it might trigger a memory.' Pearce studied Giuseppe. He was sitting upright on the chair, his legs stretched out as far as the table allowed, his fingers still tapping out a rhythm.

'Favourite tune, or something?' Pearce said.

Giuseppe stopped tapping and drew his hand back. '*Scusi.* Sorry, it is a habit, it helps me to think. Did the clerk at the railway station explain that the stranger bought a ticket to London on the afternoon of the incident? Also that he was very rude.'

'Not exactly a lot to go on, is it?' The Italian was wasting his time, he was sure of it, and yet... 'Do you think it's the same man who was rough with the Leigh brothers? Shouting at them and so on?'

Giuseppe nodded. 'Detective Sergeant, all of this is little or nothing to suggest a motive for murder. I understand that and if one of my team brought such an idea to me, I would tell them to stop wasting my time. Also, I understand I am only a visitor, not a member of your team, not even an Englishman.'

Pearce could sense the Italian was building up to something.

'May I ask, is there anything else you can tell me about the crime scene? Anything your team discovered that surprised them?'

Pearce put his hands together as if he was praying, and then he said, 'I'm not sure how much of this I should share with you. You might have been a detective once, but you aren't one anymore and certainly not in this police force.'

'I think the saying is *"Once a detective, always a detective"*. No?'

'There were several fragments of red plastic. Probably from the rear reflector of a bicycle. We have George Leigh's bike, of course, and his reflector was broken, right enough. But there were too many pieces for it to be just from one bicycle. There was glass too. Small pieces, in among the pebbles.'

'Not unusual to find broken glass on a beach? People are careless with bottles. I have known the same problem on our sandy beaches. Dangerous too, when people like to walk barefoot.'

'Maybe. But the glass was right there, beside the boy's body.'

'*Molto interessante.* Very interesting, detective sergeant. Christina also mentioned the glass. She almost put her hand on it. May I ask if you have decided on your next steps?'

'That Irishman knows more than he's saying, I'm sure of it. I'll shake it out of him if I have to.'

'I think you are right, Detective Sergeant. Someone needs

shaking, but my instincts tell me it is not Sean Murphy. But we remain hopeful until the crime is solved.'

As Giuseppe stood and moved to the door of the office, Pearce began scribbling on a piece of paper.

'My home phone number,' Pearce said, handing it to Giuseppe. 'After all, not everything happens during working hours.'

'*Grazie.*'

Pearce couldn't figure the Italian out. He closed his office door and stared at the papers on his desk, willing them to offer up answers.

CHAPTER 26
Friday, 10th July
Evening

Reginald Pearce wished that just once he could come home, plump down in his armchair and have the listening ear of his wife. And if his wishes were ever to be granted, he prayed it would be on this day more than any other.

It was Betty's constant reminder that *'work stops at the front door'* that prevented him. But wasn't married life supposed to be about sharing? Otherwise, what was the point?

He kicked his shoes off in the hallway, hung up his coat and waited. Betty always appeared within moments of him coming through the front door. 'Oh, it's you,' she'd say, as though expecting someone else. Every day the same.

To make matters worse, this evening he'd have to pretend to be interested in the inane conversation over the dinner table with the neighbours. Betty Pearce had put back the start time of the meal to ensure her husband was back from the station. As a result, the roast leg of lamb was overcooked, the vegetables boiled to an unappetising mush.

Finally, after the dessert of apple crumble and custard, coffee offered and thankfully declined, Reginald saw the neighbours to the door and breathed an audible sigh of relief as he watched them walk down the front path.

Wishing he could enjoy a cigarette, he poured himself a small whisky instead, sat in his armchair and closed his eyes. He had reprimanded his team for not coming up with answers, when really he knew he was to blame. He was the sergeant, after all. And when there's a cock-up, it's the man at the top who is ultimately responsible.

He guessed what they said about him behind his back. They all thought he was hard-hearted. No surprise, as he'd told them often enough that emotion had no place in police work. In truth, though, when he saw the Leigh boy lying on the road, crumpled like a discarded rag, he felt it in his gut. Any death was a tragedy, but when it was just a young lad, with his life all ahead of him... The anger he wanted to direct at the perpetrator, he aimed at his constables. It probably wasn't fair, but then life had rarely been fair to him.

On the face of it, the marriage of Reginald and Betty Pearce was never going to be based on romance. Neither of them were tactile. He was brought up within the strict regime of a father who saw his children for one hour a day, just before bedtime. His mother kept him and his brother clean and tidy, well fed, and above all well-mannered. But beyond that there was little by way of tenderness.

As a lawyer his father earned good money, but didn't believe in spending it. So, Reginald's childhood home was spacious, but in desperate need of repair. Windows rattled in the wind that was almost constant along Eastbourne seafront. Then, whenever it rained, he and his brother had to hurry to the garden shed to collect two tin pails to position them under the drips, one on the landing and the other by the front door. The incessant noise of the raindrops hitting the metal ate into his brain, to the point where he heard it long after the rain had stopped.

It was those memories that made him insist on as modern a house as they could afford on a constable's wages when he and Betty married.

'It might be modern, but there's no space to breathe,' Betty complained on many occasions.

She'd grown up in the countryside, the only daughter of a farming family. During their courting days, Reginald came to realise Betty's family home was more of a smallholding than a farm. Betty's parents had been given the land as part of the

172

resettlement programme during the depression of the 1930s, when men in the towns and cities were offered the chance to retrain, as industry declined and unemployment rose.

The couple rarely spoke about those early days when there had been gentleness in abundance, romance too. Perhaps it was the police work that had squeezed it all from him.

'Shall I make us a hot drink?' Betty said, returning from the kitchen, having cleared the table and stacked the dishes ready to wash them.

'We're no further on with the case. The lad who was killed on Beach Walk,' he said.

Betty sat opposite him but said nothing.

'I know you don't like me talking about work, but sometimes...'

'Hot milk, or would you prefer tea?' she said.

'Can't you just listen to me for once?' He raised his voice, immediately wishing he hadn't.

Betty moved back into the kitchen, leaving the sitting-room door open. Reginald knew she'd still be listening, although he expected no reply.

'There's a young woman, a reporter. Turns out her uncle is a retired detective, from Rome of all places.'

The noises from the kitchen confirmed that Betty was washing and drying the dishes, putting everything away and wiping down the surfaces. The routine never changed. Once the kitchen was clean and tidy, she prepared his sandwiches for the next day and then laid the table ready for breakfast. Then she'd return to the sitting room, take out the tapestry covered bag from behind her armchair and start on her knitting. Once a year she gathered all the jumpers and cardigans she'd created and donated them to the church for their Christmas bazaar. Beyond that, he knew little of her day-to-day routine when he was at work. He'd never stopped to wonder if she was lonely, if she had hopes and dreams beyond being a policeman's wife.

He poured himself another whisky, then sat opposite his wife, picking up the newspaper from a side table, before putting it down again.. He wasn't in the mood for reading about all the troubles in the world when there were troubles here in his own community that needed to be resolved. The Irish man in the caravan concerned him. Albright had interviewed him that afternoon at the station, but still not managed to get much from him. And yet Reginald was certain he knew more than he was saying.

'You say the journalist was there, she found the body?' Betty said at last. 'And her Uncle - well, if he worked for the Italian police force he must be good, mustn't he?'

Reginald watched her as she continued to knit. The rhythmic clicking of the needles and the ticking of the grandfather clock were the only sounds in the room. She didn't look up at him when she eventually spoke.

'Don't see them as competition. Use them to your advantage.'

He waited for her to continue, surprised by her insight.

'You're all after the same thing, aren't you? You want to find out how the lad died - well, that's what your Italian and his niece want too. It won't matter to that poor Leigh family who comes up with the answers, provided someone does.'

Reginald stopped himself from replying. The only response he was tempted to give was a kiss on his wife's cheek.

'I'll make us that bedtime drink when you're ready,' he said, picking up the newspaper. He was ready to read it now. After all, there would be happy stories in the news, he was sure of it.

CHAPTER 27
Saturday, 11th July

There was just a week to go before the children of Bexhill and surrounding areas broke up for the summer holidays. In recent years, to celebrate the date, many local families got together for a bonfire party on the beach. No one could remember how the idea first came about, but it had become an occasion when hundreds of people turned up, many bringing a few fireworks, as well as a picnic.

Ever since Mario and Anne opened *Bella Café* some eighteen years ago, generations of families had become regulars. The couple knew most of the locals and over the last few years it had fallen to them to take on the organisation of the bonfire party.

The bonfire was usually held near Beach Walk. Now, in the light of George Leigh's death, there was a strong feeling the gathering shouldn't go ahead. Mario and Anne had several discussions about it. Then, when Anne raised the topic with Christina, she received a clear response. 'Don't even think about it this year, Mum. Some people are terrified to go to the beach in the daytime, let alone in the evening. And I doubt the police will be happy with people tramping all across their crime scene.'

Over Saturday morning breakfast, it was Christina who mentioned the party.

'Stevie was asking about it, last night, when I was putting him to bed. I told him he's got Max to think about now. Most dogs don't like fireworks.'

'What did he say?'

'He told me that Max isn't most dogs. Then he said Tony had promised to see him at the party and that he'd bring him sparklers to hold.'

'When did Tony talk to him about the bonfire?'

'Apparently he turned up at school playtime. Stevie told him about Max, and Tony promised to come and visit so they could walk Max together. Honestly, Mum, Tony is making things really difficult, contradicting me at every turn and it doesn't help that Stevie idolises him.'

'I'm sorry you're having to deal with all of this, darling. Do you want me to have a word with Tony?'

'I don't think it will make much difference. Anyway, I told Stevie there wouldn't be a bonfire this year, so it's not something we need to worry about. And if it's sparklers he wants, then I'll buy him some.'

'I agree with you. It would be wrong to have the bonfire party this year. I'll visit Patricia Leigh, reassure her we aren't going ahead with it. I should have visited before now, to offer my condolences.'

Later that day, armed with a home-baked chocolate cake and some flowers from her garden, Anne knocked on the front door of the Leigh house.

Within moments the door opened and she was pulled into the house by a breathless Patricia Leigh, before she barely had time to say '*hello*'.

'Thank goodness you've come. I need to show someone.' She tugged at Anne's arm, pulling her towards the stairs. 'I was tidying George's room and there they were.'

She noticed Patricia's hand was shaking as she pushed open the bedroom door. For Anne it was disconcerting stepping into George Leigh's bedroom. It was like being in his private space without permission. She took in her surroundings, the posters covering the wall, the Dr Who models covering the top of the chest of drawers. Then her gaze came to rest on the neatly made bed and the diaries spread across it.

Patricia picked up one of the diaries and handed it to her.

176

'Open it up, see what he's written,'

'Patricia, these are George's private words, it doesn't feel right for me to read them.' She put the diary back down on the bed, unopened.

'I didn't know any of it. I wish I'd never found them, never read them,' Patricia wailed. Then, in a sudden movement, she pulled the bedspread to one side, sending all the diaries onto the floor.

'Try not to upset yourself, let me get you a drink of water.'

Patricia flopped down onto the wicker chair beside George's bed, doubling over as if in pain.

'Let's both go downstairs and I'll make us a cup of tea.'

Down in the kitchen Anne filled the kettle, opened cupboards to find cups and saucers. Patricia sat with her hands covering her face, rocking back and forth in the chair. Leaving the tea to brew, Anne sat and held her hand out to Patricia.

'Would it help to talk about it?'

Patricia moved her hands away from her face and stared blankly at Anne. 'He'd been watching people.'

'Watching people?'

'His dad and I thought George was a typical teenager. We always knew he was brighter than his brother, bound for university for sure. But all these writings, about emotions, about the way people think. Using words I barely understand. There's poems too.'

It was difficult to grasp what Patricia was saying, much of it was confused, as though she was still sifting through the implications of what she'd found.

'It sounds as though George was a sensitive soul, that's a good thing, surely.' Anne said.

'But he kept it all to himself. Seems like I was too busy to notice.'

'You never got a sense he was unhappy?'

'No, not unhappy. At least I don't think so. But I suppose I'll never know now, will I?'

She covered her face with her hands and started to weep, tears trickling through her fingertips, wetting the sleeves of her cardigan.

'None of us know what really goes on inside a child's head, not even the parents.' Anne said, her thoughts going to Stevie. 'You mustn't blame yourself.'

They sat for a while in silence. Then Patricia took a handkerchief from her pocket and wiped her face. 'You help to organise the beach bonfire party each year, don't you?' The question took Anne by surprise.

'Yes, but we appreciate it would be wrong to hold it this year. That's what I've come to tell you. We don't want to do anything that might upset you. I'm sure everyone feels the same. You've got enough to deal with.' Anne paused, wondering if she should say more.

'I found the entry from last year's diary, the one George wrote the day after the bonfire,' Patricia continued. 'He said it was one of the best nights of his life, how he loved seeing the whole community come together and how there were smiles on everyone's face, lit up by the warmth from the fire and the bright colours of the fireworks. Lovely words he used. What kind of mother am I that I didn't even know my own child.' She began weeping again. Then she stood, moving over to the kitchen window, turning her back on Anne.

'Oh, Patricia. I'm so very sorry. What a dreadful time for you. Have you been able to make plans for his funeral?'

Patricia shook her head. 'The police won't release his body, not yet. Which is why I want the bonfire party to go ahead. It will be a memorial for George. Everyone remembering him in the place where he lost his life, but somewhere I know that once he was happy.'

'Are you sure? With all that has happened...'

'It's what George would have wanted. I'll be there, trying to see it all with George's eyes. I'll watch for the smiles, see the colours and remember my precious boy.'

Over a second pot of tea Anne listened while Patricia spoke a little more about George.

'We had such hopes for him. Robert and I, well, we've not done much with our lives, but George had the chance to do something special, to be someone special.

Anne was about to ask about Paul. It was as if Patricia had forgotten she still had a son who was alive and having to cope with the death of his brother. She was struggling to find the right words when Robert Leigh pushed open the back door. He was carrying a canvas bag, which he opened, emptying its contents onto the kitchen table. Runner beans, a lettuce and a handful of small potatoes.

'Not much ready down at the allotment, but these should see us right for a meal or two,' he said.

'Anne's been kind enough to visit,' Patricia said.

Robert glanced up at Anne, then sat, kicking off his boots, letting small clods of earth drop onto the kitchen floor as he pulled at the laces.

'We've been talking about the beach bonfire,' Patricia continued, a hint of caution in her voice.

'Please don't tell me it's still on.' He glared at Anne, who looked at Patricia for a prompt.

'I've told Anne it should go ahead.'

'Dear God. Have these people no respect? Our son is dead and they're going to hold a party right there, just where he died.'

'Well, I'm going,' Patricia said, defiance in her expression as she held her husband's gaze.

Just then the back door opened again. Paul stood in the

open doorway, as if he was in two minds whether to come in or turn around and leave.

'Mrs Rossi has come to talk about the beach bonfire,' Patricia said.

Anne watched the warning look that passed between Robert and his son and then Paul said, 'Sounds good to me.'

'And you think that's what George would want? If it was you lying dead in the undertakers, you think George would happily go along to a party?' Robert stabbed his finger at Paul.

Then Robert put his boots back on and pushed past Paul. 'I'll have my supper at the pub,' was his parting remark as he slammed the front door.

CHAPTER 28
Saturday, 18th July

On the morning of the bonfire party Christina pulled back her bedroom curtains to reveal a vivid blue sky. It looked as though the day would remain clear and bright, with no sudden summer showers to dampen the planned event. But by mid-morning clouds had gathered, not weather clouds, but troubled discussions behind many of the closed doors in the town.

The only poster advertising the event was the one Anne had hastily drawn and taped to the front window of *Bella Café*. During the preceding week Christina had spoken to a few of the mothers when she dropped Stevie off at school and they were unanimous in not wanting to go to the event. As the days passed, so the feeling among the local community became increasingly fervent.

'It's no good the police just pinning that photofit up,' one woman said, her loud voice attracting attention. 'Waving a face in front of us isn't going to make the fella suddenly turn up, is it?'

Since Giuseppe's last visit to the police station he'd said little about the case. Most mornings he took long walks along Bexhill seafront, often not returning until mid-morning.

'I keep trying to persuade Mario to walk with him,' Anne told her daughter as they shared the breakfast washing up. 'He says Giuseppe wants to be on his own. Although I wouldn't be surprised if it's just an excuse.'

'Mum, do you know what happened to Dad in Italy? Why does he never want to go back for a visit, a holiday?'

Anne studied her daughter's face, but hesitated before replying.

'Your Dad won't speak about it, not even to me. It was

something that happened before I met him.'

'During the war?'

'I honestly don't know, darling. But whatever it was, I think that's the reason he's not comfortable spending time with his cousin.'

'Because Giuseppe knows?'

'I expect having Giuseppe here reminds your dad of everything he's tried hard to forget.'

'Seems like they have a lot in common then.'

'In what way?'

'When we were in London, I asked Giuseppe about Rosalia.'

'That's a subject left well alone.'

'I know, he's definitely loath to talk about it. But there's something else.' Christina paused, wondering whether to share what Giuseppe had told her.

'About the miscarriage?'

'No, he told me the reason he left the police force.'

Anne stopped washing up, removed her rubber gloves and waited for her daughter to continue.

'A boy fell to his death from the balcony of Giuseppe's block of flats.'

'Dear Lord, how terrible.' Anne pulled out a chair and sat, leaning forward slightly, as if Christina's news had winded her.

'It happened while Giuseppe was still a detective, but he wasn't allowed to investigate the case. It's remained unsolved because according to the coroner it was an accident.'

'And Giuseppe thinks there was more to it?'

Christina nodded, joining her mother at the kitchen table.

'So that's why he left the force early,' Anne said.

'I think it's also the reason he's so desperate to help solve this case.'

'That makes sense.'

Mother and daughter held hands for a few moments, without speaking.

It was Christina who broke the silence. 'You know that no one plans to come tonight, don't you, Mum?'

Anne returned to the sink, putting her rubber gloves back on again. She finished washing the dishes, placing them all in the drainer, before rinsing the sink for several minutes.

Mario had been covering the early morning shift in the café. Taking the opportunity of a quiet moment without customers he came through to the back kitchen.

'You two alright?' he said. 'Not had a bust up, have you?'

'We've just been talking.'

'About the bonfire party? Maybe you'll have more luck than me at explaining it to Giuseppe.'

'Because of the Leighs?'

'No, he doesn't seem to understand the idea. He kept going on about Guy Fawkes, saying, "*I thought you had bonfires in November, to celebrate the day Guy Fawkes tried to blow up your Houses of Parliament?*"'

'Well this event will be a commemoration, a way of remembering.' Anne said. 'And I'm determined we go ahead with it. We owe it to the Leigh family. If Patricia thinks it will help, it's the very least we can do.'

Christina had her own misgivings about the event going ahead that weren't only to do with George Leigh. Tony had phoned the café early evening on Friday, insisting Stevie should have the chance to stay up late to see the fireworks.

'Think about it, Chrissie. All his school friends will be there and he'll feel out of it when they are telling him about it on Monday morning and all he can say is, *I had to go home to bed.* Give the lad a chance to grow up, you can't keep him a baby forever.'

Christina was so irritated by Tony's comments she put the

receiver down without responding. Maybe there was some truth in Tony's accusation, but there was no harm in wanting to keep Stevie safe. The memories of discovering George Leigh's body still gave her nightmares. The worst ones were when George's face was replaced with Stevie's and then she'd wake up sweating, scared to close her eyes again in case the dream returned.

Nevertheless, now the day had arrived, she'd persuaded herself the event was something positive to focus on. A chance for the community to show support for the Leigh family. If George's parents were brave enough to take part, then everyone owed it to them to stand alongside them.

'I'll make a few visits this morning, try to rally support,' she said, putting her arm around her mum's waist. 'Don't worry, mum, I'm sure it will be fine. Or at least as fine as it can be, given the circumstances.'

Many of the people she spoke to on her visits around the town were tentative in their response. *I'll think about it,'* was the general response.

She left it until after lunch to tell Stevie, in an attempt to limit his excitement escalating to such a point he'd be uncontrollable by the time the evening came.

'But you will only be allowed to stay up for the fireworks if you promise to try to have a sleep this afternoon.' She told him, less than hopeful he'd be able to keep his side of the bargain, even if he agreed to it.

'How can I go to sleep in the daytime? The sun will shine in my bedroom window and make my eyes pop open.'

'You don't know until you try. Come on, we'll close the curtains and then you can pretend it's night-time.'

'But I can see the sun around the edges. Look.' He pointed to the side of the curtains, where the sunlight was creating patterns on the wallpaper.

'Well, it will be a shame if Tony brings those sparklers and you don't have a chance to have fun with them.' She left the comment hanging, moving towards the bedroom door and then turning to see Stevie screwing his eyes tight closed and pulling the covers up over his face.

A couple of hours later Stevie emerged, his face flushed and his eyes still full of sleep. The only argument now was whether Max would be accompanying them to Beach Walk.

CHAPTER 29
Saturday, 18th July

In the Leigh house there had been no arguments. In fact, there had been virtually no conversation since Patricia's announcement that she wanted the bonfire party to go ahead. Her husband had said little more than two words to his wife, speaking only when it was necessary. Paul had stayed out of the way as much as possible, coming home just in time for tea and then immediately going out again until it was dark, by which time he escaped straight to his bedroom.

Deep down, Patricia was hoping somehow the impasse would be resolved and that her husband would come round to her way of thinking. But as they sat opposite each other at the breakfast table and he lifted the newspaper up so she couldn't read his expression, she realised they would be staying on opposite sides of the divide. It wasn't anger she felt now, but a heavy sadness that sat like a lump of lead in her stomach. She pushed her plate away, having taken just one bite of the slice of toast, now likely to end up as food for the birds.

'You're not the only one suffering, you know.' She wanted to find words to shake her husband out of his silence.

Without a response, he folded the newspaper and put it on the table. Then he took his empty plate and cup and saucer to the draining board and left the room. A few moments later she heard the front door slam.

It was only when he heard his dad leave the house that Paul emerged from his bedroom and came into the kitchen.

'I haven't seen much of you these last few days.' Patricia was at the sink and spoke without turning around to look at her son. Her eyes kept filling with tears and she was loath to let her son see her crying. 'Will you walk down with me this evening? To Beach Walk.'

Paul shook his head, before realising his mother wouldn't see his response. 'I'm going down to the beach now, I'll probably stay down there, help finish off the bonfire.'

Patricia continued to wash the dishes, using her sleeve to wipe away the tears that continued to run down her cheeks. She had lost both sons and without children who was she? George had gone forever, but Paul... She dried her hands and went through to the sitting room, standing by the mantelpiece and looking again at the photos of her boys. *I sent you both out into the world to find your own way. I should have kept you close to me, kept you safe.*

While Paul was cycling down towards the beach, his mother was trying to gather the emotional strength to leave the house, to go to an event to help commemorate her son's life. This time last year both her sons and her husband were with her. The mood was light, all of them anticipating a fun evening out.

Perhaps reading George's diary through one more time would help. She sat on his bed for a while, leafing through the pages of last year's diary until she found the entry for the bonfire party. She read it aloud, trying to memorise his words, hoping she could repeat them in her mind as she watched the happy faces of all the people at the party. People who still had their families, who hadn't had their lives ripped apart.

Since George's death people had sent letters and cards, as well as small gifts, often just left on the doorstep. The community trying to make things right in the only way they could - by showing their support. Small baskets of fruit, posies of wildflowers, even freshly baked scones, had been received. At first Patricia wouldn't touch them, leaving Robert to bring the gifts into the house, storing them in the pantry so his wife wasn't confronted with them.

Straight after the accident she wanted someone to blame. She wanted to stand in front of the culprit, beat her hands on their chest, scream the most abusive words at them she could muster. But then within days she realised that knowing who had caused the death of her son would make no difference at all. It wouldn't bring him back.

She'd never been a religious person, but now she wished she had some kind of faith to hang onto. She'd even visited the local church, sitting in the back pew, staring at the altar, waiting for a feeling of comfort to wash over her. The priest had spotted her there and sat down beside her.

'I am so sorry for your loss,' he said. 'Is there anything I can do to help?'

'You can tell me why your God has taken my son away. What's the point of giving someone a life and then cutting it short before he's even reached manhood?'

The priest just took her hand and held it. He didn't speak for a while and eventually he let go of her hand and said, 'I will pray for you and your family.' And that was that.

Now, sitting in George's bedroom, she remembered the conversation with the priest and wondered what George would have made of it. Not the George she thought she knew, but the one she'd discovered from his writings, the boy who saw goodness in people and pleasure in the smallest thing. Perhaps she'd return to the church one day and seek out the priest and thank him for his prayers.

Leaving the bedroom, she walked along the landing, hovering for a moment outside Paul's room. She rarely went into his room except to leave his clean clothes in a pile on his chest of drawers. She'd given up telling him to tidy up. His bedroom was always a mess, shoes thrown across the floor, dirty socks and underpants just left where he'd dropped them. She'd asked him time and again to bring his dirty clothes down and put them in the washing pile in the scullery, but weeks would go by until finally, when he'd run out of clean clothes he'd arrive with armfuls of dirty laundry that needed a good scrub before looking presentable again.

She pushed the door open and stood for a moment, sensing there was something different. One pair of dirty socks lay on the floor beside the bed, but there no sign of Paul's slippers or plimsolls. A drawer was partly open, the jumpers pushed to one end. She pulled the drawer out fully, took all the jumpers out and laid them on the bed, then folded each one before putting them back in the drawer again. Paul's favourite green pullover wasn't amongst the pile. She tried to remember what he was wearing when she saw him earlier. *I didn't see him, I didn't even turn around.* She pulled the second drawer open to find only one tee-shirt when usually there would be six or seven.

Feeling increasingly uneasy, she stood beside the bed trying to determine what else might be missing. The duffel bag he used for his school books, usually slung on the floor under the window, wasn't there.

She moved towards the window. The curtains were still drawn closed. She pulled them back and as she did a piece of paper floated from the windowsill down to the floor. She stopped to pick it up, recognising Paul's writing.

Mum, I'm staying with a friend tonight. Maybe for a few nights.
I love you Mum and I'm sorry.
Paul

She felt almost faint with sadness. Her husband wouldn't speak to her, her eldest son couldn't bear to be around her and her precious boy, George, was gone forever.

She sat on the floor and wept.

CHAPTER 30
Saturday, 18th July

Anne spent the afternoon preparing a hamper with sausage rolls, sandwiches, crisps, and cake. As soon as 5pm arrived, she put the closed sign on the door of the café, leaving the clearing up for their return.

Arriving at Beach Walk, it seemed that Christina's attempt to persuade people to come along had worked. There were easily as many locals crowding the beach as there had been on previous years. Perhaps even more.

Some families brought deckchairs, many just brought blankets they spread out on the stones, before emptying their picnic baskets and hampers, ready for a feast. Despite what some of the mothers said to Christina earlier in the week, several of the men had prepared a bonfire, which stood about ten feet high, made up of random pieces of driftwood, as well as branches collected from the woods that ran to the north of Bexhill.

The usual arrangement was for the bonfire to be lit at 7pm, with the first fireworks set off around 8pm. Until then, families who were sitting close to each other swapped food - a pork pie for a sausage roll; a cheese sandwich for a ham one. The children ran from one picnic to the next, collecting handfuls of treats, before running down towards the sea edge where they formed their own little groups. Once the food was eaten, they were in prime position to have contests about who could throw a pebble the furthest, or who could make a stone skim across the water.

Stevie won the argument about bringing Max, and Mario lectured Christina about giving in too easily.

'You'll end up spoiling the boy.'

'What do you mean, *I* will end up spoiling him? You and

Mum are just as bad.'

'Children need boundaries. And Max would be much happier at home.'

'Max might be, but then we'll all have to deal with a moaning six-year-old for the whole evening.'

Stevie was given strict instructions about keeping Max far away from the bonfire and was told that once the fireworks began, if Max was upset in any way then Christina would take him straight home.

The Rossi family chose a spot about halfway down the beach.

'If the wind picks up at least the smoke won't be blowing in our direction,' Mario said, nodding towards the tattered flag stuck on the very top of the wood pile. 'What flag is that, anyway? I don't recognise it.'

'I think it's time you got yourselves some glasses,' Anne said by way of a gentle reprimand. 'It's not a flag at all, it's an old pair of trousers.'

Only when they laughed did they realise they'd each been on edge for different reasons. Anne was worried for the Leigh family, telling Christina she was certain when it came to it the event would be too much for them to cope with. Mario had been anxious about Max, and Christina dreaded seeing Tony.

'Room for one more?' She heard Tony's voice before she saw him, as he disentangled himself from a group of people who had chosen to sit right next to the Rossi's picnic spot.

'Have you brought my sparklers?' Stevie jumped up, grabbed hold of Tony's hand and pulled him towards the rest of the group. 'Look, this is Max.'

'Pleased to meet you, Max.' Tony crouched down and took one of the dog's paws, pretending to shake hands with him.

'Look, Auntie. Max knows how to shake hands.'

'I hope you've brought your own picnic?' Christina didn't

hold back from letting the sharpness in her voice provoke a reaction. Anne drew a breath, but Tony's response was to laugh and plonk himself down beside Stevie and Max.

'I do have some sparklers for you, like I promised. But you need to wait until it's a bit darker, otherwise they won't be so much fun.'

'Mum, look, there's Patricia Leigh,' Christina said, pointing to a woman who was walking down the beach on her own. She was dressed quite formally, in a camel coloured coat and court shoes that seemed wholly inappropriate for a beach bonfire. Her hair was pulled back into a tight bun and she was carrying what looked like a small book in her hands.

'Poor woman, I'll go and speak to her.' Anne left the others, and as she approached Patricia people turned to look.

Christina watched as the two women greeted each other. She couldn't hear the conversation, but guessed from her mum's expression that she was trying to persuade Patricia Leigh not to turn around and return home. Anne had her arm around Patricia and appeared to be reassuring her. Christina looked away from her mum, scouring the crowd to see if she could spot Mr Leigh, or Paul, but there was no sign of them.

'There's Councillor Rogers over there,' Mario said. 'I'll try and catch a word with him.'

'Dad, this is supposed to be a night off for you, and there you are still worrying about work.'

'I need to find out about these changes the Council are planning to the seafront. If they go ahead they could affect our café.'

'You worry too much.'

'Someone has to.'

As he moved away, she noticed Giuseppe had found a solitary spot on one of the groynes. His gaze was on each of the faces in the crowd and Christina guessed he was still searching for anyone who might fit the description of the elusive fisherman; the one person who might still be able to throw some light on the events that continued to unnerve the community.

Although the sun wouldn't disappear completely until nearly 9pm, it would be dark enough before that for the first fireworks to be lit. For safety's sake the fireworks were always carried down to the water's edge and lit there, first making sure all the youngsters had moved far enough away to avoid accidents. In all the years they'd held the event, there had only been one accident when old Mr Bantam was in the process of lighting the end of some rockets that had been stood in old milk bottles. Somehow he managed to trip over, tumbling into the bottles and knocking them over, which in turn meant the rockets were directed back up the beach, rather than up into the air. There was just enough time for everyone to stand well back, but even so it was a close call.

But the team in charge of the fireworks this year were taking no chances. Someone had brought a megaphone and as it approached 8pm he announced to the waiting crowd that the first fireworks would be lit in just ten minutes.

'Please stand well back and Mums and Dads, if you can keep a tight hold of your children's hands then we can avoid any unfortunate mishaps,' was the instruction.

Some of the children had formed their own groups, swapping sweets and other goodies. Stevie had been walking Max around in circles. Christina had told him he wasn't to move from her side, but the instruction was becoming increasingly difficult to follow.

'Can you stop that, Stevie, you're making me feel dizzy.' Christina said.

'Can I go and say hello to William? He's just over there, Auntie.'

'You'd better leave Max with me then,' she said, taking the dog's lead. 'But be sure to come straight back.'

There were so many people now that it was starting to feel almost claustrophobic. As the sun set and the air stilled it was apparent it would be one of those rare July evenings when there was barely need for a jumper.

Mario was still talking to the councillor. Giuseppe had wandered off, and Christina could see her mum in the distance, still standing with Patricia Leigh. So far Max hadn't shown any anxiety about the crowds, or the bonfire that was now fully ablaze. Suddenly the first firework exploded, sending a shower of blue, green, and yellow light into the sky. The crowd responded with *oohs* and *aahs* and Max pulled a little on his lead.

It was only then Christina realised Stevie hadn't returned after his chat with William. She looked in the direction he had taken, but all she could see were the backs of people who were now standing to see the firework display down by the water's edge.

Her first reaction was annoyance. Stevie was always pushing the boundaries and never considering the consequences. She started to weave her way through the people who were standing closest to her, trying not to let Max get tangled up in people's legs. She spotted her mum a little way ahead and waved to try to gain her attention, but her mum was looking in the opposite direction. Once she was close enough, she tapped her mum on the shoulder.

'Mum, Stevie went off to find his friend. I told him to come straight back and now I can't see him.' She had to raise her voice above the noise of the next batch of fireworks, which seemed to be getting louder. She could sense Max getting agitated. 'I need to get Max back to the car, but we need to find Stevie first.' The annoyance had now turned to a tension in the pit of her stomach.

'Give Max to me and give me the car keys. I'll take him home, then I'll come straight back.' Anne's voice was calm and full of authority. 'Then you can look for Stevie. Find your dad and Giuseppe, they will help.'

Christina nodded, fishing the car keys from her bag.

Patricia grabbed at Christina's arm, her face pale, her eyes wide with fear.

'Patricia, I'm going to leave you now, but I want you to find Marjorie Selmon. You know each other, don't you? She's just over there,' Anne pointed, and as she did she noticed that Stevie's friend, William, was not with his mother. 'Christina, what about Tony? Didn't he promise Stevie some sparklers?'

'I haven't seen him, not since he was here earlier.'

'Well, maybe Stevie has gone to find him?'

'That's typical of Tony. He's thoughtless. He has no idea about how to be responsible.'

'Don't start blaming him before you know what's happened.'

As the minutes ticked by with no sign of her young nephew, the knots in Christina's stomach had turned to lumps of lead. She watched her mum lead Max off to where the car was parked, back up Beach Walk, far away from the festivities. Suddenly she felt alone, despite being surrounded by people. As she pushed her way through the crowd, she kept repeating the same phrase.

'Have you seen a small boy? He's wearing a red jumper and short blue trousers.'

Most people barely turned when she spoke, perhaps not hearing her over the sound of rockets and bangers going off. A few people shook their head, their gaze following her as she continued to move on past them.

After a few minutes she saw Giuseppe up ahead of her. He'd found some space towards the top of the beach and was sitting on the shingle, paying little attention to the coloured lights in the sky. As she ran towards him he stood, immediately sensing the panic from her expression.

'What has happened?'

'It's Stevie. I can't find him.'

'He has Max? Perhaps with the noise of the bangs?'

'No, he doesn't have Max. Mum has taken the dog home and then she'll drive back to help with the search. Stevie went off to speak to one of his friends just before the fireworks started. I told him to come straight back, but he never listens to me.' She held her arms out, signalling her sense of desperation. 'Something dreadful has happened, I'm sure of it.'

Just yards away from where they were now standing was the spot where thirteen days ago she'd found the body of George Leigh.

CHAPTER 31
Saturday, 18th July

Earlier in the evening, Giuseppe had been watching the crowds gathering on the beach, but all he could see was the potential opportunity for a mishap, even a crime.

In Rome there were frequent festivals, many associated with a saint's feast day, with processions led by a choir of young children. During carnival time in February, everyone dressed up and the gaiety continued long into the night. On such occasions Giuseppe opted to do overtime, going into the office, and leaving his wife to go on her own. Rosalia accused him of being miserable, pessimistic. He countered that he was merely being realistic. It was another reason their marriage had ended - they were on opposite sides for too much of the time, wanting different things from life. He wanted peace and quiet, while she yearned for excitement. His experience was that so many people gathering in one place inevitably resulted in a disagreement, tempers got frayed. But now, with Stevie missing, perhaps it was something far worse.

He needed to focus. He wished he could sit quietly somewhere, on his own, close his eyes and think through the possibilities. The most likely scenario was that Stevie had gone to find Tony.

He turned to face Christina, choosing a measured tone, as if he was giving instructions to a new recruit. 'Now, we do not think of bad things happening to Stevie. We will find him.' He took Christina's arm. 'Your mother is right, first you must try to find Tony. It is possible Stevie is with him. Go and check and if he is not with Tony, then come straight back here.'

'What are you going to do?'

'First I am going to think.'

Giuseppe turned his back on the crowded beach and

looked towards the cottage. There were lights on in the front sitting room and the curtains were still open. As he watched he was certain he saw movement. On the morning of George Leigh's death, he and his brother had visited Rose Walker. *Is there a connection? Think, Giuseppe.*

He strode up the front path of *Rose Cottage* and thumped his fist on the front door. He heard a chain go on the door, and then it opened just a sliver. He saw Rose's face, white with fear.

'*Signora* Walker, do you have a young boy here with you?'

'You're frightening me. I want you to go away.' She whispered through the barely open door and then went to push it closed. Giuseppe prevented her from doing so by putting his foot in the way.

'It is very important you tell me the truth. Perhaps you invited the child in?'

'I haven't done anything wrong.'

'I cannot speak to you through the doorway like this. Will you open the door and let me in?' He changed his tone; gentle persuasion was needed.

She opened the door fully and stood back, her hands gripped tightly in front of her. He stayed on the doorstep and tried to detect any sounds from inside the house, but down on the beach there was still so much noise that it was impossible.

'Stevie.' He called out, certain that if the boy was in the house he would come to him.

'I want you to go,' she said.

'*Signora* Walker, you can help me if you tell me the truth. A boy has died and now a young child has gone missing. Stevie is Christina's nephew. Christina and I came here and spoke to you last week. Now she is desperately worried that something bad has happened to him. You would not want that, would you?'

She turned away from him and without hesitating he

followed her. In the front room he watched her go to the mantelpiece and pick up the photo of the boy.

Giuseppe had felt certain, almost from the first time he met Rose Walker, that she did not have a son. Perhaps it was her desperation for a child that led her to visit the school, just for the chance to watch the children play. It was clear from the way she'd spoken about the visit from the Leigh brothers that there was an unfulfilled longing in her. For a moment he thought it was that same longing that may have led her to invite Stevie into the cottage. But now he realised he was wrong.

'*Signora* Walker, you don't have a son, do you?'

'I do have a son. His name is Vincent.' She held the framed photo close to her, almost embracing it.

'Where is your son, *Signora* Walker? He doesn't live with you, does he?'

She shook her head. 'You won't be able to understand. It's too complicated to explain.'

'I would like to understand.'

Giuseppe was torn between wanting to leave to help search for Stevie and wanting to stay, in the hope Rose Walker would provide vital information. Information that may not only help them find Stevie, but could shine a light on events that led to the death of George Leigh. He was certain there was a connection.

'Are you hiding from someone? Someone you are scared of?'

Rose stared at him. It was as though she was in a trance, barely able to move.

'I thought he wouldn't find me here,' she whispered.

'Who?'

'My husband.'

'He's been here to the cottage?'

Rose wrapped her arms around herself. Giuseppe noticed

199

she was quivering. 'And does he know where your son is? Would he harm him?'

Giuseppe's mind was whirling, leaping from one possibility to another.

'*Signora* Walker, when was the last time you saw your husband?'

Giuseppe was so desperate for all the facts he wanted to shake them out of the woman, but he knew that the only way to get a frightened witness to open up was to be gentle, to gain their trust.

'Anything you can tell me will only help you to feel safer. If we can find your husband we can make sure he doesn't scare you again.' He used his calmest voice, waiting for her response and hoping he'd said enough.

'I saw him last Sunday.' This time the whisper was barely audible.

'The day that George Leigh died.'

'Yes.'

Their conversation was interrupted by a fierce banging on the front door. Rose's expression froze, colour draining from her face. 'It's him, he's come to get me. I won't go back. I'd rather kill myself.' Her voice was no longer a whisper, but a shriek.

'Try to calm yourself. I will answer the door. I am certain it will not be your husband. Trust me.'

It was Christina at the door, her face flushed, her breathing rapid, a look of desperation on her face. 'I can't find Tony and I can't find Stevie. I've looked and looked. If something bad has happened to him, it will be my fault.' She had arms wrapped tight around her chest.

'Wait for a moment outside,' he said. 'I need to speak to *Signora* Walker. I will be a few minutes.'

Giuseppe was struggling to think clearly, surrounded by all

the heightened emotion. If Rose Walker's husband had been hanging around at the time of George Leigh's death he may have been involved in some way and may now have something to do with Stevie's disappearance. How or why, Giuseppe still couldn't figure out.

He closed the front door and returned to Rose, who had taken refuge in a corner of the kitchen, crouching down as if she trying to make herself invisible.

'Can I use your telephone?' He'd seen the phone in the hallway when he arrived. He wanted the chance to speak without Rose overhearing. Mario was forever telling him that local families formed a tight-knit community, people looked out for each other. It seemed to Giuseppe the people of this seaside town had let Rose Walker down. She was vulnerable, lonely and in need of some kindness. When all of this was over he would speak to Anne.

He took the scrap of paper from his pocket and dialled the number that Detective Sergeant Pearce had written down for him the last time they met.

The phone rang several times before Pearce answered. Giuseppe imagined the sergeant grumbling as he laid down his newspaper, put his beer glass to one side and moved slowly to the telephone. Perhaps Mrs Pearce would be irritated that their evening had been interrupted.

'Pearce.'

'*Buona sera, Signor Pearce.* It is Giuseppe Bianchi. I am sorry to disturb you.'

'What do you want?'

'Stevie Rossi is missing. He is the grandson of my cousin. We were all at the bonfire party at Beach Walk when he disappeared.'

'Where are you now?'

'I am in the cottage of *Signora* Rose Walker. The

conversation I have just had with her leads me to believe the child could be in danger.'

'I will meet you there.'

Returning to the kitchen, he spoke to the frightened woman. '*Signora* Walker, I must go. I need to help in the search for Stevie, but I will come back, I promise. Keep your door closed and do not open it for anyone this evening. Unless it is the police.'

Christina was standing on the edge of the shingle, away from the crowds, when Giuseppe joined her.

'Go down to the water, find the man with the loudspeaker. Ask him to put out an announcement. Keep it clear and simple. Stevie Rossi is missing, he is six years old and is wearing a red jumper and blue trousers.'

Christina gazed at Giuseppe, trying to absorb his words, but all she could see was her young nephew, all ready for the party earlier that day, barely able to stand still for excitement.

'Go now and get the announcement made.'

CHAPTER 32
Saturday, 18th July

Shortly after Christina left, Detective Sergeant Pearce arrived.

'What can you tell me? Gatherings like this, bonfires, fireworks, it's so easy for it to get out of hand. I should have had a constable here on duty.'

'Perhaps. But this may be something else. Maybe someone has seized the opportunity of such a crowd to commit another crime. However, I am still struggling to understand his motive.'

Pearce waited for Giuseppe to continue.

'I have spoken to *Signora* Walker. She tells me her husband is a man to be feared.'

'Local?'

'No. But he was here at the beach on the day George Leigh died.'

'And you think he's returned tonight and taken Stevie Rossi?'

'I don't want to believe it, but we have to consider it as a possibility. If he caused the death of George and perhaps he thinks Stevie was a witness, then...'

Pearce held his hand up, stopping the Italian from voicing words he didn't want to hear.

'And him?' Pearce gestured towards the caravan.

'Once again the Irishman has not stepped outside his caravan. He has not taken part in the evening's events. He will say he has seen nothing, knows nothing.'

'We should rule him out at least.'

They approached the caravan, Pearce taking the lead and banging on the door.

'Evening.' Sean Murphy opened the door wide enough to show his face to the two men, but not wide enough for them to see inside.

'A child is missing,' Giuseppe said, raising his voice over the noise of the loudspeaker announcement now being repeated to the crowd.

Suddenly, the door was pulled opened as Stevie squeezed past Sean, launching himself into the arms of the Italian. 'Uncle Giuseppe.'

'Stevie, we have been very worried about you. Your aunt has been looking for you, everyone has been looking for you.'

'I didn't like the bangs.' The child nestled his face into Giuseppe's shoulder.

'Once again you are guilty of irresponsible behaviour,' Pearce said, directing his fury at Sean. 'You must have known people would be looking for the boy.'

'Don't have a go at me. If you ask me it's a stupid idea to bring a little lad to an event like this. And even more stupid to let him out of your sight.'

Giuseppe ignored the inference, instead attempting to release Stevie's grip on him. 'I must go and tell your aunt you are safe. Stevie, you stay here with Detective Sergeant Pearce until I return.'

'I guess you'd better come inside,' Sean Murphy said to Pearce, holding the door open for the detective and the child to enter.

'I've been helping Paul with the jigsaw,' Stevie announced, running over to Paul and jumping onto his lap.

'Paul Leigh. What are you doing here?'

'Jigsaws.'

'Don't try to be clever with me, lad. Do your parents know you're here?'

'What do they care?'

On the floor beneath the jigsaw table was a duffel bag. It was partly open with a couple of tee-shirts spilling out.

'Are these your things, lad?' Pearce asked.

'What if they are?'

'You'd better mind your manners and tell me what you're doing here.'

Sean Murphy stood between the detective and the boys. 'Leave him be. There's no harm in him being here.'

'I'm staying with Sean if you want to know,' Paul said, glaring defiantly at Pearce. 'It's not like I'm missed at home, so I might as well be here.'

Pearce saw an exchange of looks between Paul and Sean that he couldn't quite determine.

'You need to let your parents know where you are, Paul. If you don't, then I will. But first you can both help me by answering a question.'

'Fire away,' Sean said.

'Paul, you said there was a man who was fishing here by the shore a while back. A man who shouted at you and George. Mr Murphy here, he warned him off.'

Pearce had the attention of Paul and Sean, while Stevie was focused on picking up individual pieces of the jigsaw and studying their shapes, as if he was learning a new technique in puzzle solving.

'Yeah, I shouted at the fella. What of it?' Sean said.

'You must have seen the photofit image we put up. Do you think this is the same man?'

'It could be. Not that I studied his face that much.'

'Is there anything else you remember about him?'

'What else do you want me to tell you? I guess he was fishing for mackerel. Although I know about fishing and it was pretty clear he didn't.'

'What makes you say that?'

'Wrong gear, wrong kind of line.'

'Think carefully before you answer the next question.' Pearce snapped. 'On any of the occasions that this man was at the beach, did you ever see him approach *Rose Cottage?*'

'Maybe. What of it?'

'Did you see this man on the beach last Sunday?'

'I might have done.'

'And have you seen him since?'

Before Sean Murphy could respond, the caravan door flung open and Christina pushed forward, picking Stevie up and holding him tight to her.

'Oh, Stevie, you gave us such a fright. We didn't know where you were.'

'I didn't like the bangs. Where's Max?'

'He didn't like the bangs either. Grandma has taken him home, and that's where you and I are going right now.'

Pearce stepped outside the caravan to join Giuseppe. They stood in silence for a few minutes as they watched Christina walking back along the beach, clutching Stevie's hand.

'One happy result,' Pearce said.

'*Sì.*'

'Sean Murphy is being as evasive as ever. I could bring him into the station, try to force it out of him, but right now I think our best bet is Mrs Walker. We have the clerk's description of the stranger. It might be enough for us to determine whether this fella and Mrs Walker's husband are one and the same.'

Giuseppe nodded. 'If the descriptions match, then we will know who we are looking for.'

Pearce frowned. 'But we still have nothing to connect him with the boy's death. All we know - or suspect - is that the man is a bully. It's a bit of a stretch from that to murder.'

'*Un passo alla volta.* One step at a time.'

CHAPTER 33
Saturday, 18th July

There were several minutes between Giuseppe knocking on the door of *Rose Cottage* and the door being opened. It was only after Pearce called through the letterbox several times that Rose Walker was reassured sufficiently to pull back the chain and open the door.

'*Signora* Walker, we have found Stevie Rossi and he is fine.' Giuseppe chose a calm tone, hoping his approach would in turn lead to a calm response to the questions he planned to ask her.

'Thank God. And he's not harmed?'

'He is really fine. He was just a little scared of the fireworks and had taken refuge.' Pearce explained, matching his tone to that of his Italian counterpart.

'*Signora* Walker, may we talk to you for a few moments?'

She opened the door and then led them through to the front room, where the two men sat while she remained standing, as if she wanted to be ready should she need to make a quick escape.

'When I was here earlier, you mentioned your husband.' Giuseppe spoke slowly, knowing that any mention of the man she most feared could result in her asking them to leave. 'Do you have a photograph of him?'

By way of response she left the room, returning after a few minutes, clutching a small diary in her hand. She handed it to Giuseppe.

'You look at it. I can't. I'm sure you'll understand.'

Giuseppe opened the diary and there, tucked in-between the pages, was a small black-and-white photo of a couple on their wedding day.

'You were a beautiful bride,' he said, smiling.

He studied the photo for a few moments before passing it to Pearce.

'Do you mind if we take this photo away with us?' Pearce said.

'You think he had something to do with George Leigh's death?' Rose started wringing her hands and Giuseppe noticed her breathing quicken.

'We're not making any assumptions at the moment,' Pearce replied. 'All we are doing is gathering information.'

Giuseppe stood and moved to the window overlooking the beach. 'This is a pretty cottage. You keep it very well.'

Rose didn't respond, but remained still, watching the Italian who now turned to face her.

'Is this your cottage, *Signora* Walker?'

'I look after it, for the owners.' The words came out in a rush, as if she was defending herself against some unspoken accusation.

'You are their housekeeper?'

Pearce said nothing, shifting his gaze from Giuseppe to Rose, wondering where the Italian's questions might lead.

'Their housekeeper, yes.'

Rose clutched the edge of her cardigan in her hand. 'It was an omen, you see. The name of the cottage too. It was meant to be.'

'*Sì*, I can see that.'

'They are abroad.' Rose provided the answer before the question is asked.

'The family who own the cottage?'

'Mr and Mrs Taylor.'

'And they asked you to look after the place?'

'And Tabitha. They've got plenty of money. A place in Cyprus, as well as this cottage. They pay me a small wage, enough for food. Although I don't eat much, I never have.'

208

'And when they return? Will they keep you on?'

Rose shrugged.

'And your son, *Signora* Walker, do they know about him?'

Giuseppe had been working up to the question, but the moment he voiced it Rose moved over to the mantelpiece and picked up the photo of the boy.

'Can you tell us where your son is now?' Giuseppe said. He conveyed no emotion in his words. There was enough bubbling under the surface without providing further triggers.

'I never wanted to let him go. He made me.'

The emotion she'd been trying to keep contained now threatened to overwhelm her. She collapsed onto one of the armchairs, her hands covering her face.

'Your husband made you give up your child?'

Giuseppe was forming a picture of the man in his mind, a man who could forcibly separate a mother and child.

'It was all my fault,' Rose said.

'Are you able to tell us what happened?' Giuseppe asked.

'The trouble started when I had an idea to take a little job working in a clothes shop.' She spoke slowly at first, her voice gathering strength as the story emerged. 'It would have been a chance to get out, to meet people. Arnold, my husband, he was at work most of the time, even in the evenings sometimes. I felt so lonely.'

'Your husband worked shifts?' Pearce asked.

'He sells insurance. He was out all hours, catching people when they're at home, I suppose. Some days I didn't speak to a soul. But when I told him about me wanting a job, he was furious. *No wife of mine is going to be a shop girl*, he said. *I provide for this family and that's the last word I'll say on the subject.* But that was the problem, we weren't a family. Of course we hoped we'd be blessed with a child one day.'

'Your husband didn't want you to work?' Giuseppe said.

He had an image of the insurance salesman, a man who liked to be in control, to know where his wife was every moment of every day. Someone who was used to his tea being on the table when he arrived home from work. His thoughts went again to Rosalia. He'd taken her for granted, assumed she'd be content to be his wife, when all along she wanted so much more.

Rose was still gripping the edge of her cardigan, her knuckles almost white with tension.

'You and your husband had a row,' Giuseppe nodded to Rose to continue her story.

'I didn't argue back. I didn't dare. Instead I went out, left him to get his own tea, and I went to the pub. First time I'd ever been inside a pub without Arnold. I'll show him, I thought. But as soon as I stepped into the place, I wanted to run out again. There were no other women, just the barmaid. All the men propping up the bar, smoking and supping their pints, they all turned and stared at me.'

'I was about to turn around and walk straight out. Then this nice West Indian fella put his hand on my arm. *"You alright, miss?"* he said. His voice so gentle and musical.'

She moved her head from side to side as though she was remembering a favourite tune.

'He offered to buy me a drink,' she continued. 'Said he came from Jamaica. The way he described his homeland, it sounded like paradise. I asked him, what on earth are you doing here, giving up paradise for this place, you must be mad. He just laughed. Such lovely big white teeth he had, when he opened his mouth it was like turning a light on.'

As Rose was recounting her story Giuseppe was preparing more questions. He was beginning to guess how the story might end.

'You spent the evening with the Jamaican man?' Giuseppe

said.

She nodded, taking on a look that reminded him of Rosalia, guilt and defiance all rolled into one.

'I got a bit tiddly. I'd never had more than the occasional glass of milk stout, but he kept buying me Babychams, with a little cherry on a cocktail stick. I was having such a nice time I didn't want to go home. I couldn't bear the thought of going back to Arnold with his surly face, when I could spend the rest of the evening with this man who was so gentle and made me feel so precious.'

'But you had to go home to your husband,' Giuseppe said.

She bowed her head, making her words muffled. 'I did go home, but not until the next morning when I knew Arnold would be at work. Arnold never asked me outright, but I let him think I'd stayed the night with my friend Mary.'

'Did you see your Jamaican friend again?'

Rose shook her head. 'Such a kind, gentle man.'

'Then you and your husband had a son? The family you had always hoped for.' It was Pearce who spoke now.

'When I told Arnold I was pregnant, he was thrilled. He told me I'd made him the happiest man alive. All through my pregnancy he treated me like a queen.'

'Until the baby was born.' Giuseppe said it as a statement of fact.

Rose brought her knees up to her chest, hugging them to her as though she was a baby, nestled in her mother's womb.

'He was such a beautiful boy, big brown eyes, just like his father's. I couldn't be sure, not until the moment he was born. It was the midwife's face that told me. She could see the trouble ahead. A black baby born to a white mother. Then as soon as Arnold saw him he refused to even touch him. He called me terrible names, said I was nothing but a whore. He told me I wasn't to feed him. I pleaded with him. You'll grow

211

to love him, I know you will, I told him. But he wouldn't even speak to me, I can still see the look of disgust on his face.'

'He asked you to rehome the child?' Giuseppe said.

She shook her head. 'He made the arrangements with the hospital. It all happened so quickly. Just days after my baby boy was born they took him away, and I never saw him again.'

She curled into a tight ball, rocking a little backwards and forwards. A prickly silence descended on the room, as though each of them had something to say and yet the words had to be carefully chosen. Giuseppe's thoughts were of the boy first, and then the boy's father. Here was a child born as a result of a chance encounter who would never know his parents and never understand the reason his mother had let him go. And the gentle Jamaican didn't even know he had a son.

Rose stood. 'You can see from that wedding photo, Arnold is so fair, you see. He had real blond curls when he was a baby. People would have talked, asked questions, he'd never be able to hold his head up.'

'Your words or his?' It was too late for Giuseppe to bite back the question.

Rose went to grab back the photo, almost tearing it in her haste. 'You can't understand. None of you can. I did a bad thing and saying goodbye to Vincent forever - that was my punishment.'

'Vincent?' Pearce asked.

'I named him after his father.' She moved to the mantelpiece and took down the framed photo of the young boy, holding it close, almost embracing it.

'Where did you get the photo, Mrs Walker? It's not of your son, is it?'

'When the Taylors left for Cyprus, they said I could pack some of their ornaments away. Less dusting, they said. So I went through some of the boxes in the garden shed and there he was, wrapped in a towel.'

'Do you know who he is?'

She shook her head and put the photo back down, in the exact same spot where it had stood before.

'And all this time, your visits to the school?' Giuseppe said.

'I like to watch the children playing. There's no harm in it.'

There was a quiver in her voice, then suddenly she moved forward, picked the photo frame up again, lifted it high into the air and smashed it down with force. The three of them looking down at it, the shock of the moment stilling them all into silence. The frame landed on the edge of the fireplace surround, picture side up, the glass cracked in several places.

Pearce bent to pick up the photo and as he did a couple of pieces of glass fell onto the floor. 'Is there anyone who can stay with you? You shouldn't be on your own tonight.'

'There's no one.' She dropped down into the armchair and began to cry.

'Well, in the absence of alcohol I recommend you make yourself a hot, sweet tea. My wife recommends it for shock.' Pearce put his hand on her shoulder.

'*Signora* Walker, where did you and your husband live when you were together?'

Rose narrowed her eyes, pausing before replying, as though she was weighing up the implications of sharing her story.

'London.'

'Ah, yes. And one more question, then we will leave you in peace.'

She looked up at Giuseppe, her movements slow.

'I wish I could find peace.'

It was the saddest thing Giuseppe had heard her say during all of this evening's conversation.

'Does your husband own a car?'

'Oh no. He doesn't drive you see.'

'Perhaps he has learned to drive since you and he parted?'

She shook her head. 'Epilepsy. He suffers with it. So he'd never have been allowed.'

'But he is an insurance salesman,' Pearce said, 'he doesn't do it all on foot, surely?'

'Bicycle. He has a bicycle.'

CHAPTER 34
Saturday, 18th July

'You have a theory, don't you?'

The two men were sitting in Pearce's car, having walked away from *Rose Cottage*.

'I need to show you something,' Giuseppe said.

Pearce remained silent as they drove to *Bella Café*. Once inside, Giuseppe's first thoughts were about Stevie. 'Is he alright?' he asked Christina.

'I've learned that small boys have no concept of the anxieties of adults. He was asleep almost before his head hit the pillow.'

'*Meno male.* That is good.'

Giuseppe took the detective sergeant up to the sitting room and Christina offered both men a hot drink, leaving them for a few minutes, returning with a tray of coffees, and followed by Anne.

'I'm pleased you are here, I have something to share with you both.' Giuseppe had retrieved the wedding photo from Rose Walker after her outburst, promising he would return it to her. Now he took the photo from his pocket and passed it to Anne. 'Christina, do you have the photo Matthew Harding gave us? The photo of his sister?'

A few moments later Christina returned to the sitting room, holding out the little black-and-white photo of Matthew's sister. Christina and her mother stared at the two photos. There was little difference between the teenage girl who Matthew had tried to care for and protect and the bride who stood beside her husband. But since her wedding day Rose's experiences had added not only lines to her face, but hidden scars that could only be imagined.

'Rose Walker is Barbara. She is here in Bexhill?' Anne's tone

215

was one of incredulity. 'I don't understand. How? Why?'

'The "*why*" is perhaps to do with the kindness you and your family showed her during the war,' Giuseppe said. 'The "*how*" we need to discover.'

'Why didn't she come to see me? I could have helped her settle in, we could have been friends.'

While her mother was speaking, Christina was still staring at the photos, reflecting on the way she'd spoken to Rose Walker. Rose had been in desperate need of kindness, instead she was left alone to cope with her fears.

Giuseppe stood, taking the two photos from Christina, and passing them to Pearce.

'Let me explain. The woman in this photo,' Giuseppe pointed to the picture of the young woman Matthew had given them, 'came with her brother to Bexhill as part of the evacuation of children at the beginning of the Second World War. When they eventually returned to London, they arrived to scenes of great devastation. We don't know much about their life from then on, except to know that Rose – or Barbara as Anne knew her – eventually married. You and I heard a little of what Rose has suffered at the hands of her husband. I am guessing she tried to escape her husband, returning to live with her brother, Matthew. But then, for some reason, she felt the need to run further away and so she came here to the south coast, a place she associated with happy times.'

Pearce was listening, while at the same time, trying to assess all the implications, for Rose Walker, and for his priority – finding the person responsible for the death of George Leigh.

'Matthew Harding recently contacted Anne,' Giuseppe continued. 'He was concerned over the disappearance of his sister. She had not been in touch and in desperation he thought his friend of years ago – Anne – might help.' He turned to Anne as he spoke. 'I don't think he ever believed you could help find her. I think his real wish was to have someone who might listen.'

'I've let him down,' Anne said, bowing her head. 'I should have gone to London myself, not sent two people he had never met. Poor Barbara. Poor Matthew.'

Christina moved to sit beside her mum and put her arm around her.

'This can all be fixed. You and I can visit Rose...'

'And I will return to London and visit Matthew Harding once more,' Giuseppe said. 'We need to know more about the husband. It seems that *Signora* Walker's escape to Bexhill was not enough to ensure her safety.'

'There is little more to be gained this evening.' Pearce stood, extending a hand to Giuseppe. 'You will let me know how you get on?'

'Of course. But there is something else. I hope you do not think me impertinent. This is your case, I understand that.'

'You'd better tell me what it is, then I'll tell you if I think you are impertinent.' It was clear from Pearce's expression he admired Giuseppe's tactics, making someone else feel as though they were taking the lead, when all along they were really being led by the nose.

'Paul Leigh.' Giuseppe dropped his voice, hoping Anne and Christina weren't listening. 'Ask to take a look at his bicycle.'

There were many discussions later that evening at the Rossi home. While the others had been talking about Rose Walker and making plans for the next day, Mario had been downstairs in the café clearing up and preparing for the morning. After saying goodbye to the detective sergeant, they spent the next hour or so, bringing Mario up to date with the evening's events.

'And it's your guess this woman's husband might have

something to do with the death of George Leigh?' he asked his cousin.

'I try not to guess when I am investigating a crime. It is safer to focus only on evidence and facts.'

'I'm surprised Detective Sergeant Pearce is letting you be so involved. He does know you're retired from the police force, doesn't he?'

Giuseppe muttered something under his breath.

'If you've got something to say, then say it,' his cousin said.

'I think we are all tired and overwrought,' Anne said, before Giuseppe could respond. 'It has been a long and difficult evening and I for one want to curl up in bed and not think about any of this until tomorrow.'

'I'll second that,' Christina added.

'But I'm not sure you should be going to London on your own, Giuseppe,' Anne continued. 'I'm torn between coming with you and going to see Rose. What if Christina goes with you? I don't want you getting lost. Mario can look after the café and Stevie and Max, and I'll go to see Rose on my own.'

'Mum, I've decided not to go into work next week. I need to keep Stevie safe. All the time some crazy man could be out there, capable of who knows what.'

'We must not become hysterical,' Giuseppe said, using the calm tone he had used many times in the past with fearful witnesses and victims. 'We do not know if the husband of *Signora* Walker is involved in any way with George Leigh's death. We do not know if he is still here in Bexhill.'

It was a closing statement of fact, requiring no response and time for them all to go to their beds.

CHAPTER 35
Saturday, 18th July

It was a little after 11pm when Christina was woken by a noise. She'd fallen into a deep sleep, where the image of a giant's face was somehow connected to the sound of fireworks and the smell of seaweed and rotten fish. As she was pulled out of her dream, she couldn't decide if the banging noise was real or if it was a continuation of the imaginary fireworks.

But as the noise persisted, she tossed back the bedspread, grabbed a dressing gown, and ran downstairs. The café was in darkness, but the face at the door was lit by the streetlight. Tony.

Unlocking the door, she put her finger to her lips to urge him to be quiet. He followed her through to the back kitchen.

'What are you doing here, Tony? Threatening to wake the whole family, tonight of all nights.'

'I was worried.'

'*You* were worried.' The mix of frustration, anger and tiredness made it almost impossible for her to form any words. She moved to the cooker, filling the kettle and lighting the gas.

'I don't want a hot drink.'

'I'm not offering you one. But from the smell of your breath I'd say you could do with a strong coffee to sober you up.'

'I'm not drunk, Chrissie.'

She turned her back on him, pulling her dressing gown tightly around her.

'Stevie went missing tonight. I came looking for you.'

'That's why I'm here. To make sure he's alright.'

'No thanks to you.'

'I'm to blame, am I? Seems like I'm always to blame.'

The kettle started to boil and Tony reached forward to

remove the whistle. 'Best not make any more noise, eh?' He stood beside Christina, looking at her while she continued to look away. 'I woke you, didn't I? I can see the sleep in your eyes.' He went to touch the side of her face, but she pulled away.

'What do you want, Tony?'

'I want us to be friends again.'

'Don't you think it's a little late for that?'

He pulled out a chair and sat, his long legs stretching out in front of him, his elbow resting on the table.

'I didn't realise Stevie was looking for me. If I had then I'd have...'

'He wasn't looking for you. Despite your promise of sparklers. Good job for you he doesn't hold grudges.'

'Shame his aunt does.'

Tony picked up the salt cellar and tipped it up, letting salt trickle out onto his hand. 'You know they say if you spill salt you have to throw some over your shoulder to chase away bad luck.'

Christina watched as he threw the salt over his shoulder. There was still so much resentment boiling inside her that she wondered if she'd ever be free of it.

'Tell me again why you're here,' she said.

'I was worried about Stevie.'

'And why are you worried about Stevie?' She sat opposite him, her gaze directed at him.

'He's a great kid, I care about him. It's not a crime, is it?'

'Why do you care so much about him, Tony? Is it because you think he's your son?'

Tony laughed, but there was nothing light-hearted about the sound. He returned Christina's gaze, his expression suggesting he was deciding what to say next.

'Isn't it time to tell the truth? About you and Flavia?'

220

Christina said.

'You want to know the truth? Okay, here goes.' He stood, and for a moment she wondered what he was going to do. 'I think I'll have that coffee now.' He put two heaped teaspoons of instant coffee in a mug and filled it from the kettle, then added two teaspoons of sugar. When he spoke this time he had his back to Christina.

'You're right, your sister and I had a one-night stand. I could say she lured me into it, but I knew what I was doing. And deep down I knew what she was trying to do.'

'She wanted to split us up.'

'Yep. And she got her wish, didn't she? But ever since I've regretted that one night and that's the God's honest truth.' He turned to face Christina, his eyes searching her face.

'And Stevie?'

'I have no idea. But let's face it, your sister wasn't exactly a one guy kind of girl.'

'So why do you take so much interest in him, always wanting to spend time with him?'

'Because it means I get to spend time with you.'

Now it was Christina's turn to be lost for words. *Love and hate go hand in hand.* She'd hung onto anger and resentment towards Tony because deep down she still cared for him, still loved him.

For a while neither spoke. Tony sipped his coffee and Christina pretended to inspect her nail varnish, occasionally looking up at him each time she felt his eyes on her. It was Tony who broke the silence.

'Am I forgiven?'

'You'd better ask Stevie.'

Tony gave her a questioning look.

'He's still waiting for those sparklers.'

CHAPTER 36
Sunday, 19th July

The next day, when Matthew Harding answered the door to Giuseppe and Christina, he didn't appear surprised to see them.

'You've come to tell me to forget about my sister, haven't you? I have to accept she's chosen a new life and doesn't need her brother anymore. But I'm so grateful for what you've done, coming all this way, taking the time to listen to me. It's really helped to have someone to share it with.'

His outburst of thanks took place while the three of them were standing inside the entrance to the flats. Once Matthew finished speaking, Giuseppe gestured towards the staircase.

'We would like to talk to you, if you have some time to give us.'

Matthew's stance altered. He'd been standing in front of them, his shoulders drooping, his head bowed - a man who had accepted defeat. But on hearing Giuseppe's words he stood tall, put his shoulders back and held Giuseppe's gaze.

'Of course, follow me.' He led them upstairs, back into the flat that Christina noticed still had a lingering smell of damp.

'Shall I make us a pot of tea?' Christina didn't wait for a response, but moved over to the kitchenette area of the flat, leaving the two men to talk.

'*Signor* Harding, we have some news for you.' Giuseppe removed the two photos from his jacket pocket and laid them down in front of Matthew, on a small coffee table.

At first, Matthew didn't look at them, instead looking at Giuseppe, his eyes wide as if he didn't want to hear what the Italian was about to say. *News*. It could be good, but it could also be bad, worse than bad, and once it was spoken it couldn't be unsaid.

'This is the photo you gave us of your sister, Barbara, when she was a teenager,' Giuseppe pointed at the black-and-white photo. 'And this,' he continued, pointing at the second photo, 'is a photo of a wedding.'

Matthew picked up both photos, giving a gasp as he looked at them.

'Barbara's wedding day. I don't understand. How did you get this? Who gave it to you?'

'Your sister.' Giuseppe let the words hang for a few seconds before saying any more.

'Barbara? You've found her? She's alive? She's alright?'

Christina had been standing behind Matthew, watching and listening to the conversation, but now she stepped forward, placing her hands on his shoulders. 'You've had a shock,' she said. 'But at least it's a good shock. We've both seen your sister and she really is fine. She goes by the name of Rose Walker.' She filled a glass from the tap and set it down in front of Matthew.

Over the next hour, Giuseppe explained the events of the last few days.

'She's living in Bexhill?' Matthew asked, clearly still trying to absorb all he was being told. 'I still can't believe you've found her. Did she say why she hasn't been in touch? It was my fault, wasn't it?'

'I think your sister's actions have been based on fear, but it was not you she was scared of. She may have felt the safest thing was to tell no one of her whereabouts, not even her brother.'

'She didn't think I'd tell that brute of a husband, surely?'

'It would not be your intention, but once you had her address, it was possible he could have found a way to force you to share it with him. As it is, we fear he may have found her anyway.'

Matthew jumped up from the chair. 'Dear Lord, has he hurt her? You said she was alright. Please tell me the truth.'

Giuseppe stood, moved towards Matthew and put his hand on his arm. 'Your sister is safe. But if you can help us find her husband, then we can make sure she remains safe. Can you tell us a little more about him? How they met, perhaps?'

'I told her he wasn't right for her but she'd hear none of it. As soon as I met him I could see he was a wrong'un.'

'In what way?'

'Cruel. Nothing physical, at least I never saw any bruises on her, although I suppose she could have hidden them.'

'He treated her badly?'

'He wanted to control her. Never trusted her, accusing her of all sorts.'

'He was jealous?'

'She didn't give him any reason, at least not at first.'

'Matthew, your sister has told us about the child.'

Matthew's voice became increasingly faltering, as though he was letting his sister down just by speaking of her.

'The man is a bully. She didn't deserve the way he treated her. No surprise she turned elsewhere for comfort - I don't blame her, not one bit. But when you were here before, if I'd told you the whole story, then maybe...'

He paused mid-sentence. There was a vibration in the floor, perhaps from the door to the block being slammed. He stood and moved to the window, pulling back the yellowed net curtain.

'Are you expecting someone?'

He didn't reply at first, but put his face close to the window that was so smeared it provided little light to the room. Giuseppe and Christina exchanged a look, sensing the tension in Matthew's posture.

'Are you okay?' Christina was beside him, following his

gaze, trying to see whatever was the focus of his attention.

'He's been watching the flat again. I'm certain of it. As if it wasn't enough he made her give up the child. She turned up here late one evening, all her belongings in a little battered suitcase. He'd thrown her out.' He looked around the room as though expecting to see the suitcase lying in front of him. 'Stay here with me, I told her. We'll be fine together. We always used to be fine until that brute came along.'

He was still staring out of the window as he spoke. 'He left her alone for a few weeks, but then he started turning up here late at night, often drunk, but always raving. He'd stand on the pavement and shout obscenities, calling her terrible names. I made her stay in the bedroom, told her to put her hands over her ears so she didn't have to listen. As soon as he left I'd go into her and find her in a terrible state, shaking, crying.'

'Did you ever confront him?' Giuseppe asked.

Matthew returned to his seat, leaning forward towards Giuseppe, so focused on telling his story he didn't acknowledge the question.

'She had terrible nightmares. She'd wake screaming, I'd go into her, try to calm her down, but nothing worked. Then it got so that the days were unbearable too.'

'In what way?' Christina asked.

'She'd say things that scared me.'

'What sort of things?' Giuseppe had first-hand experience of the threats that someone might choose when they are at their lowest ebb. The arguments he'd had with Rosalia before she left often ended in her threatening to ruin his career. And then, on Saturday night he'd heard Rose Walker say she would rather kill herself than have to return to her husband.

'I should have asked for help,' he said, suddenly. 'I know that now. I should have told someone, but I was scared they'd take her away, lock her up. I've heard tell of such things, women who have babies when they're not married, locked up in some godforsaken institution. Left there for years.'

'Years ago, maybe,' Christina said, speaking quietly. 'Not now, not anymore.'

'And was your sister able to work?' Giuseppe asked, taking a sideways glance at Christina. He sensed from her expression that all of this would add another strand to her newspaper article, women living in fear, the prejudice that existed over illegitimacy. It was the same in Italy, worse perhaps. In a Catholic country religion set the rules, and anyone who broke them could be cast out.

'I earn good money as a postman,' Matthew replied, bringing Giuseppe's attention back to the room. 'I take all the overtime I can and we had a simple life. When things got really tight, and I was worried we couldn't pay the electricity bill or some such, then she'd take some casual work, cleaning mostly. She wasn't scared of hard work, it was just that it was awkward. She'd make up stories, talking about her boy as if he was still living with her and then there'd be questions she couldn't answer and she'd get upset. I couldn't bear to see her cry.'

'Your sister was ill. Illness isn't always just physical. Traumatic events affect the way we think, make us do strange things.' Christina stretched her hand forward across the table.

She could sense Giuseppe fidgeting next to her. Matthew leaned forward to pick up the glass of water that until now had remained untouched.

'Can you tell us what happened the day she left,' Giuseppe said.

'Like I say,' Matthew continued. 'She created a fantasy world, talking out loud to the boy, as though he was here in the flat with us. She had this little bit of blue ribbon. It was all she had to remind her of the baby. From a bonnet, or matinee jacket, I expect. Anyway, she'd sit for hours holding the ribbon, winding it around her fingers over and over. It got so I couldn't take much more of it. Plus, she was terrified, night and day. We never knew when her husband might turn up. We used to turn all the lights out and I'd peep through the curtains, waiting until he'd gone. He'd be there for an hour or more some days.'

'Why didn't you go to the police?' Christina's voice was raised now, not hiding her fury towards Rose's husband.

'They want proof, don't they? And we didn't have any. It's not a crime for someone to stand around outside someone's house, is it?'

'Well, it should be,' she said.

'Then three months ago it all came to a head. We had a terrible row. I told Barbara we couldn't carry on, we had to do something about him, otherwise I'd move out. I didn't mean it, I'd never have left her.' He covered his face with his hands as though he had run out of words and run out of the energy to say them. 'It was wrong of me, I know that now.'

Giuseppe and Christina exchanged a glance, wondering who should take the lead in continuing the conversation, and then Matthew dropped his hands to his knees.

'And after the argument?' Giuseppe said.

'She left, that's what happened. I went to work and when I came home she'd cleared all her things out.'

Giuseppe took a notebook from his pocket. 'Do you know where Barbara's husband lives?'

'I know where they were living when they were still together. He might still be there. It's worth a try.'

Giuseppe passed the notebook to Matthew and waited while he wrote down the address.

'What are you going to do if you find him?' Matthew asked.

'We have some questions to ask him.'

'Will you let me know how you get on? And Barbara - do

you think she'll want to see me?'

'We will find him, *Signor* Harding and when we do we will make sure the police do what they should have done a long time ago.'

'And my sister?'

'Please trust us to do what is right, for you and for your sister.'

CHAPTER 37
Sunday, 19th July

After his adventures of the previous evening, Stevie slept late for the first time in his young life. Mario waved Anne off, saying he'd keep an eye on Stevie. From the look on Mario's face, '*keeping an eye*' suggested their grandson would have a rare chance to choose from the cake display on the café counter for his breakfast, forgoing the usual cereal and toast.

Anne drove as far as the eastern end of Beach Walk, parked up and then took a slow walk to *Rose Cottage*, giving herself time to plan what she would say when she arrived and, importantly, how she would say it.

From all Giuseppe had said it was clear that Barbara - or Rose as she now called herself - was feeling scared, vulnerable and alone. Anne wished she could turn back the clock. Perhaps if she'd visited Matthew as soon as she received his letter, instead of sending Giuseppe and Christina, then maybe she would have made the connections sooner. But even then it would have only been days ago, which still meant Rose had spent several months hiding in the cottage, afraid of everything and everyone.

To reach the cottage Anne had to walk past the police notices, the photofit poster of the stranger and the very place where George Leigh had died. The same place where just the night before the event had started as a celebration of George's life and ended with fear and anxiety.

She shook her head, trying to dispel the black thoughts, then walked slowly up the front path to the cottage. The front garden was a blaze of colour. It was as if the swathes of hollyhocks and irises were trying to outdo each other.

Several moments passed between her knocking on the front door and the door being opened. Then it opened the barest amount. All that was visible were the fingers of Rose's right hand.

'Barbara, it's me, Anne. You remember me, don't you? Can I come in?'

There was silence from the other side of the door and Anne was wondering what she might say next to encourage the woman to allow her to enter.

'I didn't know you were here in Bexhill. If I'd known I'd have visited before now. You must have been feeling lonely.'

Still silence.

'We were friends back then, weren't we? Do you remember the fun times we had? That first time you saw the sea, you couldn't wait to rush straight in.'

Anne heard the chain slide across and then the door opened wide and there stood Barbara, someone she hadn't seen for over twenty years.

'Anne.'

It was the simplest of greetings and yet there was an acceptance in the way she said it. She turned and led Anne through to the front room. Tabitha was curled up on the settee. She shooed her off and brushed down the cushions, gesturing to Anne to sit.

'Would you like a cup of tea?'

If someone had been eavesdropping, they would think this was the most ordinary of meetings and yet there was nothing ordinary about what had led Rose to the cottage, and nothing ordinary about Anne's visit.

'Giuseppe Bianchi - the Italian who spoke with you last night - he's my husband's cousin.'

'And the girl?'

'My daughter. But we didn't know who you were. It was only last night when...'

'He will have told you then, about me, about why I'm here.'

Anne wasn't sure what to say. Here was a woman who'd experienced the kind of life Anne had only heard about; brutality, the loss of a child, living in fear, day after day. None of it was the stuff of easy conversation, not something to be chatted about over a cup of tea.

Rose left the room. While she waited Anne looked around the room, not really thinking about her surroundings, but remembering the days she'd spent with Matthew and his sister years before. The girl she remembered from more than twenty years ago had arrived in Bexhill as a timid child, clinging onto the hand of her brother, but two years later, when they left, Barbara was almost thirteen. She was tall for her age and ready to look the world in the eye. But seeing her now, Anne could tell she had reverted to that timid child once more. Not surprising, given what she'd had to endure.

Rose returned with a tray of tea and a plate of arrowroot biscuits.

'You've suffered a great deal.' Anne said.

Rose poured the tea, then sat and looked down at her hands, which were clenched together in her lap.

'And you chose to come to Bexhill. I'm pleased you remember this as a place where you felt happy.'

'I hadn't planned it. It was a spur of the moment thing.'

'Are you able to tell me how it happened? How you came to be here in this cottage?'

Rose took a sip of tea and for a few moments it was as if she wasn't going to speak, but then she started.

'I'd been saving every penny I could because I always knew that one day I'd have to run away. Matthew did all he could to keep me safe, but he couldn't be there all the time. Some days when he was at work I'd close myself in my bedroom, terrified about what I'd do if Arnold came knocking on the door.'

'You must have been so scare.'

231

'I couldn't bear to be in the flat, but some days I was too frightened to step outside in case he was there, just waiting for me.'

'You felt trapped.'

Rose gave the merest of nods and was quiet for a few moments.

'Then Matthew and I had an argument. He wanted me to go to the police, to tell them about Arnold. What he didn't know was that I'd been there already. But all the police officer did was to sit me down in the interview room and fire questions at me. *Why do you think your husband wishes you harm? Have you done something to give him just cause?'* They made me feel like I was a criminal.'

She paused, taking a deep breath before continuing.

'Anyway, that day, after the argument with Matthew, I waited until he was out, then I walked to the station, bought a ticket, waited for half an hour on the platform and then stepped onto the train. I'd been angry with Matthew, but once I was on the train I realised he'd helped me to make the decision. I needed to start again, somewhere new.'

'You were very brave to make such a big decision.' Anne was thinking about how cautious she'd been at the thought of going to London to visit Matthew. And all the time her friend had been dealing with so much.

'There was a man sitting opposite me, pretending to read his newspaper. He kept looking up, peering at me over the broadsheet. So I made sure I looked out of the window, keeping an eye on him out of the corner of my eye. Every time the train pulled into a station I hoped he'd get off. Then I was scared he might get off at Bexhill and watch where I went.'

'Arnold had made you scared of every man you met. I can understand that.'

'In the end the man got off three stops before me. I felt

232

such a sense of relief.'

'So you arrived in Bexhill. How did you decide where to go once you arrived here? You knew I was there at the café. How I wish you'd come to find me.'

Rose shook her head. 'I had to start over, I had to do it for myself. So, I stopped at the newsagent's next to the station and bought a street map. I couldn't remember much from all those years ago and anyway, the place was bound to look different. But then, as I made my way down the hill from the station, I smelled the sea. Oh, it was just as I remembered it. I wanted to drop my suitcase there and then and run towards it.'

'Like you did all those years ago. Do you remember what your brother shouted at you?'

Rose smiled. 'I still had my shoes and socks on. I remember calling back to him, "*I don't care*". And back then I didn't care either, I was happy to escape from London and all these years on I was just as pleased.'

'So you'd saved enough money to pay for your lodgings?'

She shook her head. 'I needed to find a way to disappear. If I'd booked into a guest house they'd be asking questions. That's what folk are like, they want to know the whys and wherefores. I walked along the promenade, thinking I'd sleep on the beach. I would have too. That's when I saw the beach huts. There was one painted blue and when I got close to it I saw the padlock was broken. I decided to wait until dusk, to be certain that no-one might be coming to use it, then I settled in there and felt so safe. Such a small space, and just one entrance.'

There were so many questions Anne wanted to ask, but she didn't want to interrupt. She was worried that at any point Rose might clam up, overwhelmed by her memories and the fears that had never left her.

'I've always been scared.' Rose said.

'You had good reason though.'

'I don't mean just because of Arnold. Even as a child I used to imagine someone could creep along the landing of our house and we'd all be murdered in our beds. You read of such things in the newspaper all the time. That's why I married Arnold. It was his job after all, protecting everyone who bought his insurance policies. Even though Matthew was against it, I had this feeling that Arnold would keep me safe.'

Anne was close to tears hearing her friend speak. Rose couldn't have known back then that one day her husband would present the very terror she'd been dreading for years.

'And then you found this cottage?'

'It was a handwritten advert in the side window of the newsagent's. *Housekeeper required. Board and lodging provided.* And when I saw where it was, right here on the beach, where I could smell the sea, listen to the waves rolling onto the shingle, well I knew it would be the perfect place for me.'

'And you chose a new name?'

'It's my middle name, Rose. So when I saw the place was called *Rose Cottage*, well, that was that.'

'And Walker? Is that your married name?'

Her face relaxed into a half smile. 'Next to the advert for the position of housekeeper, was a poster asking for walkers to join a rambling club. Silly I know, but I thought if no one knew my real name, then Arnold would never find me.'

Much later that day Anne parted company with Rose, promising to return.

'Giuseppe is a good man. He won't rest until he gets answers.' Anne said.

'I'm grateful for all of it, for him, for you and Matthew. I've caused my brother a lot of worry, when all he wanted to do was protect me. Do you think he'll forgive me?'

'He loves you, and when you love someone there's nothing to forgive. Besides, look at how brave you've been. You must know that what you did took great courage. To come down to Bexhill on your own, find somewhere to live, a way of earning money. It's more than I could do.'

'It's surprising what we can do when we are faced with few choices.'

CHAPTER 38
Sunday, 19th July

It was a day for gathering information. Giuseppe had suggested to Detective Sergeant Pearce that he questioned Paul Leigh about his bicycle. Pearce had mixed feelings about the part the Italian had played in solving the crime; irritation that Giuseppe Bianchi seemed to be one step ahead of him, but a begrudging sense of gratitude too.

Pearce waited until late afternoon before visiting the Leigh family. He wondered if Paul had returned from Sean Murphy's caravan, or if he was still hiding out there. There was a strong likelihood his parents didn't know where he'd spent the night. Pearce was weighing up what to say and how to phrase it, when Patricia Leigh opened the door.

'Detective Sergeant Pearce. Do you have some news for us?' There was a hopefulness in her tone.

'May I come in?'

She led him through to the sitting room. A needlework basket was on the floor beside one of the armchairs, with a pile of socks lying beside it.

'I need to do some darning, but I can't put my mind to it.'

During his drive to the Leigh house Pearce had been thinking long and hard about the Leigh family. He and his wife had no children. It wasn't that they hadn't wanted them, it was that it had never happened. Neither one wanted to know who was to blame. Not that anything could be done about it. It was a fact of life. But reflecting on the Leigh family, he wondered what it must be like to have two sons, so close in age, and yet - from all he'd heard about them - so different in temperament. The last time he spoke to the parents he sensed disquiet. It was beneath the surface, but apparent, nevertheless. He'd seen so many reactions to grief over the years he could write a book on the subject.

He knew what the Italian was suggesting when he mentioned Paul's bike. Giuseppe Bianchi clearly thought Paul knew more than he was saying about his brother's death. When investigating any crime Pearce had always told his team to focus on nothing but the evidence and the facts. He'd never admit it to them, but over the years he'd come to accept that intuition had a part to play as well. And right now his intuition was telling him that before the end of the afternoon he would be hearing a confession.

'Can I make you a cup of tea, Detective Sergeant?' Patricia Leigh's question brought his attention back to the present. He waved his hand by way of reply and waited for her to sit before he spoke.

'Mrs Leigh, we are still trying to establish exactly what happened at Beach Walk, the day your son lost his life.'

'You haven't caught the culprit then.' It was more of a statement than a question.

'Can you talk me through that day again? George and Paul went out for a bike ride.' He took out his pocketbook.

'That's right, yes.'

'And what time would that have been?'

She looked at him, but it was as though she wasn't seeing him at all.

'They were out for most of the day. Off straight after breakfast, but they know they have to be back for Sunday lunch. We always eat together as a family on Sundays, have done since the boys were born.'

She stopped speaking, lines appearing in her face making her age before his eyes. She took a deep breath as though doing so might give her the courage to carry on talking about a family tradition that could never be repeated.

'You had dinner together,' Pearce prompted.

'The boys stayed to help clear up and then they were off again. It's how they spent most weekends in the fine weather. They love those bikes. It took us forever to save up for them, but it was worth every penny to see their faces. Two years ago, on their birthday. No need to wrap them, I told Robert. He hid them in the garden shed until that morning. No sooner had we given them to the boys than they were off. We didn't see them for the rest of the day.'

'They already knew how to ride?'

'Oh yes, they'd been borrowing friends' bikes for ages. Always on at us they were, it was the only present they wanted.'

'Mrs Leigh, can you remember what time Paul got home that Sunday afternoon? After his bike ride with George?'

Once again she offered a blank look as though she hadn't understood the question. Pearce guessed that in order to respond she'd have to revisit that day in her mind, a day she had been trying to erase from her memory.

Before he could ask any more questions, Pearce heard the back door open and a moment later Paul appeared. He threw a duffel bag down by his feet and glared at the detective.

'Hello Paul.' Pearce held the teenager's gaze until Paul finally averted his eyes, looking instead at the floor.

Pearce watched Patricia Leigh's reaction, wondering what she might say about her son's absence from the family home the night before.

'It's good to see you, love,' Patricia said, reaching her hand towards her son as he moved away towards the fireplace.

'Paul, the detective sergeant has come to ask us a few more questions.'

'He should be out catching whoever killed George, not here pestering us.' His words were sharp but his tone quiet.

'There's no need to be rude, Paul. I'm sorry, Detective Sergeant, but we're all still feeling the strain. I'm sure you understand.'

'Paul, perhaps you can help your mother. She was trying to remember what time you got home last Sunday, after your bike ride with George.'

'What does it matter what time I got home?'

'We are trying to establish a timeline, to see exactly what time the incident could have occurred and who might have been there.'

'I was here when that policewoman came to tell us about George, wasn't I, Mum?'

His voice was no longer quiet, his tone no longer steady.

'Detective Sergeant, I'm not sure what you are saying. You're not trying to suggest Paul was involved in any way with his brother's death?'

Paul glared at his mother and then at Pearce, before picking up his duffel bag.

'I'll be in my room.'

Pearce moved towards the boy, putting one hand on his shoulder. 'No Paul. I can't let you go just now.'

'What are you going to do then, arrest me?'

'Withholding information is an arrestable offence, but I don't think you want to withhold anything anymore. I think you would feel better if you told us the truth. Paul, where is your bike?'

'What's his bike got to do with anything?' Patricia Leigh moved to stand beside her son, her eyes wide with fear.

'Shall we all go to the garden shed together? Your bike is there, isn't it?'

Paul didn't answer, instead he rushed out of the back door, not waiting to see if his mother and the detective sergeant were following. He pulled open the door of the shed and dragged out his bike, pushing it towards the detective with such force that the front tyre bumped into Pearce's leg.

'Steady on there, son. You don't want to add injuring a police officer to your list of offences.'

Pearce eased the bike from Paul's hands, moving it forwards.

'The rear reflector is broken,' Pearce said, watching for Paul's reaction.

'So what if it is?'

'When did it get broken?'

'How do I know?'

'I think you do know, Paul, and I think it's time for you to tell us exactly how it happened.'

Patricia Leigh watched the scene unfold, unable to understand any of it, not the detective's questions, nor her son's replies.

Then, as Paul started to speak, it was as if a sheet of ice had been broken, leaving both mother and son in danger of falling through to the freezing water below.

'Mum, I'm so sorry, I didn't mean it, please believe me.' Paul dropped to his knees at his mother's feet.

'What are you saying? Don't tell me, I don't want to know.' She turned away from him, clutching her stomach as if she'd been kicked.

Pearce would have preferred the next words Paul spoke to have been uttered in the police station, in a quiet interview room, where he could write it all down. But he knew enough about the effect of emotion on a witness to know he was more likely to hear the truth if he captured it at this moment, when there was no time for preparation or rehearsal.

The boy stood again, turning away from his mother and the detective, as though it would be easier to speak if he pretended they weren't there to listen.

'George and me, we had an argument. It started off as something and nothing. We'd been to see the woman in the cottage just that morning. And I told George I thought she was a bit daft. He said I was heartless, so I said he was a fine one to talk, only caring about himself, revelling in being everyone's favourite.'

'Oh Paul.' his mother went to touch his arm, but it was his turn to push her away.

'It's true, Mum. You and Dad, all the teachers, they all preferred George. He was cleverer than me, better at sport, better at everything. I told him I was sick of it, sick of him.'

'And you were on the beach while you were having this argument?' Pearce wanted to understand the exact sequence of events.

'We'd been cycling side by side, shouting at each other and then I lost my temper. I swerved, moving my front wheel towards George's bike. We both braked hard and kind of fell towards each other.'

'Both bikes were damaged, the rear reflectors smashed?'

Paul nodded.

'What happened next?' Pearce asked.

'George took the worst of the fall, cracked his head on the ground and I landed on top of him. The accident took the wind from both of us, but then George pushed me off him, shouting at me, telling me I was stupid.'

'And then?'

'I picked up my bike and rode off, that's what I did.' Paul's voice was so quiet now it was difficult to catch his words.

'You left your brother without seeing how badly he was hurt? Without telling anyone what had happened?' Patricia Leigh spoke as though she was trying to grasp an impossible mathematical equation.

241

'He was fine when I left him, I promise.' Paul turned now to face his mother. 'I know I was wrong to leave him there like that but I thought he'd just pick up his bike and follow me home. Now my brother's dead and it's my fault.'

CHAPTER 39
Sunday, 19th July

Giuseppe didn't need to hear Paul's confession. When he suggested to the detective sergeant a visit to the Leigh family might reveal valuable information, he already had a plan in mind. A plan that would uncover the truth about the death of George Leigh.

After a few wrong turns and having to ask for directions on two occasions, Giuseppe and Christina arrived at the address Matthew Harding had given them. The road was narrow, little more than an alleyway, leading onto an area of rubble, the remains of a bombed-out building that had yet to be cleared. There were a few dustbins placed randomly around what could be loosely described as a yard. In between the dustbins there was an old iron bedstead and a couple of broken bicycle wheels. It seemed as though the residents of Merchant Way just threw their discarded items out onto the street, hoping someone might eventually remove them. Some of the houses had laundry hanging from open windows, the dust and grime likely to make the clothes dirtier, in families' attempts to dry their washing.

The houses were bunched tightly together, terraced, with nothing to distinguish them from each other beyond the front doors. They knew to look out for number seven but, as far as they could see, no door numbers were displayed. Then Christina spotted a rusted sign bolted to one of the house walls, showing the number five. In the absence of any other numbers all they could do was guess which way the numbering might go and try the house to the left or the right.

'It's a fifty-fifty chance we get it wrong,' she said, walking up to one of the doors. 'Before I knock, shouldn't we plan what we're going to say? We can hardly ask him outright.

That's if he even lives here still and if he's at home.'

'I have a plan,' was all Giuseppe was prepared to say. He nodded to Christina to go ahead.

'Here goes nothing,' she said, rapping firmly on the door.

They stood for a few moments in silence, both listening out for any movement from within.

'How long should we wait?'

'We have the rest of the day,' Giuseppe replied, the beginnings of a smile lightening his face.

Then the door opened to reveal an elderly lady, wearing a floral housecoat and holding a duster in her hand.

'Yes?'

'I'm sorry to disturb you. We are looking for Mr Arnold Morton, we understand he lives here?'

'What's that?' The woman turned one ear towards Christina. 'I don't hear so well, so you'll need to speak up.'

'Mr Morton.' Christina spoke loudly, articulating each syllable.

'You don't need to shout.'

Giuseppe had remained a little way away from the doorway, so his wry smile wasn't seen by either woman.

'Mr Morton, you say. Well, he doesn't live here, luvvie. He lives two doors down - number seven.'

There was barely time for Christina to thank the woman before the door was closed, with the woman presumably returning to her housework.

Now they had confirmation of the house and of the occupant, it was Giuseppe who approached. There was still a chance Arnold Morton would not be at home, but in that case all they had to do was wait. However, luck was on their side. A few moments after knocking at the door, it was opened.

'*Signor* Morton?' Giuseppe said.

'That's me. How can I help you?' Arnold's gaze went first

to the Italian, but then in the direction of Christina.

'Insurance.'

'How's that?'

'We want to buy insurance.'

The frown on Arnold's face indicated it was not only the request that was unexpected but also the accent of the speaker.

'You sell insurance? That is what we were told.' Giuseppe continued.

'Well, yes I do. But not here from my house and not on a Sunday. It's more usual for me to come to you.'

As Arnold was speaking Giuseppe was watching him and remembering all that Rose Walker had told them about her husband. Could this be the man who Rose lived in fear of? He was of slim build and short, maybe three inches shorter than Rose. There was nothing powerful about him, not in his stature, or his demeanour. But then he reflected on what Matthew had said, that Arnold hadn't physically harmed Rose, but had bullied her in other ways, undermining her and seeking to control her.

'We have come a long way to find you. Perhaps we could come in?' Giuseppe spoke with such confidence as though Arnold would have no choice but to agree to his request.

'I suppose it's alright. But you'll have to take me as you find me.' He stepped back, allowing his unexpected visitors to enter.

The inside of the terraced house was as dismal as the outside. The decorations looked as if they had remained untouched since the house was built decades earlier. They walked along a dingy corridor that led to a tiny sitting room. Papers were strewn all around the room, covering the surfaces, and most of the chairs, bar one. Arnold gathered them up and threw them down in one corner of the room.

'Sit yourselves down. Tell me again, how was it you found

me? I don't usually give customers my home address. A man likes a bit of privacy when he's off duty.' He gave a sickly smile, revealing a missing tooth in the bottom centre of his mouth. 'Now what type of insurance are you after? Life? Sickness?'

'Life.' Giuseppe said, holding Arnold's gaze.

There was a palpable tension in the room, which was wrong-footing Arnold Morton.

'Yes, of course.' Arnold bent to pick up a wad of paper from the pile on the floor, and as he did his glasses fell forward, landing on the carpet. 'Dratted things,' he said, picking them up and putting them back on.

'Your glasses are new?' Giuseppe asked.

'No, well, that is, my own glasses got broken. I've ordered some new ones, but in the meantime I've had to go back to these old things. They've lost all their grip and they're forever falling off. Now, where was I?'

'You are going to explain to us about life insurance,' Giuseppe said. 'It is so important to be protected, is it not? One never knows when our life might end.' He paused, as though waiting for his words to take on their full meaning.

'Well now, is the policy for yourself, or your...?' Arnold hesitated, looking at Christina.

'Every day I hear terrible stories, of people who die suddenly,' Giuseppe continued. 'Just the other day I heard the saddest story of all. A young boy, in his teenage years, with all his life ahead of him. Then, *bang*, it was all over.' Giuseppe raised his voice as he simulated a bang by thumping his fist on the side of the armchair, making both Christina and Arnold jump.

'I don't like your tone. You don't want insurance at all, do you? I want you to leave right now, both of you.' Arnold went to grab Giuseppe's arm, but the Italian was too strong for him, resulting in Arnold being pushed back against the wall.

'This is my home, you've no right barging in here. I want you out or I'll call the police.'

'Yes. A very good idea. It will save me from having to call them.' Giuseppe stood close to Arnold, blocking any movement he might make to leave the room.

'Christina, you will find a telephone box just outside in the yard. Please go there and phone the police. And while we wait for them to arrive, *Signor* Morton will tell me exactly what happened that afternoon two weeks ago.'

'I've got nothing to say to you. I don't even know you.'

'You don't need to know me. It is enough that I know you. I know you were in Bexhill on Sunday 5th July and that you went to Beach Walk to try once again to frighten your wife, Barbara. While you were there you encountered a young boy. There was a scuffle of some kind. As a result, you broke your glasses and injured the boy. Then you ran away, leaving the boy to die.'

'He's dead?' With just two words Arnold confirmed all that Giuseppe had surmised.

'Yes, *Signor* Morton. He is dead.'

Arnold's mouth dropped open.

'You can't prove any of it. It'll be your word against mine.'

'I don't need to prove it. Because when the police arrive you will confess.'

'And why would I do that?'

'Because there is nowhere for you to escape to and no future for you here or anywhere. You have killed a child. You will not be able to live with yourself.'

'I didn't kill anyone. The boy got in the way, that's all.'

'I think it is time for you to tell the truth. If you didn't kill anyone, then you have nothing to fear. If, as you say, it was just a terrible accident, then it is better for you to explain, no?'

Giuseppe gestured to Arnold to sit, while he stood over

him, ready to restrain him if he tried to get away.

'It's that stupid wife of mine, she's the one who's caused all the problems. She goes off with some bloke, gets herself up the duff, then expects me to bring the bastard up. Like hell I would. So I made her get rid of the boy. But all she did was go on and on about him. I couldn't stand it anymore, so I threw her out.'

Giuseppe remained quiet, studying the man's expression, wondering what would make a man so heartless towards a woman he purported to love.

'She went running to that pathetic brother of hers. And how was I supposed to manage? Who was going to cook for me, eh? So I thought I'd get her back. She's still my wife, so she should be here, keeping house for me. Isn't that what a wife is supposed to do?'

There was so much Giuseppe would like to have said, instead he let Arnold continue.

'I watched the flat where they lived, I'd seen her go in and out. But then several days on the trot I stood outside and there was no sign of her. So I got to wondering where she might have gone to.'

'She had told you about Bexhill. About her time there as a child during the war.' Giuseppe could fill in the blanks of the story without asking questions.

Arnold nodded. 'It didn't take long to find her. I made a few trips down there, asked around, found out that someone had taken over that cottage by the beach, someone who wasn't local. All I needed to do was hang around and wait until I spotted her.'

'So you tried your hand at fishing?'

'You seem to know an awful lot about me. I still don't even know who you are or how you found me.'

'I am here to listen to your story. My story is not so

interesting. So, that Sunday...?'

'I went down there ready to have it out with her. I planned to bring her back with me, even if I had to drag her here.'

'But then there was the boy.'

'I hung around the beach until teatime. I found a good spot where I could squat down behind one of the groynes, so I could see the front of the cottage, but I couldn't be seen. Anyways, there were a couple of lads on bicycles. They were having a row, shouting at each other and the next thing I saw was one of them on the ground. The other one rode off and then all of a sudden the sea mist came in. Real quick like, so thick it was, worse than some of those smogs we get up here.'

'So you thought you could take your chance, under cover of the mist. You could force your wife out of the cottage and there would be no one to see you do it.'

'I hadn't reckoned on the boy recognising me. I'd seen him before and the other one. They'd been throwing stones down by the water when I was fishing. I'd given them a piece of my mind and some Irish fella came running out of that caravan that's parked up, poking his nose in.'

'Did George Leigh confront you on that Sunday afternoon?'

'The lad came at me out of the mist. Said how I didn't ought to go round shouting at people. How I'd scared his brother.'

'I told him I'd do more than scare him, talking like that to me. I told him to clear off.'

'But he did not *clear off*.' Giuseppe was thinking of the gentle boy his mother had described, wondering how much of Arnold Morton's story was fact and how much a version he had concocted to shift the blame for the events that unfolded.

'He rushed at me, pushing me. I lost my footing and my glasses. Smashed on the ground they did.'

'George Leigh was shorter than you, *Signor* Morton. Are

you saying a young boy, some twenty years younger than you managed to overpower you?'

'Who said anything about overpowering? I stumbled is all.'

Giuseppe was certain that by defending his actions the man would eventually admit to the truth of the fatal blow that killed his young victim.

'It was his own fault. Accosting me like that and right close to the railway crossing. I could have stumbled right into the path of the train. He deserved everything he got.'

'And what did he get, *Signor* Morton?'

'I pushed him, yeah, that's what I did. Shoved him good and hard. He fell over, must have banged his head on the ground.'

'And then?'

'What was I expected to do, eh? Not likely to hang around for him to have another go at me, was I?'

'So you ran alongside the track to the railway station. You were rude to the ticket clerk, staring at him in a strange manner because you had lost your glasses. Then you caught the train back to London, caring nothing for the boy you left lying on the ground.'

'How was I supposed to know he was going to die, eh? The kid banged his head is all.'

As Arnold Morton stopped speaking, the door to the flat opened and Giuseppe watched as Christina led the police into the flat. Giuseppe too was silent. The sequence of events were as he had surmised, but there was little pleasure in knowing he was right. A boy had died. His family would get justice. But that justice would not bring the boy back to life.

Giuseppe took one of the police officers to one side, giving him a summary of the confession he had just heard.

'*Signor* Morton will provide you with all the details, officer. He can no long run or hide from what he has done.'

Giuseppe gestured to Christina for her notebook, writing out his contact details, tearing the sheet out and handing it to the officer. Then they watched Arnold Morton being led away. Giuseppe's thoughts were not just of the Leigh family, but of Rose Walker, another victim, but one who thankfully had not lost her life. Her life to date had been diminished, she had lived in fear for so long, but now she had a chance to live the rest of her years out of the shadows.

On the journey home Christina was quiet. Even with his eyes closed Giuseppe sensed she wanted to talk.

'You have much to add to your article,' he said. He opened his eyes, smiling at her questioning look. 'You have seen how a person's life can be destroyed by cruelty and oppression.'

'And narrow-minded thinking.'

'To live in harmony, we have to respect boundaries, to know what is right and what is wrong. It is the crossing of those lines that results in all criminal behaviour.'

'It's more complicated than that, surely? It's not just about the law, is it?' Christina sat forward in her seat. 'It's about so much more.'

'Many people believe their own opinion is the only one, the right one. But opinions are coloured by experience.'

Christina looked away, avoiding Giuseppe's gaze. He continued, 'I have made mistakes, as has your father...'

'And me? You think I'm wrong to judge my sister?'

'I cannot know what is in your heart, but we have all crossed lines we should not have crossed. Sometimes the mistakes we make can't be undone. We can't always go back to the way things were.'

He was thinking now about his own life. He could not put off his return to Rome forever, but he wasn't ready to go back home, not yet. Giuseppe closed his eyes and they continued the rest of the journey in silence.

CHAPTER 40
Monday, 20th July

Giuseppe went alone to the police station the next day, while Christina accompanied her mother on another visit to Rose to reassure her the man she feared was now behind bars. As he waited for the desk sergeant to ring through to Pearce, he looked around the entrance area, comparing the British police station with the building that had been his own place of work for so many years.

His working life had given him structure, he'd been glad of it. He'd come to rely on it, so much so that as he counted down the weeks and then the days to his retirement, he was often gripped with a sense of panic. There were moments when he'd be sitting, closed off from the rest of his team by the glass wall that divided his private space from the larger office. His colleagues were chatting, swapping anecdotes, laughing. He could see it all, even hear it in muted form through the glass partition, and yet it was as though he was watching a film at the cinema. It was happening around him, and would continue to happen despite him, once he took his leave. It was then he started to feel his heart rate increase, his palms sweat and a throbbing at his temples. In those moments, even a cigarette didn't help. He learned that if he sat very still and cleared his mind, the sensation subsided. Once he was calm again, he left his office and visited the small kitchen area, poured himself a glass of cold water and sipped it slowly, until every drop was gone.

These were the thoughts that occupied him as he followed the desk sergeant down a dark corridor into Pearce's office. The room was dark, making him look towards the window to see if the blinds were closed. The walls were yellowed with nicotine, the furniture battered and old. The only item in the room that gave it any personality was a large rubber plant that stood in the corner. But then his office in Rome was hardly colourful, although he benefited from having a large window that shed almost permanent sunlight straight onto his desk. Sometimes he'd move his hands around the desk, feeling the warmth from the rays on the backs of his hands, while his palms enjoyed the smooth walnut surface.

Giuseppe was uncertain as to the reception he might receive. No one liked to be beaten by an outsider. The detective sergeant stood when Giuseppe entered and went to shake his hand.

'You did well.' Pearce said.

'Perhaps. But much was luck.'

'No, not luck. You followed your instincts and it paid off. The Metropolitan Police have been in touch. They're sending an officer down to take statements, but they say it should be an open and shut case. Morton has made a full confession.'

There was an awkward moment. Neither man spoke. Then Giuseppe asked, 'And Paul Leigh?'

'You won't be surprised to know he and his brother had an argument. There was a bit of a scuffle, resulting in George banging his head. But the lad swears his brother was fine when he left him.'

'And so, the second blow to his head, when Arnold Morton pushed him - that was the fatal one.'

Pearce took a packet of cigarettes from his desk drawer and offered one to Giuseppe.

'We have both stopped smoking, Detective Sergeant, have we not?'

Pearce gave a brief nod.

'And yet you keep them in your desk?'

'To test my resolve.'

'Ah, *si.*' Giuseppe thought about the strategies he had put in place since Rosalia left, to force him always forward, to help him find a new way of living.

There was silence for a few minutes as the two men mulled over what had been discovered and what was yet to be resolved.

'You will speak to the Leigh family?' Giuseppe said. Although, on the face of it, his question sounded like an instruction, it was quite the reverse. He was waiting for the detective sergeant to lead the way.

'The lad was certain he was to blame for his brother's death. I am guessing the conversations in that household after I left can't have been easy.'

'But now you can reassure them he was not at fault?'

'It won't be that simple. I doubt he'll be able to shake off that feeling of guilt, not for a long time. Maybe never.'

Giuseppe nodded his head slowly. 'Guilt is a heavy load to bear, no matter what age you are.'

Throughout the investigation into George Leigh's death Giuseppe hoped that by solving one crime it would help assuage his guilt over the event that caused him to leave his job, even his country, fleeing to England to forget. But the feelings were the same, the guilt was still there, hovering. Perhaps it would remain the same until he returned to Rome and faced his demons, but what was the point of returning to an empty flat, an empty life.

'There is someone we haven't yet dealt with,' Pearce said, interrupting Giuseppe's thoughts. 'At least not to my satisfaction.'

'The Irishman?'

Pearce gave a wry smile. 'Perhaps I will leave you to advise him as to where we are with the case? I'm sure you will be able to make him understand how difficult he has made it for us.'

Giuseppe stood and extended his hand to Pearce.

'*Grazie*. You have been very generous allowing me to...' He paused. By acknowledging his part in solving the crime it might appear he was bragging.

'Do you have many days left of your holiday?' The detective sergeant cut in before Giuseppe could continue.

'I have no fixed return date.'

'Then I may see you again? But I hope not in such troubled circumstances.' Pearce pulled open his desk drawer, took out the packet of cigarettes and tossed it into the wastepaper basket, before following Giuseppe to the door and watching him leave.

A bus ride and a short walk later and Giuseppe was knocking on the door of Sean Murphy's caravan. When there was no response, he knocked again and then decided he had chosen a rare moment when the Irishman was not at home. He sat down on the caravan steps and looked down the beach towards the shoreline. Now the schools had broken up, a few families had taken advantage of a dry, warm day to spread themselves out on the shingle and enjoy the sunshine. Perhaps their decision to come to the beach on Saturday evening for the bonfire party had chased away their fears about an unsolved crime. Although the poster depicting the man Giuseppe now knew to be Arnold Morton was still pinned to the post beside the railway crossing.

People's behaviour continued to surprise Giuseppe. So many of the holidaymakers wore nothing but a bathing costume, when he was still in need of his jacket. He closed his eyes and tried to imagine that instead of an English beach he was sitting outside a beach bar overlooking the Mediterranean, with the sun so hot he needed to seek the shade of a beach umbrella.

'Got time to relax now, have you?' Sean Murphy's voice

caught him by surprise.

'*Signor* Murphy.'

'Waiting for me? Well, if you'll budge off my steps, then I'll open up and we can go inside. I'm guessing you want to talk to me?'

Giuseppe stood, stretching out the stiffness in his back. Once inside the caravan Sean Murphy put the shopping bag down on the sofa and began emptying it.

'I'm spending more money on that blessed cat as on myself.' He held up a tin of cat food before putting it away under the sink.

'The police have asked me to let you know they have arrested someone.'

'For the lad's death?'

'*Si.*'

Sean pushed the empty bag onto the floor and sat on the sofa, picking up his pipe and lighting it. 'What will happen to him?'

'He will go to court and then, perhaps, to prison.'

'Prison?'

Giuseppe watched the Irishman's expression, wondering how long Sean Murphy could hold out before asking the question that would in turn indicate the part he had played in the events of that Sunday afternoon.

'He's just a boy.'

'Paul Leigh?'

Sean nodded, but then studied Giuseppe's face as if he was trying to read his thoughts.

'*Signor* Murphy, I think it is time now for you to tell me what you really saw that day. It can only help everyone involved.'

'I saw nothing. That's what I kept on telling you and the police, but, like I said before, no one wants to listen to my answers. I saw nothing, but I heard something.'

'An argument?'

Sean puffed on his pipe and held Giuseppe's gaze. 'You already know, don't you? Well, then you don't need me to tell you.'

'That is where you are wrong. I know what Paul Leigh has said, now I need to hear what you have to say.'

'How come it's you asking me these questions, anyway? Shouldn't the police be here?'

'We are all on the same side, are we not? On the side of what is right and just.'

Sean stood, moved past Giuseppe so he could stand in the doorway of the caravan, looking out towards the shore.

'I tend to stay inside mostly, when the beach is busy. I have enough of a chance to enjoy the place when I've got it to myself. So that Sunday afternoon there were crowds, as usual, but just before that sea fret came rolling in it got real chilly. Everyone packed up their stuff and headed home. I'd made a start on the jigsaw, a real tricky one it was, the first one I've done with a thousand pieces and all I'd managed all morning was to do the frame. So, I planned to spend the afternoon working on the sky, get that out of the way before I made my tea. A bit of a challenge.'

'You were working on your jigsaw and the door was closed?'

'That's right. It wasn't warm enough to have the door open, plus I like my privacy.'

'And you heard something?'

'The Leigh brothers. They often come cycling this way. In fact, I'd seen them that morning, going into that woman's cottage. But later on in the afternoon they must have come back. Like I say, I didn't see them, but I recognised their voices.'

'You know them quite well. They have been into your

caravan several times?'

'Paul more than George, but yes. Paul is spirited, but there's no harm in him. Seems to me he's lived his life in the shadow of his brother.'

'Why do you say that?'

'It's clear to anyone that George was the brainy one, sensitive too, I'd say. But Paul is quick-witted. He likes to hear about my years at sea, fishing and so on. Although there are some stories I'd never tell him.' Sean's voice tapered off and he looked away.

'Did you hear what was said? What the brothers were arguing about?'

'No, just raised voices.'

'And you never looked outside once to see what might have been happening?'

'Look, the way I see it, I don't want folk poking their nose into my business, so I keep my nose out of theirs. Simple as that.'

'Perhaps if you had "*poked your nose*" on this occasion you may have saved a boy's life.'

Sean turned to face Giuseppe. 'Oh no you don't. You're not going to pin this one on me.'

'When you heard George Leigh was dead you thought Paul may have done more than just argue with his brother?'

'I wasn't going to drop the lad in it. Whatever happened, I can't believe he meant any harm.'

'*Signor* Murphy, not only have you made the investigation of this case more difficult, but if you had looked out of your caravan that afternoon, looked away from your jigsaw for a few moments, you may have seen George Leigh on the ground, having suffered a blow from falling off his bike.'

'Is that what killed him?'

'Some time after that fall, after Paul had cycled off, hoping his brother would follow, George Leigh suffered a second blow to his head.'

'A second blow?'

'*Sì.*'

'Now you've got me. So not Paul, then?'

'No, not Paul. The man who caused the second blow was the man you saw fishing down by the seashore. The man who shouted at the boys and who you shouted at in order to defend them. It is a great shame *Signor* Murphy that on this occasion you did not manage to defend them. Perhaps George Leigh would still be alive and his brother would not have to live the rest of his life burdened with guilt.'

'You've no right to judge me. Can you stand there and tell me, hand on heart, that you've never made a mistake in your life?'

It was Giuseppe's turn to look shame-faced. He said nothing, but then Sean continued.

'My son died and it was my fault.' Sean paused, his expression pained. 'I was a skipper on a fishing boat. Joe had been out with me dozens of times. Trouble was, he thought he knew as much about the sea as his dad did. But he never saw the danger. He fell in, I jumped in after him, but it was no good. I couldn't save him.' Sean leaned forward, staring at the floor. 'I left Ireland and came here, thinking that looking at a different sea might help.'

'I am truly sorry.'

Sean's friendship with the Leigh brothers, his concern that Paul had somehow been responsible for his brother's death, all now made sense to Giuseppe.

'The boy has taken a bit of a shine to me,' Sean said.

'Paul?'

'Maybe his dad doesn't have much time for him, but whatever it is we seemed to have hit it off. You know he turned

259

up here Saturday afternoon, announced he'd left home. Told me he wants to live here with me until he can get a job on a fishing boat.'

'What did you tell him?'

'I let him stay Saturday. Then there was all that kerfuffle with the little kid. Anyway, Sunday morning I told him to go home and tell his mum and dad the truth, that his brother dying like that was an accident. I understand, you see. I have to live with the guilt of my son's death every day.'

Giuseppe thanked Sean for his honesty and shook hands before leaving, taking a slow walk back to the bus stop.

During his time as a detective he had often come across witnesses who chose not to come forward, who were loath to get involved for fear that some of the guilt might rub off on them in some way. On this occasion the Irishman wasn't worried for himself, but for the young lad he had befriended. It was, perhaps, the wrong thing done for the right reasons.

CHAPTER 41
Sunday, 26th July

One week on from the bonfire party, and three weeks after the death of George Leigh, life had begun to return to normal in and around Bexhill. This time, when Stevie pleaded with Christina, suggesting an afternoon on the beach, she was able to give him a definite *Yes*. It would be a family outing, but not just for the Rossi family.

Giuseppe had phoned Matthew Harding, telling him he would be met at Bexhill station. During the train journey to Bexhill Matthew felt like a young boy again, although this time his sister wasn't there to hold his hand. He looked out of the window, marvelling, as the drab confines of the city were replaced with green fields where lambs suckled their mothers, and cows took shade under trees. He could almost smell the freshness of the air. It stirred up a longing in him he'd forgotten.

His life as a London postman meant walking the dusty streets every morning, weighed down by a heavy sack of mail. Now, sitting on the edge of the train seat, he was free of all weight. His sister was alive, she was well and soon he would be with her again.

As the train pulled into the platform, he slid the window down and put his hand out to grasp the door handle. Suddenly another hand held his and there was a familiarity about the face. Memories from years ago, and a striking likeness to the girl who stood beside her.

'Matthew,' Anne said, her voice just as it was more than twenty years earlier.

'It's very kind of you,' he said, looking in turn at each member of his welcoming party.

Christina led the way, with Stevie tugging at her hand in his impatience, not helped by Max straining at the lead. Anne took Matthew's arm, while Giuseppe followed behind, as the group made their way along the platform.

Matthew was used to the frenetic activity of the capital city, people bumping into him as he worked his post round. But here, as they emerged from the station concourse, he was struck by the quiet. A man was sitting on a nearby bench, reading a newspaper. A woman cycled past and then another older woman crossed the street, pushing a pram. He wondered where all the residents of Bexhill could be. The last time he'd taken a train south the platforms were crammed full of people, children made to leave their families, adults looking anxious as they took on the responsibility for a stranger.

They led him towards two cars, parked side by side. He sat in the back of the Hillman Imp, with Mario at the wheel and Anne beside him. Giuseppe squeezed himself once more into the passenger seat of Christina's Mini, with Stevie and Max on the back seat. As they made their way from the station along the seafront, Matthew felt like a child again, catching the first glimpses of the sea. He wound the window down and breathed in the fresh sea air - such a contrast to the usual smells of London, the dust and fumes from cars and buses, intermingled with the occasional waft of a breakfast fry-up.

They approached the cottage and the people accompanying Matthew hung back. This moment was for him alone. There was Rose on the path, ready to greet him, holding her arms out, apologising to him, as he apologised to her.

'I'm so proud of you,' he said.

'Because I ran away?'

'No, because you've taken the first step towards a new life. You're braver than you know.'

The beach was busy with families enjoying a proper July day where the sun was high and the sky was cloudless. The others found a quiet spot to sit, leaving the brother and sister to talk. Giuseppe muttered under his breath about the discomfort of English beaches and propped himself up against one of the groynes, while the women sat nearby.

'What will happen now?' Anne asked Giuseppe.

'To Rose?'

'I can't stop thinking of her as Barbara. At least that brute of a husband can't hurt her now. He'll go to prison, won't he?'

'I cannot speak for your English justice system, but yes, I think so. After all, he has admitted his guilt.'

'Do you think she'll choose to go back to London?'

'Her brother's life is in London. If she stays here, she will be on her own,' Giuseppe said.

A cough alerted them and looking up they saw Matthew and Rose approaching, walking hand-in-hand.

'We have much to thank you for,' Matthew said, looking at Anne.

'I've done nothing.'

'Your family were kind to us before, and now they have helped to bring us back together.'

Anne studied the face of her friend. It was as if she'd shed years in the space of a few days. The constant tension in her expression had been replaced with small smile lines around her mouth and her eyes. Her hair was tied back with a coloured ribbon, matching a brightly patterned summer dress.

'You are safe now, Barbara. And you have friends around you, you aren't on your own anymore.'

Rose smiled, still holding tightly to her brother's hand.

'Do you think you might try to find your son? Your Vincent?' Anne asked.

There was no need to voice what they were all thinking. Little Vincent might have been adopted, already receiving love from a new family.

'Right now there's just one thing my sister wants to do and this time I'm going to be right there beside her,' Matthew said.

It was as if Stevie had already guessed what the plan was, because he and Max started running towards the sea, Max's yelps of delight echoed by Stevie's laughter.

Following them close behind were Rose and Matthew, with Anne's shout of, 'Your shoes and socks,' barely heard, as the waves pushed the shingle up the beach and the seagulls swooped overhead.

Author's note

The decade of the 1960s has long held a fascination for me. It was time of such change across all countries, all social classes and all ages. When I planned this story I chose to set it in 1964, as this was a year when some of the most radical changes took place, affecting people's everyday lives. Young people delighted in the idea of the 'swinging sixties' but many older people struggled to keep pace.

In Britain, television sets were just appearing in people's houses, leading Mary Whitehouse to rail against the black and white images brought into sitting rooms across the country of the new 'permissive society'.

Some families continued the life they had lived since the end of the Second World War, in damp, cramped homes, surrounded by buildings left derelict from the bombings. While for others a new life beckoned, in a modern home, filled with labour-saving devices and Habitat-styled furniture. But London was seeing overcrowding on such a scale that the Government announced plans to build three brand new towns in south-east England.

Pop and rock music blasted out from transistor radios, teenagers clamoured for Mary Quant fashion, and clashes between Mods and Rockers disturbed otherwise sleepy seaside towns. Further out to sea, pirate radio began broadcasting from a ship anchored off the Kent coast. People were finding their voice for the first time in a generation, while others were being silenced.

It was in June 1964 when twelve-year-old Keith Bennett went missing near Saddleworth Moor. The phrase 'stranger-danger' filtered into public consciousness. It would be years later before Ian Brady and Myra Hindley were found guilty of his murder, together with the murders of many more.

Across the Atlantic thousands more soldiers were sent to fight in the Vietnam war and the Warren Commission met to investigate the murder of US President, John F Kennedy.

All the contrasts between light and darkness were there in the headlines. Contrasts that we see as Giuseppe Bianchi and Christina Rossi set about investigating the death of a teenage boy on a quiet stretch of beach in Sussex.

Isabella Muir
June 2020

About the author

Isabella rediscovered her love of writing fiction during two happy years working on and completing her MA in Professional Writing.

Aside from her love of words, Isabella has a love of all things caravan-like. She has enjoyed several years travelling in the UK and abroad. Now, Isabella and her husband run a small campsite in West Sussex.

You can discover more about Isabella's books and characters on her website, or download a free novella when you sign up for Isabella Muir's newsletter and you can follow Isabella on Twitter: @SussexMysteries

By the same author

THE SUSSEX CRIME MYSTERY SERIES
BOOK 1: THE TAPESTRY BAG
BOOK 2: LOST PROPERTY
BOOK 3: THE INVISIBLE CASE

THE SUSSEX CRIME MYSTERIES: A Janie Juke trilogy

SUSSEX CRIME NOVELLAS
DIVIDED WE FALL - 1st in the series
MORE THAN ASHES - 2nd in the series
WAITING FOR SUNSHINE - 3rd in the series

THE FORGOTTEN CHILDREN - a mother's story about the search for her child

TWELVE AT CHRISTMAS - an anthology of twelve Christmas-themed short stories

Thank you

I first met Christoffer Petersen and Sarah Acton while the three of us were studying for our MA in Professional Writing with Falmouth University.

Since then they have continued to support and encourage me with my writing, while going on to achieve great things with their own creative work.

My special thanks go to them now for their generous advice during the drafting and editing of *Crossing the Line*. Without their cajoling, Giuseppe Bianchi may never have seen the light of day.

But now I've met him I have a feeling he's here to stay.

Isabella Muir
June 2020

Lightning Source UK Ltd.
Milton Keynes UK
UKHW041123060720
366103UK00002B/97